WHO DONE HOUDINI?

T0159602

Also by Raymond John:

The Cellini Masterpiece (2006)
Mix, Match, and Murder (2010)

WHO DONE HOUDINI?

A New Adventure of Sherlock Holmes

By

Raymond John

NORTH STAR PRESS OF ST. CLOUD, INC.
St. Cloud, Minnesota

Published by
North Star Press of St. Cloud, Inc.
P.O. Box 451
St. Cloud, Minnesota 56302

northstarpress.com

PREFACE & ACKNOWLEDGEMENT

Books, stories and rumors about Harry Houdini's death have been rampant from the day he died on Halloween 1926. TV documentaries speculated that his death might actually have been a homicide, one concluding that Bess, Houdini's wife, was the most likely perpetrator. For this reason alone *Who Done Houdini* includes information already covered. Other material about Houdini's personal life and his fight against fraudulent Spiritualists come from the splendid biography by William Kalush and Larry Sloan, *The Secret Life of Houdini: The Making of America's First Superstar.*

      Houdini's feud with Sir Arthur Conan Doyle regarding Spiritualism is an extensively covered area. The opportunity to have Sherlock Holmes and Sir Arthur together in the same story was irresistible. So was the opportunity of having Sherlock's main Baker Street Irregular, Timothy Wiggins, now a middle-aged reporter for the *Detroit Free Press* the narrator.

CHAPTER 1

"Special Delivery for you, Tim. From New York."

Caught in the middle of a sentence, I jammed my typewriter keys at the interruption and cursed as I snatched the large manila envelope from Mike Grant's hands. "My name is Timothy, Junior," I said with as much venom as I could muster. "You can call me Mr. Wiggins."

He scowled and turned away, and I glowered after him. Damned whippersnapper! Pimply-faced copy boys should be more respectful of their elders.

When I looked at the envelope, my heart began to pound. I hadn't heard from "Doctor Trevor Claybrook" under any name for years, and, as far as I knew, he had never been to New York. I shoved my stricken typewriter out of the way. My article about the murder of an elderly recluse in Hamtramck would have to wait for another few minutes.

I attacked the large envelope in a frenzy with my scissors and shook the contents onto my desktop. To my amazement, all that fell out was a single sheet of paper with a red wax seal monogramed ACD and franked with a green British stamp.

A letter from Sir Arthur! I could hardly wait to see why "Dr. Claybrook" had sent it to me.

3 November 1926

My Dear Holmes—

As you undoubtedly have heard, Harry Houdini is dead. Though his death is publicly attributed to a ruptured appendix and peritonitis, it is also

1

being investigated as a possible homicide. To my consternation and amazement, the police suspect me of complicity. Your assistance is urgently requested.
> *As Always,*
> *Your devoted and admiring friend, Conan Doyle*

So, my dear friend Mr. Sherlock Holmes had sent me a puzzle. From the New York posting address, he was clearly already in America. But why had he simply sent me Sir Arthur's letter? Where were the other pieces?

How silly of me. I fished the larger envelope out of the wastebasket and reached a hand inside it. *Aha! A note.*

Wiggins,

On my way to Detroit. Arriving 8 November on the Michigan Central train at 9:43. Please meet me. Sorry about the short notice. H.

That was tomorrow morning! Even though he apologized, I could imagine how delighted he must be to make me twitch like a puppet on a string to arrange my schedule. He was my best friend, but I have always been aware of the air of competition that hung between us from the first day of my employment as a Baker Street Irregular. Almost like a jealousy, and I had never understood what caused it. I have never admired anyone nearly as much to this day. I know his feeling for me is mutual. Regardless, I was scheduled to attend a meeting with the mayor and the commissioner of police at the same time regarding a series of burglaries in the Woodbridge Neighborhood, and I couldn't reschedule.

I picked up my notes and headed for Charlie Hoffman's desk in the next room. I knew he was there because our rooms were full of tobacco smoke. Even when I opened my window, the haze from his chain-smoking always managed to reach me. Charlie wasn't a lead reporter, but had subbed for me off and on and knew the crime beat well. The son of Wisconsin farmers, he was nearly bald, fully barrel-shaped, and had jowls that nearly drooped to the desktop when he was at work. I found him hunting and pecking at his typewriter. He looked up, and his jowls hoisted into a grin.

Rising from his chair, he bowed. "Lord Wiggins. To what do I owe the honor?"

"My pigsty needs cleaning," I said.

Charlie nodded. "Okay."

It was a silly code we used to ask each other for help. "How soon can you get around to it?"

"Depends on what the pigs have been eating."

"Just the usual," I said, handing him my notes.

Charlie's eyes moved over my notes from the police investigation. "Shouldn't be any problem. Why can't you finish it yourself? Something come up?"

"Yes. An old friend from across the pond is coming to town and I have to send Violet to meet him."

He frowned. "I don't get it. What's so terrible about that? Violet knows how to get to the station, doesn't she?"

I bent closer to him. "I can't explain here. When I get nervous, I don't think, I connive. Can you break away from shining the silverware for an hour or so? We need to make a tour of the wine cellar."

Snatching up his hat from his desktop, he said, "As long as you're furnishing the wine, m'lord."

CHAPTER 2

The heater in the Chevrolet hadn't even had time to warm up by the time we reached the Stone House. The oldest bar in Detroit, the Stone House was located on the near east side, on Ralston Street across from the fairgrounds. With Prohibition in full swing, it probably was the best place to get a drink in the city. Instead of poisonous homemade hooch, one could find genuine Canadian whiskey and pretty much any other kind of alcohol desired, compliments of the Purple Gang, who owned and operated the place. They had their headquarters in the basement. Everyone I knew from the *Free Press* referred to it as the wine cellar. I could actually get a decent Beaujolais there, if I wanted.

The door was locked.

I rapped. A panel at eye level slid open and a pair of eyes stared out at me. Then the door opened.

"What're you doing here at this time of a day?" an accented voice asked. "One of the boys get picked up?"

Slomo Weinberg knew me, and he knew I was the crime reporter for the *Free Press*. As such, our paths crossed constantly without problem. If one of the gang got arrested, we'd wave at each other as he got hauled away in the paddy wagon. Mo also knew I'd never tip him off about an up-coming raid, and I even assisted the police in arresting one of the gang members. We lived in separate worlds, and respected the fact. The biggest difference—my world didn't include dead bodies lying in the streets.

I flashed him a grin. "Not today. We just need a quiet, friendly place to talk."

"So you just want to schmooze, eh? No problem. I'll go upstairs and kick one of the girls out of her room. It's a quiet day. No one'll get upset."

"You don't have to do that. We can use a booth."

He beat back my protest with his palm. "It'll be my pleasure, believe me."

True to his word, he came down minutes later behind a filmily dressed young redhead. As she passed, her robe fell open, presenting us with an impressive view of cleavage. With a coquettish smile, she found a place in a booth.

Mo gestured to the stairway. "First room on the left. I'll kick you out if we get busy."

"Thanks. What do you want to drink, Charlie?"

THE ROOM REEKED of perfume, but the bed appeared unused. I seized a dainty chair that looked like it could collapse under my weight, leaving the bed for Charlie. I had enough troubles as it was, so I didn't want to reek of perfume when I went home to meet Violet. Charlie had no such worries. He was a bachelor.

We had barely settled in when Mo appeared with our bourbon waters. He saw me reaching for my wallet. "On the house," Mo said, handing a glass to me. "My son's having his *bar mitzvah* tonight."

"*Mazel tov.*"

Mo threw me an admiring look. "You're the only *goyem* who talks Yiddish when he sees me. I never said it before, but I'm truly touched."

"A rabbi and his wife used to take care of me once in a while when I was growing up. Thanks for the drink."

"*L'cha-yihm*," Mo said. He took two steps toward the door, then turned to us. "Did you hear what that *mamser* Henry Ford said yesterday?"

News about another statement from "that bastard auto maker" was a constant topic at the Stone House. "No. What did he say this time?"

"That all Jews are Bolshevists. That we're trying to take over control of America and the rest of the world. According to him, we Zionists almost succeeded in taking over Germany, except there's some rising star who's going to save the country. Some schmuck named Adolf something. I've never even heard of him. According to Ford, we go around stirring up labor trouble, and when the government tries to stop us, we cause strikes. When people get mad enough at the government, we take over. He has proof. It seems one or two of the congressional representatives from New York are Jewish. Ford says they're just the first stones in the avalanche to come."

"Mr. Ford will say just about anything," I said with a sigh. "I don't think many people are listening. I'm not even sure the *Dearborn Independent* has more than a few hundred readers even though he sends copies to all his dealers. His paper really is just a joke."

"It isn't a joke if you're Jewish. But if you want to hear a *witz,* I'll tell you one. As much as all the high-mucky-muck automakers hate us, we supply the liquor when they put on one of their parties. Ford never touches the stuff, of course."

"Just goes to prove he's *meshugena,* right."

"Yeah." With a faint smile he bent toward us, and in a voice barely louder than a whisper said, "We sort of pay them back. Even though they know they could get fired for doing it, half of the workers in their plants come here to drink."

All I could manage was a sad smile. Raising my glass, I said, "*Dank aich,* Mo."

"Don't mention it. Let me know if you want more to drink."

We watched him leave the room.

"What's up?" Charlie asked

"I really don't know where to begin. You kid me about having come from England, like I'm some kind of aristocrat. Nothing could be further from the truth."

"You mean you're not from England?" Charlie asked with a twinkle in his eye.

"I mean I'm anything but an aristocrat. I lived on the street in London until I was twelve."

He looked shocked. "Impossible. You're pulling my leg."

"What a repulsive thought. No, I'm telling the gospel truth. Believe me. I was telling Mo why I knew Yiddish. It was because the wife of a rabbi caught me when I was filching her milk off her doorstep one morning. I always hid in waiting until the milkman came, then snatched a bottle before the owner opened the door. Well, that morning Mrs. Bernstein wasn't feeling well. She opened the door just as the milkman arrived and caught me red-handed. I started to run away but she told me to come inside and she would give me something to eat. It was the first real breakfast I had eaten in more than two years. Mrs. Bernstein lost her only son in the Afghan Wars, and said I could visit anytime I wanted to."

"How else did you feed yourself?"

"I always had a good supper. I knew every pub in a ten mile radius, what they were serving, and when they threw out their food. I was a genuine trapper. If anyone ever tried to cut in, I'd kick him in his whirlygigs and send him on his way."

Charlie broke into loud laughter. "Whirlygigs? I've never heard them called that before. I thought you Brits called them royal jewels. What else did you do?"

"I eavesdropped, played hide and seek with the peelers and learned how to be a magician. I finally knew enough about sleight of hand I could steal a banana with one hand and a strawberry with the other with a greengrocer watching every move. I always wore a jacket with loose sleeves. Luckily for me, I couldn't fool everyone."

"Lucky? What do you mean?"

"Not what. Who. You wouldn't believe me if I told you who I mean. I used to regularly do my shopping—if you want to call it that—at a greengrocer just a block off the Strand on Artillery Road. I was strolling away with an apple when suddenly I was hoisted off my feet by the nape of my jacket. I was sure a peeler had nabbed me and I was headed straight to the Vick. Whoever grabbed me turned me around and stared me in the face. The man's eyes bored all the way to the back of my head, and I really was starting to wish a bobbie had been the one to catch me."

I paused long enough to finish my drink. We both raised our glasses in salute at the pounding on the wall between us and the next room and a woman's delighted screams.

"On with it," Charlie said. "What happened then?"

"He told me we were going back to the greengrocer and pay for the pippin. I told him I didn't have any money, and he said he'd pay for it, and I could work it off. That scared the bejabbers out of me. I was sure I'd be sent somewhere to sort coal in a colliery like so many other boys of the time. Instead, I nearly fainted when he told me how much he would pay me. A shilling a day."

"That doesn't sound like very much to me. How much was that in those days?"

"About a dollar."

"A dollar! I don't make that much myself. What did you do?"

"Nothing more than what I had been doing for the past two years. The only difference was I wasn't allowed to steal."

"So, in other words, he wanted you to be a spy."

"Precisely, though I never thought of myself in that way. I was very well paid for my work. Besides the daily shillings, I earned regular bonuses for the quality of my information, and became so affluent I even had a bank account set up so I could make a weekly withdrawal. When I sailed for America, I had more than one hundred fifty pounds in my pocket. That would be more than a thousand dollars today."

"That's a lot of money, but not enough to put you through college."

"Once again, the generosity of my benefactor and his brother provided for me. They both spurned my offers of repayment when I finished."

"Enough with the suspense. Who are you talking about?"

"You know him as Mr. Sherlock Holmes."

Charlie snorted. "You brought me here to tell me that?" He got to his feet. "What do you take me for? Thanks for the drink and wasting my time."

"I know how this must sound, but I'm being perfectly honest with you."

"You're a graduate of the University of Michigan. They don't take street urchins."

"Mr. Holmes had a close friend who was a headmater at Harrington. The headmaster made sure I got the best tutoring and I always did well on the exams. I'm sure my classmates wondered who Timothy Wiggins was when they never saw him in class. My grades were high enough that I was able to get into just about any college I wanted to attend. Mr. Holmes and his brother paid my tuition."

I could tell from his tight smile he still didn't believe me. "If what you're telling me is true, you don't have a thing to worry about."

"You're very wrong. Violet thinks I'm the son of a vicar in Bayswater. What's she going to think if she meets Holmes and finds out my real background?"

"I don't know, but I wouldn't be concerned about it."

Charlie's words floored me. "Are you daft? How can you possibly say that? She thinks I'm an entirely different person."

"Are you?" Charlie asked with a sly grin.

"Of course not."

"Okay, how long have you been married?"

"Twenty wonderful years, and I want at least twenty more."

"Has your wife been happy, too?"

"I certainly think so."

"Then she'll think your childhood was romantic. What you are now is all that matters. This isn't England, for Pete's sake."

"How would you know? You're a damned bachelor."

He downed the last of his whiskey and got to his feet. "I just do. You're wasting my time. You've got nothing to worry about, so I'm going to give you your notebook back. Stop conniving and start thinking again. Write your own damn story."

I brooded over the Hamtramck article for the rest of the day and finally finished it before the deadline. When it got to be time to leave, my stomach was tied up in knots. Charlie might think I was over-reacting, but he wasn't the one who had to face Violet.

She had fixed an excellent piece of Coho salmon for supper, broiled in the oven and served with a baked potato and tossed salad with mandarin orange slices.

I finally gathered up my courage while washing dishes.

She gave me a slant-eyed look as she passed me a plate to wipe, "And just who is this Trevor Claybrook I'm supposed to meet at the station?"

I took a deep breath before. "Trevor Claybrook is the name Mr. Holmes used to book passage from England. From what I had been told, it might even be his real name. He's a very old friend I've known all my life."

"Are you sure he's not the great detective Sherlock Holmes?"

At the words, the plate slipped out of my hand and shattered on the floor. "What?"

"Sorry. I should have told you I found your diary. I thought you were writing a novel. It's so good I was sure you'd get it published some day when you finished it. Then I discovered your first edition *A Study in Scarlet*. Autographed to Timothy by none other than Sherlock Holmes. Imagine my surprise to find your name in the story. I had no idea Vicar Douglas and his wife let you live on the street when you were a child."

She already knew! And she was smiling. I could barely believe my fortune. "You're not angry?"

"Of course I am. I'm absolutely furious. What if you discovered I'd been a lady-of-the-night twenty years after you married me? Wouldn't you be mad, too?"

"No. Then I'd know how you learned your tricks."

She kicked my shin. Hard. It hurt, but it seemed to be small enough punishment for twenty years of deception.

We'd met in a nineteenth-century English lit class at the university. She came into the auditorium late one spring day and the only vacant seat near the door was next to me. I liked the wavy blond hair under the bonnet, and the way her nose wrinkled when she smiled. She slipped out of her sandals to show off her very small feet. Noticing my interest, she brazenly asked me to have coffee with her in the union after class. We married in our senior year. She proposed to me.

"I'm sorry I deceived you. I was afraid you wouldn't want to marry me if you knew my real background. I'm certain your parents would never have approved."

"I wouldn't have cared how you grew up unless you had robbed a bank or killed someone." She stopped. In a worried voice she said, "You didn't, did you?"

"Of course not."

"Then you had nothing to worry about. I love our life, and I couldn't care less what my parents might have thought of you."

"Um," I said. Not knowing what else to do or say, I stooped on my haunches to pick up the pieces of the plate.

"Don't. You'll cut yourself." She handed me a broom and dustpan. "None of this makes any sense whatsoever to me. How can Sherlock Holmes be a real person? Everyone knows he's just a fictional character."

"Everyone else is wrong. He's very real. It's just that Sherlock Holmes is not his real name. No one knows what it is. Not even Sir Arthur himself. He invented the name when he wrote his stories telling about the real detective's assistance to the police."

"What about Dr. Watson?"

"That dear fellow also exists, but the chronicler in the Sherlock Holmes stories was Sir Arthur himself."

She dug her fists into her hips and cocked her head. "You're just teasing me, aren't you? Why would anyone go to all the trouble to change names? Is Holmes a spy or something?"

"No, but his brother Mycroft was, and still is, a high-ranking member in the Admiralty Office. He feared that if his brother's exploits were publicized, his own identity would become known. The Office learned of Sir Arthur's plans to publish the great detective's adventures and demanded that the names in the stories be changed. Sir Arthur agreed. The Diogenes Club is the name the Admiralty Office took for itself. They were always looking for credible information from reliable sources. In other words, honest men."

Her scowl gradually disappeared as I finished sweeping up the shards of the plate. "Were you as good a detective as you appear to be in your diary?"

I unintentionally broke into a grin. "You'll have to ask Mr. Holmes about that. All I know is that he always relied on my information when he was involved in a case. He and his brother provided most of the money that sent me to the University of Michigan."

The scowl returned. "I can't believe you never told me this. It sounds as if you have as many secrets as the Holmes brothers themselves."

I wondered if she knew how close to the truth she had come. "Not nearly as many, my dear. All I'm asking you to do is meet Mr. Holmes at the train station and see he gets to the Royal Palm Hotel."

"How will I know him? Will he be wearing a cape and deerstalker cap?"

"I doubt it very much," I said with a laugh. "He'll recognize you. You'll be carrying one of Cameron's U of M pennants and wearing a beanie. I wired the train office to pass on the message, so he'll know what to look for. Go Wolverines."

She giggled. "Then you'll have to leave the Chevrolet for me."

"Not on your life," I said. "You don't even know how to signal your turns and someone will crash into you. I have the trolley schedule."

"I do too know the signals. Arm up is right turn, arm straight is left turn, and arm down is stop. So there." She stuck her tongue out at me.

"N-O."

"Spoil sport," she said. Unlike every other woman I knew, Violet wanted to drive. She pestered me about it. Only one of the unfortunate consequences of her being a feminist I had to endure. "Oh, all right."

I gave her a hug. "Thanks m'dear."

CHAPTER 4

Next morning, the phone rang as I was at my desk writing up my meeting with the mayor. "Wiggins."

The phone crackled, then cleared for a long-familiar voice. "Good morning, my good man. Hard at work, I suspect."

"Holmes!" I blurted. I said it loud enough I was sure others could hear me, but, looking about, no one seemed interested. "Where are you?"

"In the lobby of the Royal Palm Hotel. Can you break away for a midday repast sometime soon?"

The clock on the wall behind my desk said 11:15. "I can leave right now. Should I meet you at the Royal Palm?"

"Yes. I've bought a copy of your newspaper. You will find me sitting behind it in the lobby. Your piece about the progress of the police inquiries into Houdini's death is quite excellent. I can hear your voice very clearly in it."

"High praise indeed. I'll see you in ten minutes."

THE DOORMAN OPENED the door to the hotel lobby. Passersby on the parkway must have been surprised to see a middle-aged man in suit and tie dashing down the street, quite unable to understand why I didn't take a cab. After daubing my forehead with my handkerchief, I took a quick look at the denizens of the lobby. Only one was hidden behind a newspaper.

As I approached, the paper lowered and a familiar face appeared. "For shame, Wiggins. You are more than four minutes early. I should have guessed you had a better grasp of the distance and time than that."

I answered in a firm voice. "Ten minutes was walking time, sir. As you can plainly see, I didn't walk."

"Ah, yes, of course. My mistake. I'm flattered by your obvious desire to see me. Other than your dampness, you don't appear to be any the worse for your sprint. I do see you've added a few pounds about your middle, and your hair has added a hint of gray. Otherwise you look much the same as the last time I saw you."

"As do you." I dropped into the chair next to him and gasped in a deep breath before continuing. "Remarkably so, I would say. How was your voyage?"

Mr. Holmes raised the newspaper and held it in a position to shield our conversation. "A bit rough at mid-ocean, but pleasant enough otherwise. Unfortunately, I barely slept on the train. Tell me, have you heard anything from Sir Arthur recently?"

"No. Should I have?"

"I talked to him and suggested he contact you. A letter may still be in the mails. When last I spoke to Sir Arthur just before I sailed, he said he's very sorry for Mrs. Weiss's loss, and he regrets his falling out with her husband."

"Mrs. Weiss? I had heard that Mr. Houdini and Sir Arthur had had a falling out, but Sir Arthur must be very angry indeed if he's using Houdini's real last name."

"Perceptive as ever, I see," Holmes said.

"Houdini's denial of his own supposed supernatural gifts infuriated Sir Arthur. Worse, the magician's insistence on exposing other mediums as frauds finally drove our friend to distraction."

I shook my head. "I still can't believe how poor Sir Arthur could continue to believe in Spiritualism after Houdini and other investigators showed every proported medium to be a charlatan."

Holmes nodded somberly. "Quite so, but it seems Sir Arthur's standards for being a medium are a bit different from most. He doesn't require them to prove physical contacts with the dead as evidence of spiritualistic power. Even the resorting to trickery doesn't necessarily disqualify someone. To his thinking, twenty percent genuine contacts is more than enough."

"Do you know how much he's paid to the mediums he's visited?"

"Not in exact sums, but I know from his published contributions it is not an insubstantial part of his fortune. I believe it is all because he takes great comfort from the purported messages his son Kingsley sends to him from the beyond. Sir Arthur has attended hundreds of séances. One can only wonder why Kingsley hasn't had a bit more to say other than that all is well, he is happy, and that he misses his father very much."

I nodded. "Hasn't the poor man required some sort of proof? I could fob myself off as a medium, couldn't I? How would he know?"

"A very good point, Wiggins. Many of the mediums were said to have produced messages containing facts and events that only Sir Arthur and his son could have known. It invariably turned out they came from sources our friend didn't know about."

I could tell from his expression that he shared my low opinion of the ghouls that feasted on people's grief. We both knew Sir Arthur has dreamed for years of combining science and religion. We both feared that his agonized quest for contact with his dead son and others he had lost finally overcame his critical faculties regarding Spiritualism.

Holmes lowered the newspaper and folded it. Laying it on the table in front of him, he said, "Well, Wiggins, it's time to get something to eat. I avoided breakfast on the train and I'm famished. We can continue our conversation over our meal. I will trust to your judgment where we should eat."

"We needn't go far. The hotel restaurant has excellent food."

ORDERS TAKEN, HOLMES rubbed his hands together. "Now, give me all the details of Houdini's last show. I'm very pleased to hear you were there."

"I wish I could say I felt the same way. You are quite correct, however. Violet and I were at the Garrick Theatre on Halloween eve. Everyone was in a festive mood, and the band was playing the Houdini's theme song, *Sweet Rosabelle*, for all it was worth. But from the moment Houdini took the stage, I knew something was wrong with him. He performed badly from curtain-up, and seemed terribly distracted. His stage career deserved a better ending."

"Indeed it did. And so did his life."

"Yes, but in a perverse way, I felt that his death on Halloween day seemed to close an eerie circle. You are probably aware that among his last words was the promise he would communicate with his wife from beyond the grave."

"He must have believed in what Spiritualism stood for, if not in mediums. And has Sir Arthur contacted Mrs. Houdini? Like it or not, she's joined the ranks of the Spiritualists herself."

"True, but I have no idea. We hardly even know each other."

"Ironic, isn't it? Both Sir Arthur and Houdini believed in communication from the departed. The only difference between them is Houdini could never be satisfied with the results of his attempts, and Sir Arthur was rarely dissatisfied. What happened after the show?"

"A doctor examined Houdini backstage and discovered he had a 104 degree temperature."

"I expect he was taken directly to the hospital, then."

"Unbelievable as it may seem, the Houdinis returned to their hotel. Dr. Leo Dretzka had examined him before the performance. The examination in and of itself is a very curious event. From what Bess Houdini says, Dretzka asked the magician if he wanted to perform that night or go directly to the hospital. Houdini was running a fever and should never have waited so long, though, from what I hear, it wouldn't have mattered a whit. The poison from the ruptured appendix had spread too far."

Mr. Holmes nodded, his eyes taking on a familiar sparkle. "I see. This is turning out to be much more interesting than I originally imagined. Continue."

At his words, years melted away and I began to feel we had become colleagues once more.

"At the hotel, Daniel Cohn, the new doctor on duty, called for an ambulance and one showed up almost immediately. I caught a glimpse of Houdini's face when they wheeled him out. It was drenched in sweat, but he lay quietly on the stretcher. We on the street watched the ambulance as it drove to the end of the block and turned left. I remember the wail of the hand-cranked siren sounding for a several seconds after it disappeared from sight."

"Did you go to the hospital?"

"Not that night, but I was there at six the next morning. I was told that Houdini had had two surgeries during the night and now lay clinging to life. No one but Bess and his brother were allowed to see him. I wrote his obituary for the *Free Press*. 'Died: Harry Houdini at 1:26 PM in Room 410 Corridor D, in the John R. wing of Grace Hospital at the age of 56.' I still feel a genuine sense of loss. We both came from humble beginnings and worked our way up. He was probably the greatest illusionist and showman that ever lived, and I'm sure no one will ever equal him."

"I agree." He looked at me. "You look pensive. Is something troubling you?"

"I just realized he was only fourteen years older than I am. I know I have been aging, but I didn't realize I had gotten so old."

Mr. Holmes reached out to pat my arm. "Ridiculous, Wiggins. No matter how old or young Mr. Houdini was, you will remain the same brilliant, mischievous boy forever."

At a loss for words, I took a quick bite of my filet mignon.

Holmes' Beef Wellington remained untouched. I reminded him that it was getting cold, but he waved me off and pushed on with his questions. *Fur Elise* playing from the piano in the corner of the restaurant made our close conversation seem intimate.

"Are there any other eye-witness accounts of what happened at the theatre?"

"Len Hopkins wrote a feature article. I'll happily get you a copy of it, but it doesn't vary much from what I've told you."

"I see," Holmes said, cutting the first piece of his lunch. "Is the hospital where he died near enough to walk?"

"Yes. But I have to get back to work to finish my article, so we'll take a cab. Why do you want to go there?"

"I'm amazed you should ask, Wiggins. I want to talk to the attending physician and the others present at the surgery. Perhaps it wasn't peritonitis that caused his demise. Did you know that Houdini received nearly a hundred death threats last year?"

"No, but I'm not surprised. Every medium in the country feared him. He invited them to his show to perform their tricks on stage after his magical performances. Only one ever came close to fooling him. Mina Croydon, also called Margery. I'm sure you must have heard of her."

"Ah yes. The White Witch of Lime Street. Sir Arthur has been touting her as the greatest medium in the world for years. Absolutely sterling credentials, he says."

"Not quite. Houdini showed how she performed every one of her tricks, or at least he said he did. Some say there were other phenomena he couldn't explain away."

"Be that as it may, his assertions infuriated Sir Arthur so much that he broke off all communications with Houdini. Sir Arthur isn't the only one of that opinion, either. Some very important psychic researchers regard her highly, too. We shall want to visit her, but, from what I have heard, that may not be easy."

I stopped in mid-sip of my water. "We? She lives in Boston. That's halfway across the country from here. This isn't Britain where we're only a few hours away from anywhere. It would take days, and I'm not sure I can get away."

Mr. Holmes tapped at the side of his nose. "That has already been taken care of, my good man. I contacted the owner of your newspaper by telephone, and Mr. Scripps is absolutely delighted to find a possible front-page story that his rival Mr. Hearst knows nothing about. He has agreed to put you on special assignment at my expense. Mr. Hoffman will be assuming your beat until we are finished."

I could barely believe my ears. A chance to investigate a story involving two of the most famous personalities in the world would make me the star reporter on both sides of the Atlantic. And to be able to associate with Mr. Holmes again to do it made it a joy beyond belief.

"If you want to talk to Margery, I expect we may have to pay for a séance," I said.

Holmes paused to cut off a piece of his Wellington. "She doesn't charge for them, and even if she did, it would be money well spent. Especially if she isn't aware of who we are or why we're there."

Our waiter appeared at our table and noticed my friend's full plate. In a worried voice he asked, "Is there something wrong with the food, sir? If so, we will happily replace it with another dish."

"I have no complaint. The meat is excellent, though not quite as succulent and well-aged as that which we serve in Britain. I hope you get an opportunity to try our Angus beef from Scotland someday. It truly is incomparable."

The waiter suppressed a smile. "I'm sure it is, sir. Your food is cold. Would you like me to warm your plate?"

"Unnecessary. We will be leaving in a few minutes--unless you would like some more mineral water, Wiggins. I thought it quite good."

"Nothing more for me, thank you."

Left to his own designs, Holmes dispatched the rest of his lunch in a few larger than gentlemanly-sized bites. The waiter returned to remove the plate. "Would you like dessert?"

"Might you perchance have Spotted Dick?"

The waiter's mouth gaped.

I stepped in before he could reply. "It's not what you may think. It's an English dessert made out of suet. I'm sure you've never even heard of it."

"I'm afraid we don't, sir," the waiter said.

"Too bad. It is quite delicious," Holmes said as he took out his wallet. Handing the man a twenty-dollar bill, he said, "I hope this is enough to cover our food. It's more than four pounds sterling."

I took the banknote from the waiter and passed it back to Mr. Holmes. Taking out my own billfold, I handed the young man five dollars. "Please keep the change."

CHAPTER 5

In a matter of minutes we were on our way to Grace Hospital. In Detroit, the downtown folds in on itself along the river, and nearly everything is within walking distance, though more people seem to be driving motor cars every day. Lusty young people crowd the saloons on Friday and Saturday nights, and weekend days attract whole families. I always find it amazing that a one-time site for a circus, now long abandoned, should become such a bustling gathering place. The Statler Hotel, where Houdini stayed on his last visit, was near the hospital, less than a block from the Garrick Theatre.

In the cab, Holmes sat forward in his seat carefully observing his surroundings. My friend's remarkable facility to instantly take in every detail, then as quickly forget it when it is no longer of any importance, remained strong as ever.

"I expect Houdini's ambulance followed much the same route on the fateful night."

"Yes. It's the quickest way."

"Why do you suppose he put off seeking professional help for so long? The pain must have been excruciating."

I shook my head. "I have no idea, though I know he lived with pain from his escapes most of his adult life, and seldom saw a doctor. He had hundreds of imitators, in Europe especially. Quite a few even claimed to be him. He hunted them all down."

"The best always have their imitators."

"Even worse were the ones who tied him so tightly with wires they broke through the skin and muscles, all the way to the bone. Then there were the ones who used locks with plugged keyholes and fouled mechanisms so he couldn't pick them. The poor man broke an ankle in Albany in mid-October and had to perform on it for all his final shows. Imagine standing for three hours a night on an aching foot."

Holmes shook his head. "His ankle wasn't his biggest problem, it would seem."

"I wonder if he felt he was coming to the end of his stage career and wanted to make sure he made the most of his performances."

Holmes cocked his head back and closed his eyes in contemplation. "Hmm, yes. I suppose that's possible. Were there any individuals of particular importance in the audience that Saturday night?"

"Good question. I know Mayor Smith and his wife were there, as were Mr. and Mrs. Henry Ford and son Edsel. I think I heard that Governor and Mrs. Green had come in from Lansing. Any others, I can't say offhand."

"I see."

I recognized Holmes's expression. It was the same whenever he worked through a vexing puzzle. We didn't talk for the rest of the ride.

We entered through the hospital's heavily paned main entrance. A woman wearing a crisp nurse's hat and friendly smile greeted us. When I showed her my press card, the smile vanished, and she turned her back to us. After an over-the-shoulder look in our direction, she picked up her phone. The call lasted longer than I expected, and Holmes and I traded quizzical glances. At last she hung up and returned. "Mr. Beaufort is on his way here to talk to you. He's the hospital administrator."

"Administrator?" Holmes echoed in an angry voice.

"Yes. He'll answer all your questions."

I shook my head. "We were hoping to talk with the people who were here when Mr. Houdini was brought in."

"That won't be possible," said a deep baritone voice.

Andre Beaufort, more than six-feet tall and solidly built, stood before me. The perfect palace guard, I expected to see him cross his arms across his chest. Instead he greeted us with a cautious smile and welcoming hand.

Mr. Holmes refused to shake it. I did, and nearly got my fingers broken.

"What do you mean that's not possible?" Holmes asked sharply. "Aren't they on duty at this time?"

"I'm truly sorry, but I can't respond to that, either. All I can say is that the hospital is not allowed to answer any further public inquiries, only those from the police."

"Has there been an inquest?" I asked.

"That's something you'll have to find out from the authorities. I'm puzzled by your belated interest in Mr. Houdini's death, Mr. Wiggins. He passed away more than a week ago, and we've kept your paper abreast of all the developments."

"Your reports have been sketchy, at best." I said.

"I'm curious as to why we can't speak to his care providers," Mr. Holmes said. "Is there some concern the hospital may face some liability for Mr. Houdini's treatment here?"

Beaufort glared at him. "None whatsoever. We did everything we could to help him. Unfortunately he was well past saving when he arrived. And to make things clear, it's Mrs. Houdini who's responsible for the suppression of information, and not Grace Hospital. Mr. Houdini was removed from here the day after his passing. From what I understand, no one has viewed the body since he died."

"Why such secrecy?" Mr. Holmes asked. "It sounds as if someone is trying to keep something from the public."

"Make of it what you will. I've heard that Mr. Houdini's brother has taken possession of all of the stage props and books, and Mr. Houdini's body was sent back to New York in his stage coffin. As to what happened after the show Saturday night, that information will have to come from the police."

"Thank you," Mr. Holmes said in an icy tone. "We appreciate your help. Come along, Wiggins."

Beaufort stood in place and watched us leave the hospital.

"Things get more intriguing all the time, don't they?" I said lightly.

Mr. Holmes squinted. "Indeed, but if good Mr. Beaufort thinks we can't come up with other ways to find out what we need to know, he's sadly mistaken."

AT 4:30 THAT AFTERNOON, I was at my desk finishing my article for the morning edition when the teletype machine in the next room came to life. As a beat reporter for the *Free Press,* I had a direct link with the downtown police precinct. I immediately turned on radio station KOP for further details. *The Detroit Free Press* and *Detroit News* also have their own stations, WCX and WWJ respectively, and I once jokingly asked why people would pay a nickel for our papers when they could get their news by radio for free. The first reports of Houdini's illness came over KOP at eleven o'clock at night on Halloween Eve.

The new alert had more than the usual interest for me.

Officer McDaniels reports elderly man—I smiled at the words—*unconscious on sidewalk in front of Vinton Building at Woodward and Congress. Subject poorly dressed and has no identification. Emergency vehicle called to scene. Subject taken to Grace Hospital Emergency for observation.*

I had the number for the hospital in my desk index, but I knew it by heart, having called it so often. GLendale 0090.

"Hello, this is Timothy Wiggins of the *Free Press.* I cover the police and crime beat. I just got a report of an unidentified elderly man being taken to your hospital. Has he been admitted?"

"Yes," a female voice answered. Luckily it didn't sound like the woman who had greeted us on our afternoon visit. "Do you know who he is? He doesn't seem to be able to tell us."

"I think it may be my uncle. Does he have an English accent?"

"Yes. Sort of like yours."

"Then I'm sure his name is Ralph Howard—at least that's the way it's spelled. It's pronounced 'Rafe.' He left the house without telling us where he was going this morning, and we haven't heard from him since. We've been worried about him. What's his condition?"

"He's awake and alert, though he seems quite agitated. We thought he might have had a heart attack or stroke, but all his vital signs are fine."

"Would you kindly ask him if 'Rafe' is his name? I'm sure he'll answer to it. If it is, please call me back, and I'll be down to pick him up later on this evening."

"His doctor wants to keep him under observation for the night, but we should be able to release him sometime tomorrow."

I paused before continuing. "I'm sure he won't want to spend the night alone, and he can be rather difficult. Assuming it is Uncle Ralph, would it be permissible for me to stay overnight with him?"

"I'll have to ask the doctor, but I'm almost certain it will be. May I have your phone number?"

"RAndolph 8911. Please see he gets a private room. I'll bring a draft for the hospital charges with me when I arrive."

Ten minutes later I got the call. The elderly man was indeed "Uncle Ralph." The doctor said I'd be welcome to stay the night with him.

After handing my article to Harold Mitchell for final editing before going to press, I called Violet to let her know I wouldn't be home that night. I knew what would happen. She tee-heed in excitement and demanded I tell her everything to the tiniest detail when I returned. My shin still hurt where she kicked me, so I promised I would.

Remembering the receptionist might still be on duty and recognize me, I pulled the slouch hat I kept at the office low over my eyes, then bundled myself in the bulky Chesterfield to help to disguise my size. Charlie Hoffman covered his mouth and snorted when he saw me.

The weather had turned colder since that afternoon, but not yet wintry. I hoped I wasn't too conspicuous. Strolling at a leisurely pace to kill time, I still got to the hospital in fifteen minutes.

I sighed in relief when I found a different receptionist at the desk. A young blonde woman, well-doused with Evening in Paris, snuffed out a cigarette before handing me a clipboard and pen. A new-fangled tall radio set behind her desk blared out a turkey trot. It was the first time I had ever heard music over the airwaves and wondered if this would be a major part of that fascinating invention's future. Turning down the loudness, she said, "Your uncle is in E wing, room 611. Please sign in on line five."

I scribbled a signature, making it as illegible as possible. I didn't want Andre Beaufort to be able to read it if he checked the guest roster. I knew I would likely become *persona non grata* at the hospital if he discovered it was me. That'd end my crime beat with the paper for sure.

"I'll have an attendant escort you, Mr. . . . Uh . . . I'm sorry, what does that say?"

I smiled. First hurdle cleared. "Higgins. Jimmy Higgins."

She held the board closer to her eyes and turned it from side to side. "Oh, yes. Mr. Higgins it is. You won't be able to get to his room alone. Visiting hours haven't started yet."

As she spoke, the door behind her opened and a young man in white appeared.

"Allen, please escort Mr. Higgins to 611."

A long walk and an elevator ride later, Allen pointed to a closed door, his finger to his lips. "He may be sleeping. I'll look in on him first."

He gently rapped on the door and opened it. Seconds later he gestured for me to follow.

"Uncle Ralph" lay propped up on the bed in a sitting position. He threw me a sharp look and set the copy of the *Saturday Evening Post* on the bed next to him. "It's about time you got here, nephew," he said in a suitably irascible tone.

"Hello, uncle. You had us worried."

"Nonsense. There's nothing wrong with me. Why are they keeping me here over night?"

"Don't you remember being brought here by ambulance?"

"I have no idea what you're talking about."

Allen shuffled his feet nervously. "Have a good night," he mumbled before ducking out.

I shut the door. "So far, so good."

Holmes rubbed his hands together. "Better than good, old friend. The ambulance attendant was in a chatty mood to ease my ride to the hospital. He says he was with Houdini when he was brought in. He also told me Dr. Charles S. Kennedy, Houdini's surgeon, is the attending physician tonight."

"How do you expect to learn anything from him?"

"Professional pride, dear fellow."

I wasn't sure if I knew what he meant, but at that moment the nurse came into the room. "I'm nurse Preston and it's time to take your temperature, Mr. Howard." She made a gesture in my direction. "You'll have to leave for a minute or two."

Impossible to hide a smile, I got up from my chair. The nurse pulled the curtain around the bed.

Seconds later, Holmes bellowed, "What do you intend to do with that?"

"I'm sure you must have had your temperature taken before, haven't you? Roll over on your stomach."

"I will not! I'm perfectly capable of taking my own temperature. Now give that to me."

I heard sounds of a scuffle.

"Don't. That's not . . ."

I couldn't suppress gagging and laughing at the same time, so I made a dash for the hallway. After several peeps through the door I finally saw the curtain pulled away from the bed.

Both Holmes and the nurse were beet red.

"I apologize for my uncle," I stammered. "He isn't used to hospitals. It's too bad all the patients aren't as nice as Mr. Houdini was."

It was a shot in the dark.

"He was. Everyone in the hospital was excited that he was a patient here. I'm sure we all must have looked in on him at one time or another."

"Were you ever his nurse?"

"No." Her voice turned wary. "And I can't tell you who was. We've all been sworn to secrecy."

"I can understand that," I said. "I'm sure the poor man must have been in terrible pain."

"We all felt sorry for him. After surgery, he woke up early in the morning and tried to get out of bed, saying it was important to get back on stage to finish his act. He was so agitated when he heard everyone had already left the theater, it took three attendants restrain him."

Eyebrows raised, Holmes and I traded satisfied glances. Nurse Preston had managed to maintain medical confidentiality and at the same time tell us all we wanted to know.

"Is there anything I can get for you?" the nurse asked. "Do you need some fresh water?"

"I'm quite fine, thank you," Holmes said.

"Then . . . I guess I'll be on my way . . ." she said in a halting voice. "Let me know if there's anything you need." She paused and averted her eyes. "I'll have to get another temperature later."

"I'll be counting the seconds to your return," Holmes said dryly. "Have a good rest."

We both held our breath until she left the room.

"What do you make of that, Wiggins?"

"Incredible. We know he did finish his act . . . unless . . ."

Mr. Holmes arched an eyebrow. "Unless what?"

"Unless he was planning to expose another fraudulent medium and hadn't been able to get to it."

He beamed at me. "Exactly what I was thinking, dear fellow. If so, I would very much like to know who that may have been."

I felt my blood rising. Everything so far was working better than we could have hoped for. "So would I. We have hours ahead of us. Do you play backgammon? I brought a board and some checkers."

"I've heard of the game, of course, but I'm afraid I've never played. I'm sure I can learn it if you explain it to me."

I laid the checkerboard in front of me and turned it over to reveal a backgammon board. I put the red pieces in their proper places. "Set your checkers as a mirror-image of mine. I'll get out the dice."

Learning the movements of the men by the roll of the dice and the building of safe points took but a few rolls. Within fifteen minutes he was playing with the skill of a veteran player.

On our first play with one die each, he rolled a six and I a one.

"Aha! Six-one. I see I can build my seven point. Just try to leap now."

I didn't like his tone of voice. Some rolls later he had a lock-out, all six contiguous points in front of him built, and I had one of my pieces sitting helplessly on the edge of the board waiting for a chance to come back in. It was every backgammon player's nightmare.

I glared at him. "You haven't been truthful with me, Mr. Holmes. I can tell you've played the game before. Undoubtedly many times."

"I have not, but there's hardly anything to it. All one needs is a rudimentary knowledge of mathematical probability and an eye for the strategic deployment of pieces, but—mostly—a large dose of luck. The element of luck alone makes the game no match for the skills required to play chess."

Blood rising, I asked, "What about the occasions when you have alternatively good options? Or alternatively disastrous?"

He shrugged. "Those are out of my hands. Do you wish to concede?"

"Absolutely not! Play on, MacDuff."

He did, and I got gammoned. All my pieces were still on the board when he removed the last of his. I'd been playing the game for years and didn't like being beaten so easily by a rank beginner. In my anger I didn't tell him I had just lost a double game.

"Beginner's luck," I growled. "Place your pieces. I want a rematch."

"This all seems rather pointless," Holmes protested. "I can see no reason for a player to resign, no matter how hopeless his game may be. All he need do is play on and hope for a miracle."

I decided it was impolitic to tell him about gammons and backgammons, or the use of the doubling cube that raised the price of losing exponentially every time it was turned, or that contestants usually played for money. Though he was obviously bored, we played on. I won the occasional game. His evening meal arrived at 6:30.

He took one look at the salad greens without dressing, chicken broth, gelatin dessert, and tea and ordered me to fetch him something substantial to eat. The best I could do was a ham sandwich on rye from the automat in the hospital restaurant. I delivered it in a napkin when I returned to his room.

He grumbled with every bite, then finished his tray after he was done with the sandwich. "Hardly enough to feed a partridge."

"I don't remember you being such a hearty eater," I said.

"I get bored when I'm away from my laboratory. When is that damnable physician supposed to be here?"

His mood didn't improve when I suggested we go back to our backgammon games.

"An utter waste of time, Wiggins."

"Checkers, then?"

His nostrils flared. "An even bigger waste. I learned all the move combinations years ago so every game will end in a draw or a victory for me. I'm surprised you haven't done so, too. Why didn't you bring your chess set?"

I didn't want to tell him it was because I never could beat him, so I turned on the radio next to the bed. I had been told every single-patient room in the hospital had a radio. With a derisive snort, Mr. Holmes rolled onto his side to catch a nap.

It lasted but a few minutes, ending with a knock on the door.

Not wanting to be seen by someone who might recognize me, I made a dash for the loo. I was glad I did when I heard the voice.

"Good evening to you. How are we feeling this evening?"

"Our dear queen and I am quite well, thank you. Are you Dr. Kennedy?"

Dr. Kennedy sounded as though he was taken aback. "I am. And I take it you are Ralph Howard."

"The same. I understand you were Harry Houdini's surgeon."

I hadn't expected Mr. Holmes to move in for the kill so quickly. Obviously, neither had Dr. Kennedy. Caught off guard, the doctor stammered. "Uh, that's what it says in the papers. And that is all I will say about it."

"You may be required to be a bit more forthcoming in the future, Doctor. Continental Life Insurance has a sizable policy on Mr. Houdini that must pay a double benefit for accidental death. You can understand that we want to be very sure his death was indeed accidental."

"Is that so?" Dr. Kennedy said icily. "Then I'll certainly lodge a complaint with your company. You gained entry to our hospital by feigning illness and now accuse me of malpractice. Your gall astonishes me."

Mr. Holmes's tone softened. "I'm making no such accusation, Doctor. I've heard rumors from the police that Mr. Houdini's death was not caused by a ruptured appendix, but may be the result of a homicide. Poisoning, most likely."

I could imagine the doctor's eyes widening in astonishment. Finally the pot boiled over. "I'm not supposed to talk about this, but that rumor is patently false. There's no doubt in my mind that he had peritonitis caused by the bursting of a septic appendix. His whole stomach was inflamed. We flushed it several times with saline solution to clear it."

I waited for the next exchange. Finally Mr. Holmes said, "Is such inflammation common with peritonitis?"

"It can be."

"What happened to the appendix after it was removed?"

"I sent it to the hospital laboratory."

"And they confirmed your diagnosis?"

The doctor sighed angrily. "Absolutely. Now I have nothing more to say."

Holmes didn't quit, "Why did you perform a second operation?"

"No comment."

I heard Mr. Holmes swing out of his bed. I was also sure I heard the doctor take a step backward.

"You knew Mr. Houdini was struck in the stomach between performances in Montreal. Would the blow have been sufficient to rupture the appendix?"

After a moment's silence, Kennedy, still angry, said, "Possibly. I've never heard of such a thing though. All I know is Mr. Houdini should have been hospitalized long ago. By his own admission he had been sick for more than two weeks when he arrived in Detroit."

"I'll make my report," Mr. Holmes said. "You can be sure your name will not come up as the source of my information. As things stand, I can't see how we can come to any other conclusion than that Mr. Houdini's death was accidental."

In a voice so icy it nearly froze me, Kennedy said, "And I will write in my report that you appear to have recovered and should be released tomorrow morning if nothing occurs during the night. To be honest, I'm very tempted to throw you out on your ear right now. I also want it clear I never want you to come within a mile of this hospital again, and will call for your arrest if you do."

"Quite understandable. I shall not."

I heard the door to the room slam closed, and stepped out.

"Looks as if you can go back to your nap."

Still in ill humor, Mr. Holmes turned on his side and soon began to snore. I listened to the radio for a while and slouched in my chair. I must have dozed off myself for I awoke some time later with Mr. Holmes, dressed in robe and slippers, shaking me.

"Wake up, Wiggins. We have work to do."

I came to with a start. "What time is it?"

"Eleven-thirty. I have heard no one in the hall for nearly an hour."

I stretched and got to my feet.

"I expect you know where the records are kept?" Holmes said.

"I do. I've gone there to get information for my articles on numerous occasions. We do have a trek ahead of us, though."

"Then let us begin," he said.

The hallway outside the door was dark. A ways ahead, a light indicated the nurse's station. I took the lead in case she suddenly appeared.

Fortunately she wasn't at her desk, and we took the stairway down to the first floor. Opening the door to the hallway, I suddenly didn't re-member which way to go.

"Is there a problem?" Holmes asked in a near whisper.

"A small one."

I caught sight of a linen-covered window. Pulling back the curtain, I saw the lights along the Detroit River. "This way," I said heading to the right.

We followed a dimly lit hallway between doors with gilded letters on their windows.

"These are obviously the business offices," Holmes muttered. "Do we need to worry about security?"

"Somewhat. The hospital has a guard who makes regular rounds. One of his stops is here." I pointed to a keyhole in the wall next to a door marked "Bursar."

"I take it you brought your tools, Wiggins. I hope you haven't forgotten your skill with locks."

Before I could answer, I heard whistling beyond the door to the lobby. It seemed to be coming towards us. I dashed for one of the unmarked doors and turned the knob. Locked. Grabbing my astonished friend by the arm, I pulled him toward the second unmarked door. This one opened. I pushed him inside, with me a step behind. The door to the janitor's closet closed just as the door to the hallway opened.

The whistling stopped.

Had I left something behind?

In a panic, I grabbed the door knob just as whoever was in the hallway tried to turn it. Luckily the knob was at its locked position and it didn't move with me holding it in place. The guard, or so I assumed, tried two more times before giving up. Then, once again, the person returned to whistling "I'll See You in My Dreams."

Rather badly off-key, I have to say.

I kept my ear pressed closely against the door and took tiny breaths for several minutes, listening for movement in the hallway. Finally I heard the door to the lobby open and close.

Even though the coast was clear, I waited in silence another two minutes before turning the knob and stepping out.

Mr. Holmes's disposition remained testy. "That was uncomfortably close. I shouldn't like another such fright again tonight."

"It was no stroll in the park for me, either, my dear sir. I hope we can finish our task without further incident."

Pressing my ear against the lobby door, I heard a radio playing. It had to be the one next to the reception desk. The guards, all members of the Detroit Police, kept it tuned to KOP in case emergencies were referred during the time they were working at the hospital. It undoubtedly had announced Houdini's arrival on the fateful night. Most likely, the officer was just a few feet away.

"This won't do," I mumbled.

"Shall we return to the room?" Mr. Holmes asked.

"No. I have a better idea."

He watched as I took out my pick from my pocket. I chose the door marked Public Relations and unlocked it.

The room had a large square desk, several filing cabinets, and walls full of photographs. The phone was all that interested me, and I dialed the hospital number.

To my relief, the guard answered. "Grace Hospital Security Desk."

"Hello. This is Doctor Wheeler. I'm on third floor and I thought I heard a strange noise in the hallway. Would you mind coming up to investigate?"

"Not at all. I'll be right up."

Mr. Holmes stood leaning against the door. I joined him.

The radio turned off. I waited until I was sure he had time to get on the elevator and cautiously opened the door.

The lobby was empty, and the records office stood ten feet away.

Mr. Holmes patted me on my back. "Well done, Wiggins. I see you haven't lost any of your ingenuity over the years."

"Thanks, but we won't have much time. I have no idea how to find the chart we want."

"Hopefully it will be located in alphabetical order."

As feared, the door to the records office was the least of our problems.

The shades to the office were drawn and the room as black as a priest-hole at midnight. I fumbled for the light switch. Turning it on, I let out a groan. I had forgotten the battery of files standing six feet high around the entire office.

Finding the right file drawer for the "Hs" by trial and error took longer than I hoped. The "HO" section ended with "Hopkins."

"Any suggestions?" I asked.

"I see there are many records sitting on top of the cabinet. Perhaps the one we want hasn't been put away yet."

I doubted it would be among them and, unfortunately, was proven correct. We had wasted more than ten minutes, and I wondered how long it would take for the guard to return.

"Maybe the hospital doesn't keep his file with the others," I said.

Mr. Holmes had moved to another cabinet. "These are files for the various physicians. You don't suppose . . ."

He stopped short at the sound of someone moving in the lobby. My worst fears were confirmed with the sound of the radio. Not only did we not have Houdini's medical file but we were trapped in the office until the guard made another inspection round.

After remaining frozen in place for what seemed an eternity, I tip-toed to stand next to Mr. Holmes.

The first drawer creaked when we pushed it back in.

With a shrug we opened the drawer beneath it. A large manila marker with the name Leonard Kennedy stood at the front.

I squatted and began to finger through the files. One was turned backwards. Turning it around showed the word *Confidential* in block letters on the front. Instead of a name it had 10/30/26 written at the top.

There was no disguising whose file it was.

We both whirled at the sound of the door opening in back of us.

CHAPTER 6

 blue-shirted officer stood near the door, a revolver in his hand. "I thought I heard noises in here. Put your hands up." We did.

"Let's go to the desk so I can call the station."

I took a step forward, then stopped in my tracks. At first I had been too frightened to recognize the voice. Then I did. "It wouldn't be Officer Michael O'Reilly, now, would it?"

The officer looked startled. "How do you know that?"

"I'm the one who cleared you when your former partner was smuggling heroin in from Canada and tried to blame it on you—"

O'Reilly stepped forward to take a closer look. "Wiggins? What are you doing here?"

"My job. We're trying to find out what really happened to Houdini before he died."

"The coroner says he died of an appendicitis attack."

"We think he may have been poisoned. There's only one way to know for sure."

"Fine, but you know very well this isn't the way to do it. You have to leave."

"We don't have any choice. Someone put out a gag order."

O'Reilly motioned toward Mr. Holmes. "Who's this?"

"Dr. Trevor Claybrook, Timothy's uncle," Holmes said.

"What do you intend to do with the file? I can't let you walk away with it."

Without waiting for permission, Holmes opened the folder. "Give me five minutes. No one will ever realize it's been disturbed."

36

O'Reilly looked hesitant, then holstered his weapon. "Five minutes. If any of this ever gets out, I'll be fired. If I do," he gestured toward his holster, "I'll come looking for you."

"I promise you, it won't get out," I said.

I found a place to sit on a sturdy pile of unfiled medical records. A short time later, Mr. Holmes set the file back into the cabinet. "Very interesting," he said. "There is much to consider here."

O'REILLY LED US to the elevators. I thanked him and he left us. I expected to get a report whilst we waited, but Mr. Holmes refused to speak until we were back in the room.

"Are you going to tell me now, or are you going to make me wait some more?"

"No need to get feisty, Wiggins. I merely wanted time to digest all the new information. Would you pour me some water, please?"

Grumbling under my breath, I filled the tumbler from his table and handed it to him.

"Thank you. To begin with, most of what Dr. Kennedy told us and what appeared in your paper is correct. Mr. Houdini's appendix was inflamed. Whether it had burst naturally or was affected by the blow to the abdomen are other matters entirely."

My ill temper disappeared immediately. "Why do you say that?"

"There's a photograph of the appendix in Dr. Kennedy's file. It appears to be normal to me."

"Not to denigrate your innumerable skills, but you're not a physician."

"Quite so. That's why I took the picture out of the file. I'll have Sir Arthur take a look at it for me."

"You're going to mail the photo to him? We won't hear from him for quite a while."

"He's waiting for us in Boston. I wired him the first night I was aboard ship. He isn't too happy about it, but he agrees it was in his best interests to make the trip. In the meantime, we can pay a visit to Dr. Cohn in the morning. He has an office not far from here."

CHAPTER 7

With all the excitement of the day, I barely slept. The indefatigable Sherlock Holmes snored heavily the entire night. When he woke, he had the nerve to say I looked peaked. His ill humor had left him. Now I had it.

Breakfast of bacon, toast, scrambled eggs, and orange juice arrived at seven o'clock. Mr. Holmes wolfed it down without offering any to me. An hour later, the nurse arrived and told us we were free to leave. All that was left to do was to stop at the teller's window to pay for the ambulance and hospital stay.

I grimaced when I saw the bill. Fifteen dollars was an outrageous tariff, at least ten times what a hotel room would cost.

Mr. Holmes must have noticed my expression when I wrote out the check.

"Why such a long face? You can be sure I'll reimburse you from my cache of gold sovereigns as soon as I can get to a bank."

"If you're going to a bank, you better change your clothes first. You look like you've slept under a bridge. You'll be arrested for theft for certain."

"Good point indeed. I hadn't considered that."

"I'll loan you the money. I haven't shared with the needy for quite some time."

A quick walk brought us to Bond's Department Store where I outfitted him with a flannel shirt, trousers, suspenders and an earflap cap for two dollars. A heavy fleece-lined jacket set me back an additional ten.

Arms bulging with my purchases, I led him to the dressing room and waited for him to come out.

I was more than happy to see him without his tweeds and told him so. Mr. Holmes had nothing to say about that but was less than enthusiastic about the cap. I told him it helped him fit in with the local population.

Jaw set, he nodded and put it on his head. Earflaps dangled.

I kept a straight face, but I pictured Mycroft falling over laughing.

Our next stop was 321 West Lafayette Avenue and the top-floor office of Edward W. Scripps. Though Mr. Scripps was busy in conference, his secretary handed me a letter confirming that, as Mr. Holmes had told me, I was indeed on special assignment for the paper and promised a thousand-dollar bonus if the results were as newsworthy as expected.

I began planning a trip for two to the Bahamas as I read it.

My boss, Harold Mitchell, came to wish me luck, ignoring Holmes. He had been the managing editor for only a short time, replacing my one-time drinking mate Phil J. Reed, but we got along well. He had an affinity for me as a devotee of true crime stories and envied me my position.

"Mr. Scripps told me to do whatever you need to get your story. He wants to keep everything under wraps."

"I understand," I said. "It would be a great help if I could use you personally as a clearing house for messages. We can have messages sent here and pick them up by telephone for response."

"Great idea. No one else would need to know."

Mr. Holmes was anxious to get to the bank and left me at my desk. I used the time to fill in Charlie Hoffman on my routine. When he asked why I would be gone, I answered, "Violet and I are taking a vacation. I haven't been away from my desk for two years. I've always heard Nassau is smashing at this time of year."

"Then I take it you're still together."

"Yes. I've got a sore leg though."

"You got off light. I would have thought you'd be wearing a truss for your whirlygigs for the rest of your life."

"You're the cat's pyjamas, Charlie."

Holmes returned and I handed Charlie the key to my desk. "Feel free to help yourself to anything except the cigars. They're Cuban, and I counted them so I'll know if any are missing."

When he answered "Yes, m'lord," Holmes threw me a puzzled expression.

In the street I stopped to take a long look at the many windows of the *Free Press* Building glistening in the sunlight. Albert Kahn had created a marvelous work of art when he designed the structure, and I could almost see myself sitting at my desk, third window, fourth floor from the corner on the west side. Why did it seem as though I never would be coming back?

Holmes patiently waited until I turned away. "Shall we go to Dr. Cohn's office now?"

"No. The Downtown Grill. You seem to forget I haven't eaten yet."

DANIEL COHN, MD, had a small office above a Kosher delicatessen on Woodward Avenue just north of downtown. I passed the building every day on my way to work. The doctor was a new face in the neighborhood, just finishing his residency. The aromas from the business below followed us up the wooden stairway to his office. Did the fumes make his clientele hungry—or merely nauseate them? Either, I supposed, depending on their condition.

Unlike Dr. Kennedy, Dr. Cohn was more than happy to speak to us, especially when he heard I worked for the *Free Press*. Gesturing for us to sit on his examination table, he started in.

"I just hung my shingle out here a month ago, and every day I'm getting requests for interviews from all over the world. Everyone in the neighborhood has been in to see me and a journalism student from Ann Arbor came in to interview me. The article in the *New York Times* mentioning my name has made me famous."

I nodded. "I'm sure you deserve all the attention you get. I understand Mr. Houdini came to see you on the twenty-sixth complaining of stomach pains."

"I gave him some bicarbonate of soda. It seemed to make him feel better. He also said his feet burned. I said that wouldn't be too surprising since he had a broken ankle. He said they both burned. I gave him a bottle of aloe balm. Later that night, he came back and thanked me for my help. Then he asked me if I wanted to join him for 'Farmer's Chop Suey.' It's a Jewish dish the delicatessen makes of vegetables and sour cream. I had them send some up to us. I'm sure he liked that I'm Jewish."

"Did you see him again on the thirtieth?"

He nodded. "It was a Saturday and he called me at my home. I met him in the office. He had a 101-degree temperature, and bicarbonate didn't give him any relief. He had a grayish pallor. I told him he should check into a hospital."

"Did he give you any reason why he wasn't going to do that?"

"He said he was used to pain and that he had some important things to do on stage that night."

I took a deep breath. "Do you have any reason to suspect anything other than peritonitis caused his death?"

"Absolutely not. I saw the appendix after Dr. Kennedy removed it. He had all the symptoms."

Holmes and I traded glances. Why did Sir Arthur think the police suspected him of being involved in a homicide? I'd heard no rumors of it from any of my friends on the force, though they all were discussing his death.

"Have you had any contact with Mrs. Houdini or his brother?"

Dr. Cohn's face lit up. "They both wrote to thank me for my help, and his brother singled me out in his interview with the *New York Times.* They were both pleased I was at Mr. Houdini's bedside when he died."

"Do you recall his last words?"

"Yes. He said, 'I am weaker. I guess I've lost the fight.'"

"It sounds as if he was resigned to his fate."

"Very much so. He was a most cooperative patient the entire time he was in the hospital."

"Was his wife with him throughout?"

"She was in another room with what was diagnosed as food poisoning. Houdini's brother, Theo, was there throughout."

The room suddenly was filled with the aroma of corned beef.

Dr. Cohn inhaled deeply. "Ah, they're making Reuben sandwiches. One or another of the Weinstein family comes in to see me nearly every day with some complaint or another. This morning I gave the daughter some aspirin for a headache. My payment is always a sandwich and chicken soup. I haven't had to lay out a thin dime for lunch since I started here."

"A very pleasant arrangement," said Mr. Holmes. "Do you have any idea why Mr. Houdini was so anxious to perform that night?"

"No. When I asked him, he asked me if I ever saw his movies. I told him I hadn't." He said, 'You'd understand why if you had.'"

Holmes looked at me quizzically.

"My wife and I have seen them all," I said. "They're mostly about him being a spy and working for the secret service. The stunts were exciting, but some of the audience booed when he had to kiss his co-star."

"He was a master showman," Dr. Cohn said, "but he did seem shy in that respect. I've never seen anyone of any age in better physical condition, and he said he had trained every inch of his body to help him perform his tricks. To prove it, he took off a shoe and sock and wrote out and signed his check to me with his good foot. He said he would have been happy to sew a button on my smock, too, but he couldn't do it with a broken ankle. We both got a laugh out of that."

"I'm sure I would have liked him." said Mr. Holmes. "Do you have a card? I may have some more questions for you later."

"Right here. I just got my new ones back from the printer."

He handed one to each of us. At the bottom of the card were the words, "Attending physician to Harry Houdini in his last days."

I wondered if the good doctor realized the words could be taken in more than one way.

CHAPTER 8

We caught the northbound trolley on Woodward Avenue just outside the doctor's office. There were few riders, and we settled into a cane-back seat by ourselves. I always enjoyed riding the trolley, though I hadn't used it much lately because I was so excited about my new auto. I still enjoyed watching the people and listening to the clanging of the bell when it started and stopped. The main library was on Fifty-Fourth and Woodward, just a few steps away from Wayne State College and not far from our home on Adelaide Street. Violet said she was roasting a beef rump for supper.

Conversation turned to Dr. Daniel Cohn. We both found him likable and felt he had a fine future. Whether we had learned much of value about Harry Houdini from our visit was debatable, though I thought it might be important Houdini considered himself to be a spy.

Mr. Holmes had no doubts. "He was acting as one nearly every day of his adult life. Just as someone else I know did for some years."

I snorted.

"If he were investigating someone, obviously it must be a local. I expect I might find the name in the social columns of the papers."

"Excellent thinking, Wiggins. I also suggest you should contact the theatre. He may have arranged for free tickets for his newest 'victimizer victim.' I have a considerable amount of research to do on my own. I'm sure there must be scores of eyewitness accounts of what happened at the performance." He paused. "Though none as accurate or as well-written as yours, of course."

"That goes without saying," I replied. From anyone else, his compliment could have been taken as a satirical dig.

The ride ended near the front of a large Italianate building. Holmes stopped in his tracks, amazed. "This is a library?"

I had to explain it was less than four years old and the pride of Detroit. Much of the funding came from Andrew Carnegie, but local business and civic leaders contributed additional funds far beyond the original grant to make it as impressive as any of the buildings in our nation's capitol. The lengthy façade resembled a portico, and its seven tall, arched windows ensured an abundance of natural lighting. Violet and I proudly contributed two hundred dollars of our own money to the building fund.

"This is a great city," I said. "Detroit is London two hundred years ago. Some day, everyone in America will own an automobile and Detroit will be bigger and richer than Chicago—or New York, for that matter."

"We do live in exciting times," Holmes mumbled. "I just wonder how long prosperity will last."

"Some think forever."

"What do you think?" Holmes asked.

"I hope so."

"I do also. Mycroft says the whole world is in great peril if it doesn't. He thinks the Great War did nothing but create a cancer that is eating at Europe's entrails, and that it'll burst forth to consume the whole body someday. The only thing holding it in check is a booming economy." He paused. "Enough of that. Let's see if the library's contents match its appearance."

At least in my estimation they did.

We sat at opposite ends of the table in the periodical room. Stories about Houdini already filled three large scrapbooks and Mr. Holmes sat studying them, every so often looking away, only to nod his head and return to his reading.

As a boy, I remember him sitting in his armchair at 221B Baker Street with the same expression, pausing occasionally to sip from his teacup. He always made sure Mrs. Hudson had milk for me, and at times took my glass to pour some into his Oolong. In all my visits I never once saw him with his violin, let alone playing it, and rarely found him smoking his pipe.

In other words, I was a victim of a deprived childhood.

My own endeavours bore little fruit. Mitzi Cornwall, the spiritualist who had gotten the most newsprint, regularly called upon a "familiar" named Oswald. Oswald was a rogue spirit who had been shot dead during a bank robbery and had a bad habit of running a ghostly hand up inside the dresses of the ladies present. Participants always knew of his presence by the screams, although, surprisingly, some women remained silent. Despite his British name, Oswald spoke Polish and frequently visited Hamtramck in his forays around the spirit world.

Houdini would never have bothered with her.

A more likely candidate was A.J. Baker. According to an article in the *News,* his customers had to wait a week before being allowed into the séance room after making an initial payment of seventy-five dollars. That was almost as much as I made in a month. I'm sure the extra time was used to make a full investigation of his victim's background before the actual performance.

According to Mitzi, customers paid another fifty dollars on the night of the seance . They were then led into an empty room, seated at a table and told to wait. According to the reporter who attended the séance, Baker made his appearance by "walking through a wall" to occupy his decorative chair. Though she doubted her own eyes, Mitzi could find no semblance of a hidden door or other entrance where he had emerged.

In the course of the séance, Baker's turbaned head fell back over the top of the chair and his mouth opened. Then a ghostly voice came from his stomach. The voice addressed each of those present, answering questions from his assistant that only the participant could know. After that, each was given a message from beyond, and all the attendees left the session happy. No one ever seemed to think they had been flummoxed.

In other words, Baker fit Houdini's bill for exposure perfectly.

I pushed my stack of papers aside, then stood and stretched. "Will you be much longer? I'm finished now."

"I expect I've seen all I need to see, also."

"I'll call Violet. There's a payphone in the foyer."

VIOLET HAD DECIDED to make Mr. Holmes feel at home with a beef roast with Yorkshire pudding, browned parsnips, and rocket salad. I got seeds for the spicy greens in Britain and she grew them in our garden. She had even whipped up a trifle for desert.

I always wondered at American women's thinking. Why would a visitor want to eat the same food he could get at home? Wouldn't a true Yankee dinner be more interesting? After serving him his food, she scarcely gave him a chance to eat a spoonful, regaling him with non-stop questions.

The first one was inevitable. "Are you really Sherlock Holmes?"

"My alter ego. I barely remember my real name anymore."

Arms firmly planted on the tabletop, she coyly rested her chin on her knuckles.

"Have you ever been married?" she asked sweetly.

"No, by choice."

"Have you ever been in love?"

"If you call deep respect and fond feelings love, yes. I've never been sure what exactly it is."

Violet's third degree continued. I let her continue for ten minutes before stepping in to remind her to let him eat.

Now it was my turn to be grilled. I answered her questions about the adventures in the hospital as she asked them, but did not find myself duty-bound to answer with my mouth full.

"Do you really think you would have gone to jail if Officer O'Reilly hadn't been on duty?"

"No. They know me well enough at the station. I'm sure they would have sent me home instead of arresting me. At least one or two of them would be interested in what really happened to Mr. Holmes."

"I can't even tell you how exciting all of this is for me," Violet twittered. "I started a scrapbook and saved all the news accounts." She paused and continued in a conspiratorial tone. "I've even noticed something that may be important to you."

Holmes and I stared at her.

Giggling, she got to her feet. "I'll be right back."

"What a delightful woman, Wiggins."

"Yes. She is."

Violet returned with a large scrapbook. She had pasted a picture of Houdini on the cover. Fingering through the first pages, she stopped.

"Here. This is a picture taken of him eight weeks before he died."

Mr. Holmes and I studied it for a few seconds.

She paged ahead to where she had loosened an article with a similar portrait. Removing it, she returned to the first one and set them side by side.

"Do you see any difference between the photographs?"

Both showed full-face snapshots. I studied them, then shook my head. "I don't. How about you, Mr. Holmes?"

"They appear to be identical to me."

She giggled again, this time in triumph. "Look at the hairline in the first picture. He is nearly bald to the crown of his head, but you can see there is a fringe showing at the very top."

We bent forward to take a closer look. "I see what you mean," said Holmes.

"Now look at the newest one. It was taken the night of the performance."

Holmes and I looked at each other again. "It's gone," I said. "Maybe the camera angle is different."

"It's exactly the same," Holmes said. "The picture is clear enough to show that Mr. Houdini appears to have lost some hair. Excellent observation, Mrs. Wiggins. Timothy, find your card with Dr. Cohn's phone number."

I drummed my fingers impatiently against my pant leg until Dr. Cohn answered.

After identifying myself, I said, "I apologize for bothering you so late, but there's one question I'd like to ask you about Mr. Houdini's visits."

"Ask away," he said, sounding entirely genial.

"Did you notice any hair loss?"

"Yes. As a matter of fact, some fell out while we were eating and he had to brush it off his shoulder so it wouldn't fall into his food. I remember he had curly hair and kept it well-trimmed."

"Did he mention his hair loss to you?" I asked.

"No, and I probably wouldn't have noticed it at all if it hadn't fallen out while we were eating. I completely forgot about it. Did I miss something?"

"No. Absolutely not. Thank you for your assistance."

Mr. Holmes's face was aglow. "Our first major clue." He turned to Violet, who looked equally pleased. "Well done, my lady."

I was the one to kiss her, though I suspect she had hoped to get one from him, too.

Though it was against my better judgment, I had Violet drive when we picked up Holmes in front of the Palms the next morning. He was in a foul mood, cursing the entire way to the library because he had forgotten to bring his notebook on poisons with him.

"Inexcusable, Wiggins. I knew we would need it. I can clearly see my age has caught up with me."

"Nonsense. You can find what you need in the library."

"A needless trip."

"Not at all. I wanted to research some poisons myself. I assume arsenic isn't the culprit, but it's the only poison I can think of associated with hair loss."

"The logical choice, but that would be too easily detected. What I remember about the poison I'm referring to is that it's a fairly rare element in the boron family and is sometimes used as a rat poison."

"A metal?"

"Yes, indeed. Very good. Your memory is undoubtedly better than mine. All I need is a book with the periodic table in it. I know I'll recognize what I'm looking for as soon as I see it."

MR. HOLMES DASHED through the door and found his way to the Reference Room. Hands shaking, he opened a folio-sized chemistry book and laid it flat on the table. "Aha. Come here, Wiggins."

His index finger flew over the symbols and stopped on the right side of the chart. "Here it is."

I looked down. "What's TL?"

"Thallium. It comes from the Greek word for 'green twig,' because Sir William Crookes discovered a green line in his spectroscope while analyzing ore samples for the presence of gold. He was expecting a yellow line from tellurium, which is a common alloy produced in mining. It turned out to be a new element." Holmes slapped his forehead with both hands. "I'm amazed I couldn't remember it. What else have I forgotten?"

I sympathized, knowing from personal experience what he meant. "Your mind is a vast library, Mr. Holmes. You may not remember everything you've read at one time or another, but the most important thing is you still know where to find what you need to know."

He looked unconvinced.

"Okay. You forgot thallium. Tell me about tellurium."

"Tellurium isn't a poison, so I haven't paid much attention to it," he said with a dismissive wave. "It was discovered by a Rumanian scientist who was the chief inspector of mines in that country. Tellurium is produced in the mining of gold. Von Reichenstein thought it was antimony but realized it was something else. I don't remember how it occurs naturally."

Finished, he made a face and shook his head. "Mere elementary chemistry, Wiggins. Hardly of any importance whatsoever."

"On the contrary, sir, it is of extreme importance. Perhaps not to our investigation, but still highly important. Despite what you may think, your mind is as sharp as it ever was. Time has just put a nick or two in the blade."

He still looked unhappy. "I appreciate your words of comfort, Wiggins. Be that as it may, I have a few more references to look up, then we can be on our way."

My colleague's mood had improved markedly by the time we were at the bus stop, waiting to go home. Better still, he showed signs of genuine excitement I hadn't noticed from the time of his arrival.

"We're on the right track, dear friend. Hair loss and peripheral pain are two of the main symptoms of Thallium poisoning. I can easily understand why the doctors who treated him were unaware of what was causing his agony. Thallium sulfate is a particularly insidious type of poison. It's exactly the same size molecule as potassium and metabolized as such. It interferes with processing sulfur. It's unfortunate Mr. Houdini didn't realize what was happening to him. He could have been cured with Paris Blue if he'd been treated early enough."

"He was buried on the fourth of November" I said. "We could contact Mrs. Houdini to see if she would agree to have him exhumed for an autopsy. The information we've uncovered should be sufficient to warrant one."

Mr. Holmes nodded with enthusiasm. "Excellent suggestion. I'll wire her immediately. However, she may be unwilling. The results, if positive for thallium, would prove he didn't die an accidental death, and that could cause some problems for his estate."

"Should we contact the New York Police Department, then?"

"The official cause of death on the certificate is peritonitis. I doubt they'd execute an exhumation order without more evidence. Inquests are expensive, and Mrs. Houdini would most likely have to pay for it . . . along with possible insurance issues."

"One thing I don't understand. Why would Sir Arthur say the police suspect him as an accomplice to murder?"

"That is something we will have to find out from him."

Our trolley ride ended in short order and we got out at Adelaide Street. Like many of the streets crossing Woodward, both sides were walled off at the intersection to resemble a gate. We lived in the third house on the south side.

The Chevrolet awaited us beside the house. I could hear the hum of a vacuum cleaner within our house. Violet was at war with her mortal enemy. Dust.

As I expected, Mr. Holmes got in on the driver's side, and I offered him the key.

He got out with a harrumph. "Why do you silly Americans persist in driving on the wrong side of the road?"

I saw my opening to avenge my humiliation playing backgammon. "We drive on the right to honor the French, our allies when America gained independence. They drove their teams of horses with the driver sitting over the leftmost horse. You drive on the left because knights on horses carried their weapons in their right hand. I'm amazed you didn't know that."

Eyes glittering, Mr. Holmes's mouth opened, then closed without a word. I heard him grumble as he slid next to me. "I trust you know how to get to this A.J. Baker's séance parlor."

"He's in St. Clair Shores. It's more than ten miles from here."

"I'm surprised he lives so far from the city."

"I think he wants the privacy. Anyone who comes to see him must have a strong incentive to do so. Mrs. Henry Ford reputedly visited him a while ago. As you know, the wealthy do not like to throw away their money."

"Quite true. Would you mind stopping somewhere on the way? I would like to purchase a newspaper."

I let him read until we arrived at our destination, interrupting him only once on the way to point out the superstructure of the giant rollercoaster at Jefferson Beach now under construction. The first dip was supposed to be more than two hundred feet.

Holmes seemed impressed. "Amazing. The one at Blackpool is much smaller."

"Have you ridden on it?"

"Of course. I wanted to find out what all the screaming was about. I found the whole experience incredibly boring."

"Boring? You didn't feel an adrenalin rush when you started to hurtle downward? Cameron and I drive to Flint to ride the roller coaster at least two or three times a month. We both love it."

"*Chacun a son gout, mon ami.* But I'm delighted you have a son, Wiggins. I regret it is one of the pleasures I'll never experience."

Regret. I didn't know that word even was in Holmes' vocabulary.

"How far are we from our destination?"

"We're almost there."

Less than a mile, it turned out. Just north on Eight-Mile Road and off a long driveway leading to a house not visible from the thoroughfare. The location was unmarked, and easily passed unless a driver had a map, furnished by Baker himself, to find it.

The house itself was immense, dark and gabled. Foreboding in daylight, it had to be terrifying at night. Unlike most mediums, Baker obviously wanted to scare his clients. The easier to deceive them, perhaps.

I gathered the press camera from the trunk and followed Mr. Holmes to the door.

The door knocker, a dragon head and wings, was welded tightly against the striker plate. I pushed the button next to the door and a bell sounded somewhere deep within the bowels of the establishment.

Moments later, the door opened. A young ebon-haired woman wearing a silk dress, shawl, and sandals greeted us.

"Good morning, gentlemen. You must be the reporters from the *London Times*. Please come in."

I followed Holmes inside, still wondering how he had pulled off the ruse so easily.

"Mr. Baker isn't here right now, but he asked me to show you the séance room and answer any questions you might have. Did you see the article about us in the *Detroit Times?*"

"I read it on the way here," Holmes said. "Very impressive. I'm sure that's why my editor was willing to pay the expenses to get a story. I heard a dog bark when we got out of our auto. Does it belong to Mr. Baker?"

"Yes. He doesn't want trespassers on his property. We haven't had much trouble, but students from the high school occasionally come here for thrills."

"I can quite understand that. How long has Mr. Baker been in business?"

"More than ten years."

My eyes flitted quickly about the room. This had to be the business area with a tiger-maple desk, flowering banana plant and a calendar with a picture of snow-covered mountains beside it.

"When did Mr. Baker discover he had a gift?"

"When he was twelve. His older brother, Sidney, had drowned and contacted him in a dream one night. Sidney knew Albert felt responsible for his death because Albert had challenged Sidney to swim under a diving platform on the lake. Sidney hit his head and drowned. Albert cried himself to sleep for months afterward."

"How tragic," said Mr. Holmes. "That must have been very difficult for him."

"Yes. But Sidney came to visit his brother on the night before Albert's next birthday and told him not to mourn because he knew it was just an accident, and he still loved him very much. Sidney also said he had a birthday gift for him and that he'd find out what it was very soon."

I had to force myself not to smile. *Surprise, surprise. What could that be?*

"The next day Albert told his mother about his dream, but she said she didn't believe him. When he repeated Sidney's name, Albert immediately went into a trance. Sidney and his mother had a long, loving conversation, and, when they were done, Sidney promised to come back whenever she wanted to talk to him. After that, his mother gave all her money to Albert and told him she wanted him to make full use of his gift to contact the dead because everyone had experienced the death of a loved one and needed comfort. From that time on, Sidney would come at any time he was called and would answer questions the living had for the departed loved ones in the spirit world."

Good speech. She must have repeated it hundreds of times.

"Mr. Baker charges a substantial fee for his services," Mr. Holmes said. "What does he do with the proceeds?"

"He's saving to start a school of spiritualism. The building and equipment will be very expensive. All of those who have used his services will become fiduciary partners and share in any financial profits the school might make."

Fiduciary? Even Holmes's brows raised at the word.

"Very generous," Holmes said. "Does he have a date when this school might open?"

"Hopefully within a year or two. Would you like to see the séance room now?"

"Actually, I'd like a picture of you at the entrance of the house first," I said. "Would you mind?"

"Of course not."

She followed me out to the vestibule and stood in the open doorway. I made her take as many poses as I could without arousing her suspicion. I finally chose one with the ivy on the side of the house framing the picture nicely. Though I didn't need the flash, I used it anyway.

"Now turn sideways as if you welcoming me to come in."

She had a nice smile.

"One more," I said with my most appealing expression.

I took two more snaps of the front of the house with her standing in the doorway. As we walked inside, I hoped Mr. Holmes had made good use of the precious seconds alone I had bought him.

"Back so soon?" he said. "Show me what happens on séance night."

"I welcome them at the door and ask them to take off their footwear. After that they are requested to put their coats and purses in the closet."

She pointed.

"Then I lead them into the visitation room."

The word sounded like it referred to a reviewal area in a funeral parlor. Most appropriate, somehow.

Holmes was already in the séance room. Our hostess walked to a table just inside the door. An Edison phonograph with a wind-up handle came to life playing a scratchy version of Wagner's overture to *Parzival*.

Unexpected, but certainly better than Chopin's *Funeral March*. The mood changed from frightening to dramatic. Baker definitely wanted his victims to know who was in charge.

"We leave the lights off until Mr. Baker makes his appearance. Guests sit around the table facing his chair at the rear."

Though dimly lit, there was enough light from the hallway that I could see the chairs. "May I take a picture, please?"

"Certainly."

The room exploded in light, and it took several seconds before I could see again. I could hardly believe I would make such a stupid rookie mistake to not close my eyes.

"The article in the *News* says Mr. Baker makes his appearance by coming through the wall," Holmes said. "Which one?"

She walked to the one at the right. "He enters dressed in a red silk Persian tunic and trousers and hands a rose to everyone in attendance."

Holmes continued. "Where does he come from?"

"I don't know. It really isn't any of my business."

"Perhaps he was in the garden picking the roses. There's nothing on the other side of this wall but the outside of the building."

She shrugged.

"I'd like a shot of the wall," I said. "I know our readers will want to see where he appears."

"Go right ahead. Mr. Baker won't mind."

This time I closed my eyes.

"Where are you whilst the séance is in progress?" Mr. Holmes asked.

"Sitting at the table next to Mr. Baker. I ask Sidney the guests' questions."

"Interesting. Why is that?"

"I have to read them to him. The only ones who speak during the session are Sidney and me."

"Is it true Sidney's voice comes from Mr. Baker's stomach?"

"Yes. It's quite frightening, though Sidney is always very polite and cares very much for the ones who have come to visit him."

"How does he come onto the scene?"

"Mr. Baker calls him, then he goes into a trance."

"I see this is an oak floor," added Mr. Holmes. "Ten foot long sections, I'd say."

"Yes. This is a very old house. One of the first in the township. Mr. Baker inherited it from his parents."

"Does it have a basement?"

"If so, I'm not aware of it."

Mr. Holmes threw her a sharp-eyed look. "Was Mr. Baker invited to Harry Houdini's performance on Halloween eve?"

"I don't know. I do know he didn't have a séance that evening."

"Are you having one tonight?"

"Yes. We always start just after dark."

"You've been most helpful. I do wish I could have spoken to your employer in person, but you have answered all my questions admirably. Thank you, Miss . . . I don't believe I heard your name."

"Van Dyke. Myrtle Van Dyke. I live in the village."

SHE STOOD ON THE PORCH and waved as I backed around to return to the highway. I was anxious to hear Mr. Holmes's findings, but he told me to wait with my questions until we were well away from the mansion.

"Why so mysterious? Certainly she can't hear us here."

"My mind is still digesting the results of our findings. I can tell you for certain that Mr. Houdini would most definitely have been very anxious to expose Mr. Baker's shenanigans. Do you know the location of the registrar of deeds for the city?"

"It's in Port Huron, I believe. I'll take you there."

I dropped him off at Grand River Avenue. He was so lost in thought I knew I'd only be intruding on his concentration, so I told him to meet me at the coffee shop around the corner when he was finished.

The doughnuts were frosted and a very good buy for seven cents. Unfortunately the coffee was way overpriced at a nickel. I considered ordering a tea bag; their version of coffee was mere hot water.

I was nearly finished with my second doughnut when Mr. Holmes sat next to me in my booth.

I offered him what was left of the pastry, but he ignored me. "Finish up quickly, Wiggins. We have to get back to your library."

CHAPTER 11

Holmes didn't speak for much of the return trip. Finally unable to control myself, I said, "Your silence is rude and intolerable. I demand to know what you've discovered or I'll deposit you at the nearest train station and let you find your own way back to your hotel."

"My apologies, Wiggins. I see I've operated alone far too long. To be truthful, I have only but a glimmer of an incomplete picture. One thing I can definitely say, Mr. Baker is a fraud."

"I gathered that much. How do you know?"

"For one thing, he doesn't walk through a wall into the séance room. He comes from somewhere in the house, undoubtedly the basement. I expect your photos will give us a clue as to where to look."

"I'll get them developed immediately. What about Sidney?"

To answer, Mr. Holmes's head dropped back over the seat and a strange voice came from his stomach. "Don't run off the road, Wiggins."

"How did you do that?"

"Ventriloquism, dear fellow. It's a trick many so-called mediums employ. You can purchase a pamphlet about how to throw your voice for twenty-five cents from an advertisement in *Popular Mechanics*. I got my book from an ad in the *Daily Mirror.*"

"So Baker is a charlatan like all the others. What difference does it make? Did he poison Houdini?"

Mr. Holmes sighed. "He did not. In fact that's the only thing we know for sure. Thallium-induced hair loss doesn't begin until at least two to three weeks after ingestion, so the poisoning had to have happened while he was en route to Detroit. This is fortunate for our investigation in narrowing down the time frame, but it does eliminate Mr. Baker as a suspect."

"So why did you want to look at the tax records for the house?"

"To trace ownership, of course. Good Mr. Baker's original surname isn't Baker, it's Becker, another spelling for the German word for baker. Albert anglicized it. I want to see if there's some reason why he did so."

"I'm sure I already know why. Many German-Americans were openly pro-German when the war started. When the U.S. entered the war on the Allied side, these supporters became worried they'd be considered traitors."

"For good reason," Holmes said." Anything sounding anti-American could get them beaten, jailed or even murdered."

"Yes. Before we joined the war, we ate 'sauerkraut.' After, we ate 'victory cabbage.'"

"Very well put, Wiggins. Most German-Americans decided they were Americans, but some decided they were still Germans. I have reason to suspect our Mr. Baker may have been one such a person, and may still be."

"Even if that were true, it wouldn't be a crime now. The Germans no longer are our enemies."

"No. But they certainly aren't our friends, either. Many Germans think the generals and the Kaiser's government betrayed their country by signing the Versailles Treaty. Not only are they angry, they want revenge. Mycroft's certain they intend to get it. He says all they need is a leader and a cause, and they'll create the greatest menace the world's ever faced."

"So why are we returning to the library?"

"I need to confirm some things about our spiritualist. I also need to get a copy of *Frankfurter Zeitung* and some other German newspapers. If what I suspect is correct, we will be making a return trip to Baker Manor tonight."

I waited for further elaboration, but he didn't say anything more. I stopped in front of the library. "If you're looking for a German newspaper, there's a newsstand just around the corner from the Free Press building.

"I may be a bit late. I have to find a carpenter before I come to meet you."

I blinked. "A carpenter? What on earth for?"

"Security, dear friend. Security."

We agreed to meet in the paper's morgue when he finished. The paper's receptionist would tell him how to find it.

When I got to the third floor, Andy Norris, our photography expert, immediately took the camera with him into the darkroom. Andy had been instructed by Mr. Scripps to give top priority to any photos I gave to him for processing.

That left me with time to begin my first notes for my article or articles about our investigation into Houdini's death.

Charlie Hoffman had moved into my desk so I garnered an unused reporter's notebook from the storeroom and found a place to sit in the morgue. No dead people, just old newspapers.

An hour and a half later, Mr. Holmes rapped on the door. If possible, his face was even darker than it had been when I left him. "As I feared, we have work to do, Wiggins," he said with a sigh.

VIOLET WAS MORE than happy to play her part in our "work-to-do" by calling the social editors of the *Free Press* and the *News*.

I listened in bemused silence to an entirely new voice as she spoke. "Yes, Miss Warren, this is Myrtle Van Dyke, Mr. Baker's secretary. We're holding a very special séance tonight, and we'd like you to send someone to cover it. We guarantee it'll be very newsworthy."

Short silence.

"You will? Thank you so much. We'll be expecting you."

She hung up. "There you are, Mr. Wiggins," she said in the same voice. "Both papers are sending representatives. Please may I go, too?"

"Do you have a hundred and twenty dollars squirreled away you haven't told me about?"

She stuck out her lower lip and reverted to her own voice. "You know I don't."

"Even if you did, I really don't think you'll want to be there tonight, my dear. Mr. Holmes and I will be very busy, and I regret to say you'd only be in the way. It's too late to get you a seat, anyway."

"Why is he looking so unhappy? He hasn't said a word since you got here. All he does is sit and read the newspapers he bought."

"He won't say. It has something to do with Mr. Baker's past and what he may be doing with the money he's taking in from the séances. He promised me I'll know everything by the time the night is through."

"Then you'll absolutely have to tell me, too."

WHEN THE SUN SET at 4:47, we were parked along Eight-Mile Road just beyond the driveway to Baker Manor. Complete darkness was still half an hour away and none of the guests had arrived, though they would shortly.

I felt both foolish and excited in my black sweater and trousers. The black mask sitting in my lap reminded me of the infamous hangman, Jack Ketch. Luckily, no one could see us. The closest houses were beyond sight of where we were waiting. Across the road, a heavy copse of trees covered the side and back of the manor.

I opened the trunk for Holmes to remove his equipment. He said he had dealt with dogs many times before and knew how to handle them. Even though I trusted his word, I wasn't thrilled at the thought of meeting an angry guard dog charging at me.

After making sure the coast was clear, I slipped my mask on, then crossed the road to enter the woods. We met some cranky brambles and annoying low vines on our way, but we were able to get within sight of the manor before complete darkness.

At the edge of the clearing surrounding the house, we heard the first barks.

Holmes coolly began to extend the sections of his telescoped metal pole before stepping forward.

Apparently, we already were unwelcome. A dark form charged toward us, barking.

"It appears we've been noticed, Wiggins."

Under other circumstances, the understatement would have been laughable. I found nothing funny about the dog. It stopped some ten feet in front of us, pacing back and forth and warning us to leave with growls and increasingly menacing barks.

I didn't have to be an animal psychologist to know the German shepherd realized mere threats weren't working. The growls got louder.

I threw a nervous glance in Holmes's direction. He calmly lowered the pole and removed a noose from one end. He was still puttering with his device when warning turned to action.

The dog rushed at me, tensing to leap.

"Hurry!" I shouted.

The dog's feet left the ground. I backed away, raising my arms and closing my eyes, waiting to be knocked to the ground and feel sharp teeth tearing into my flesh. Then I heard a strangled whine and the sound of something dropping heavily to the ground.

"Got you," Holmes said.

I opened my eyes to see the dog on the ground at my feet thrashing its head from side to side.

"Hurry, Wiggins. Put the muzzle on before it breaks free."

My heart pounded. In the near-darkness I could see the animal getting back on its feet, desperately trying to free its head from the noose around its neck. The pole in Holmes's hands bent forward in a writhing arc.

"For God's sake, Wiggins, hurry."

I straddled the dog and gripped its neck tightly between my knees. The animal dropped to the ground, trying to free itself from my grip with hoarse gasps for breath. I waited until it stopped struggling and lay its foam-covered head on the ground.

Now barely breathing, the luckless German shepherd put up no resistance when I pulled the leather muzzle over its snout.

Holmes handed me the end of a rope. "Slip this through the collar. I'll tie the other end around a tree."

My heart went out to the helpless creature doing nothing more than trying to protect its owner. I ran a consoling hand over its head.

"That's how the constabulary does it in Sussex," Mr. Holmes said, barely breathing hard. He telescoped the rod back into its handle. "Now let's find our way into the basement."

We heard sounds of autos pulling into the driveway and saw headlight flashes that somehow had sneaked around to the back of the house.

We found only two windows on the rear side. Both were above my head and I couldn't see how we could get in through either of them. The door was securely locked. On further inspection, I noticed a small door at ground level. I pushed on the latch, but it wouldn't open.

"Can you pick a lock in the dark?" Mr. Holmes asked gesturing at the slot in the round hole.

I raised my head haughtily. "That is an insult, sir."

Though somewhat rusty, the lock gave up in short order. The door opened to show three steps leading down into total darkness.

"After you, Wiggins."

We tottered forward, baby steps at a time. Every so often we heard the rustle of cardboard as we brushed against boxes. Otherwise our path was remarkably clear. As we continued on, we heard sounds coming from somewhere ahead and slightly to the left.

My shin brushed against something hard, but it didn't move and there was no sound. "Careful," I whispered.

Another few steps ahead, a bright yellow line on the floor stretched from the next room. Trembling with every step, I stopped when my outstretched hand encountered a door.

We stood in silence for a very long time. Then we heard footsteps and muffled voices from guests arriving above us.

How was that possible?

Unable to crouch any longer, I stood. At that moment, the narrow yellow line disappeared.

"He turned off the light. He's getting ready to go upstairs," Holmes whispered.

We heard a very slight whir of machinery that lasted for a few seconds, and then abruptly stopped.

"Open the door, Wiggins. We don't have much time."

A low-wattage light bulb burned from a socket in the wall in one corner of the room. A heavy metal column, the base of a lift, stood near the opposite wall. A panel with a single button protruded from the wall next to the pole.

Mr. Holmes pushed the button. Seconds later, a platform began a slow descent from the ceiling.

"I'll go up first," he said. "Push the button when the lift stops. It'll come back down to you."

Pushing the button again, the platform slowly began to rise.

It stopped and I heard Holmes's voice. "Good evening, ladies and gentlemen. Forgive the interruption, but I'm here tonight to finish the job Harry Houdini was unable to complete."

"Who are you?" an angry male voice demanded. "What's the meaning of this?"

"I recognize the voice," Myrtle said. "He was one of the men who said he worked for the *London Times.*"

"I apologize for my ruse," Mr. Holmes said. "And I want you to know I'm sure you know very little about your employer. However, my identity is of no consequence. All that matters is that Mr. Baker is nothing but a fraud."

Barely able to stand the wait, I pushed the button and the platform started down.

"How dare you!"

"For years, Mr. Becker, who now calls himself Baker, has been conducting séances. You all saw him appearing to walk through a wall when he came into this room. It's an illusion, and easily explained. I used the same elevator to join you, and if someone would turn on all the lights, you'll see my associate appear shortly."

The lift stopped and I got on.

"If you listen carefully, you'll hear the sound of machinery," Holmes said.

I heard a low cacophony of muttered voices.

The lift stopped, and I was greeted with wide stares from the guests. Holmes stood next to the table with the attendees in front of him and facing Becker and Myrtle.

"Now, let's continue with our so-called séance."

Myrtle got up from her chair. "I'm calling the police."

As she tried to move around the table, one of the female guests took her by her arm and made her sit. "Don't. I want to hear what he has to say."

"I do too," said a second. "I paid a lot of money for this séance."

"Mr. Becker reputedly conducts his séances with the assistance of his dead brother, Sidney," Holmes continued. "As I understand it, Mr. Becker calls Sidney's name and goes into a trance."

He turned toward Myrtle. "If you'll kindly give me your chair, my dear."

Myrtle's captor jerked her to her feet.

"Thank you. I will now introduce my own dead brother Nigel to our gathering."

He settled into the chair and closed his eyes. "Nigel, please make your appearance."

"I am here, dear brother." The guests traded gasps at the ghostly voice seemingly coming from Holmes's stomach.

"That was not Nigel. There is no such entity, living or dead. That was me. Like Mr. Becker, I also practice ventriloquism. It's a common magician's trick. Very effective in this setting."

The murmur of voices got louder. Becker jumped from his chair and reached for Holmes. I caught his arm and twisted it behind his back before he could take two steps. His two-hundred pound bulk had no sinew, and he couldn't elude my grasp, though the silk fabric of his costume did make him hard to hold.

"How does Mr. Becker answer the questions from his guests?" asked a woman with wisps of gray hair escaping from under an enormous feathered hat.

"First of all, he has a week to learn as much about you as he can. To answer the specific question you ask, he uses a well-known magician's trick. His assistant will give 'Sidney' the question, then she will ask you to whisper the answer to her. The first words in the questions and answers she has for Sidney will spell out the information he needs."

"Is that true?" the woman demanded with a glare in Myrtle's direction.

"I—I have nothing to say."

I watched Myrna Warren and the reporter from the *Times* scribble madly into their pads. Myrna looked up and grinned at me. Tomorrow's *Free Press* would have a very juicy story on its front page. So would the *Times*.

"Now that we've shown how you deceive your clients, Mr. Becker, would you be so kind as to tell your guests where the money raised at the sessions is really being spent?"

Becker again struggled to get free. Perspiration slid over his painted-on mustache, and his sharp brown eyes blazed. "Everyone knows the money is being spent to build a school of spiritualism," he shouted. "I've answered that question numerous times. Now leave immediately. You have no right to invade my property and interrupt my business. I'll certainly sue you for this intrusion and the harm you must have done to my dog to get in here. As to the rest of these ridiculous charges—"

"They are not ridiculous, and you're welcome to try to use any legal recourse available to you," Mr. Holmes said mildly. "By then the truth will be out."

Becker snarled and tried to break my grasp.

"Just to set the record straight," Holmes said. "Birth records indicate you are an only child."

Becker growled in anger, and Mr. Holmes continued. "I was very surprised to see the Spartan condition of your business and the frugality of your lifestyle, considering the large sums of money you bring in. Your explanation that you're intending to start a school of spiritualism could indeed be true, but I think there may be another reason. Your parents' names were Alfred and Heidi Becker, were they not?"

"I refuse to answer any questions from a worthless Jew."

"You don't need to answer, my good man. They are on record as having owned this house. During the Great War, they remained strong supporters of the Kaiser, claiming that all the reports of German atrocities were no more than Jewish lies."

"My parents only spoke the truth," Becker mumbled.

"They not only spoke their version of the truth, they wrote about it. They published a newspaper from the basement here advocating that either America withdraw from the war, or that it switch sides to defeat France and Great Britain. Isn't it true they were ultimately prosecuted under the Sedition Law?"

Becker glared in silence.

"Whether or not you choose to respond, I can cite the case for you. *U.S. versus Becker and Becker.* They were convicted, but because of their age, they were given suspended sentences and deported."

Becker shouted. "It broke their hearts. They both died less than a year later in Berlin. They loved this country as much as they loved the Fatherland."

"What they were advocating was illegal, but far less reprehensible than their publicizing of their intense hatred of Jews and Negroes. Did they ever participate in lynching one, as they said all true Americans should do?"

"Of course not."

"Would you?"

Silence.

"Tell me. Why didn't you go with them when they left the country?"

Becker didn't respond, and Holmes continued. "Is it because they wanted you to stay behind and continue their campaign of hate from here?"

Holmes paused for only a moment. "When the war ended, you wanted to help build a new Germany. There's nothing wrong with that, and it could very well be of benefit to everyone. Unfortunately, that's not what you want, is it? You want Germany to occupy and rule the whole world, and there are millions of Jews, Poles, and Russians and other 'inferior' races taking up space. Tell me, why do you have a copy of *Mein Kampf* on the table in your foyer?"

Sneering, Becker asked, "Why not? It's an important book. I want everyone to know about it and read it."

"I doubt your guests know anything about it. Tell them who wrote it."

"A great patriot who will someday lead Germany. His name is Adolf Hitler. He's determined to steer the beloved Fatherland back to its deserved greatness."

"As I understand it, Mr. Hitler wrote his book from prison."

"He's a martyr to the cause. His internment has been a great contribution to his resolve."

"Indeed. His resolve to rid the world of Jews."

"That's just part of his crusade. He knows they started the war, and their days are numbered for their crimes."

"Thousands of Jewish men died during the war fighting for Germany."

Becker snorted. "They were fighting to take over the Fatherland for themselves."

"Do you have Jewish clients?"

"Several."

"Do they know of your feelings about them?"

Becker caught his breath. "I like the Jews I know and will see no harm comes to them. The guilty ones are in Germany and the rest of Europe. They deserve their fate."

"Hitler had Jewish friends also. They gave him very generous prices for his drawings before he went into politics. Do your Jewish friends know the money they spend with you is being used to fund beatings, murders, and destruction of Jewish citizens' property in Germany?"

"The leader does only what's necessary. The Communists are doing the same things. Even more so. The Jews intend to hand the Fatherland over to the Russians. Hitler won't allow that to happen."

"I've read many German newspapers recently. The National Socialist party has received large contributions from the United States, mostly through the Deutscher-Amerikanischer Freundschaft Bund. When I first came to your manor, I noticed several calendars with that organization's name on it."

"That means nothing. And even if I may have made some small contributions through the Bund, I have done nothing illegal."

"True. You're free to contribute to any organization you choose, but your contributions have been anything but small. *Frankfurter Zeitung* names you as one of the largest American donors, not under the name Baker, of course, but B A-umlaut K-E-R. Your original German spelling."

Becker stuck out his chin. "Becker is a common name. That's someone else."

"Of course. There must be hundreds of others with the same name living here in St. Clare Shores. Frankly, I'm surprised you want to hide your identity. You should be proud of what you're doing."

Becker hissed.

"I understand you were invited to Houdini's opening night show at the Garrick. Did you attend?"

"Of course not. He was the enemy of everything I stand for. He was like all Jews, a cheat and a liar."

"Then it must have been a great relief, even a joy to you, that he died before he had the chance to expose your trickery. I consider it an honor to finish his work for him."

With a scream, Becker broke out of my grip and charged. "All filthy Jew lies! Now you'll have to look over your shoulder for the rest of your life."

Holmes deftly side-stepped. I jumped on Becker from behind and knocked him to the floor.

With that, the attendees slowly got to their feet and began to leave the room. Only his assistant remained beside him.

"Don't go," Becker pleaded. "Can't you tell he's lying to you?"

None turned around, and I refused to let him up until everyone but the four of us had left the room.

"*Ich bin nicht allein!*" Becker screeched. "*Der Fuhrer* has eyes, ears and knives all over the world. I promise you and all your other Jew conspirators will be punished."

"Perhaps," Mr. Holmes said in a quiet voice, "but it'll take more than the likes of you to silence me. Maybe I shouldn't dislike you so much. You're a product of your parents' hatred. But yours is far greater and far more dangerous."

"*Fichst dich, juden! Du bist todt!*"

"On the contrary, sir, I'm still on my feet and alive, and I intend to stay that way for many years to come. Furthermore, I may be older but I still can defend myself against rape. Lastly, I'm not Jewish."

Nearly foaming at the mouth, Becker made a last attempt to get up. I pinned his head to the floor. Finally he stopped struggling and lay gasping for breath. He reminded me of the German shepherd, except I felt nothing but loathing for Becker.

Holmes apparently had the same idea. Standing over the stricken German, he said, "The only regret I have about this evening is having to restrain your dog. You'll find him unharmed behind your house. It's heartbreaking that he should have you for a master. Such a loyal animal deserves a far better fate. Now get up."

"Let me help you," I said.

My association with the police has taught me how to grasp a man's arm so as to incapacitate him. Holding him by his right wrist with my left hand, I stretched Becker's arm out straight and tucked my right arm under his elbow. Any attempt to break free or swing at me would result in a painful broken joint. All I had to do was jerk upward under his elbow while pushing sharply on his wrist.

Myrtle watched with an open mouth as we frog-marched Becker through the front door. He dragged his feet, all the way shouting. I knew enough Yiddish to recognize the obscenities. As I held Becker, Holmes went for the car.

Holmes got out, faced Becker and brandished the animal-capture rod like a lion trainer's whip. "Let him go."

I did, and Becker immediately made a dash back toward the house. "Our man appears to have had enough for one evening," Holmes said. "But I still suggest we get out of here quickly."

I agreed, and we were soon speeding away down the road.

"Excellent work, Wiggins. I'm sure we've clipped Mr. Becker's wings for good."

"At least we've put him out of business. But why are you making such a big issue of exposing a secret supporter of some obscure German political party?"

"He's far more than that, Wiggins," Holmes said with a sigh. "And Mr. Houdini must have realized it too, if he was so determined to expose him he got up from his deathbed for the performance. Hitler is civilization's worst nightmare. I told you earlier that Mycroft says there's a great cancer growing in Europe. I'm sure you realize whom I'm referring to. Sadly, the German people do have much to be angry about."

"You mean because they were forced to accept blame for starting the war?"

"That and the reparations they've been forced to pay. But most of all they're victims of the great inflation that left whole populations penniless. Germans are a proud people. Their poverty hurts them deeply. It's not surprising Hitler's message is so powerfully seductive. It offers them hope for the future and someone to blame for all their troubles. Unfortunately, his plans can only lead to war."

"And suffering for the Jews," I muttered.

"More than we can even imagine, I fear. The key is that the League of Nations is required to return the Rhineland to Germany in eight years. When that happens, Germany will have almost unlimited power to build weapons. When they finally go to war, they'll be determined to win, no matter what they have to do to achieve a victory, and their weapons will be far more deadly."

"If even half the stories about the atrocities against the Belgians are true, they'd rank among the cruelest warriors of all time."

"The next great war will be many times more horrible than the last. I hope I won't be around for it. My heart can't stand to be broken again."

I didn't like the downbeat tone.

"I'm worried about Becker," I said. "Do you think he'll try to carry through on his threat?"

"He might very well if he's able to find out who we are. My references to Houdini may be our undoing."

Conversation ended, and I drove on in silence until we were approaching downtown Detroit.

"I'm sure you're enjoying your stay at the Royal Palm, Mr. Holmes, but it's an unnecessary expense. You're more than welcome to stay with Violet and me. We have a bedroom we've never used."

"I appreciate the offer, Wiggins, but old habits die slowly, and I prefer my solitude. Moreover, we're done with what we can accomplish here. I know I should have told you earlier, but I've booked passage for us to New York on the eleven o'clock train. We have someone to meet in Brooklyn."

"Eleven o'clock? That's impossible I can't even pack that quickly. And Violet will never agree to my leaving so abruptly. If you want me to come with you, she'll have to come too."

"That would be awkward."

"To use an old expression. You made the bed. Now lie in it."

"I see I've once again forgotten I'm not traveling alone. Your charming wife will be more than welcome to join us. I'll pay her fare when we're on the train."

Clothes flew as we packed, and Violet was sure we would never make it in time, but somehow we appeared, bleary-eyed and yawning, at the station at 10:45. The train was already waiting there with puffs of steam coming from beneath the cars, and boarding doors standing open. Though resentful about the short notice, Violet was far too excited about the trip to complain.

"I still can't believe he's taking me with, too," she said with girlish glee. "I've never been to New York before."

"You must have impressed him somehow."

A cold wind bit at our ears and noses, and we were shivering when Holmes showed up three minutes later.

"Good morning," I said. "I see you're back in your tweeds."

"The rest of my clothes are in my bag. Everything, that is, except the winter cap with the earflaps you so kindly bought me. I left that in the hotel room."

His sharp look told me that my attempt at a little harmless humor at his expense was at an end. I smiled, a bit sheepishly I fear.

He glanced at our bags, then turned to Violet. "You were able to pack a few things, I see."

"Just barely," Violet said with a smile.

That was a lie. Screaming at the top of her voice, she tore everything with hooks from her closet and laid them on the bed. "I have no idea what to bring," she had sobbed, flinging herself on top of the pile.

I had fewer things to pack and finished less than half an hour later. She was still jamming things into her suitcase on the way to the train station, and barely got the bag to close.

Holmes, of course, knew nothing of this, and being a bachelor, couldn't even guess. "And a very good evening to you, my dear," he said. "Let me apologize for such short notice. Though at first I admit I wasn't overjoyed at the prospect of having another individual join us, I quickly realized you are every bit as observant as your husband and will be an excellent addition to our party. My only concern is that sleeping arrangements may be a bit awkward."

"I'll pay for our separate rooms," I said. "We can use adjoining quarters for our conferences."

"Don't be ridiculous, Wiggins. I will be more than happy to pay for Violet's expenses. Especially since they are all my fault, anyway."

A porter came by and lifted our bags into the car. Holmes gave the man two gold dollars without batting an eye.

The porter's eyes lit up at the unexpected windfall. "Thank you very much, sir."

"You're very welcome." Turning to us, he said, "I booked first-class accommodations. After a few hours' sleep we can enjoy a leisurely breakfast and be in New York by early evening."

"Whom are we going to meet?" I asked.

"One of Houdini's employees. Her name is Rose Mackenberg. I called her long distance yesterday morning. She investigated Albert Becker's operation for Houdini, among many others. I'm sure she'll have much to tell us."

We joined Holmes in the dining car at 8:30. The clattering of the wheels and the jostling kept me awake for a while, but I drifted.

Six hours later, we awoke at Holmes's knock and doused our hands and faces before heading for the dining car.

THE BREAKFAST OF SHIRRED EGGS, toast, American fries, and orange juice went down easily. After we finished, Violet insisted we play three-handed whist, also known as Widow Whist. I always assumed the husband of the inventor of the game had died leaving only three people to play the four hands. Whether I played my own hand or took the widow, I inevitably came up with my usual assortment of sixes and sevens and an occasional facecard

I always seem to get dealt. Good enough to win my three or four necessary tricks on rare occasion, but invariably the suits were too evenly distributed to bid nullo and attempt to take no tricks at all. Violet on the other hand played like a demon, making four nullos in a row to win the game for the third time.

"I see we're in the presence of a card shark, Wiggins," Holmes said. He pointed an accusing finger at Violet. "I know when I've been swizzled, young lady. Either you give me back my three dollars or I'll have the conductor throw you off the train at the next station."

Violet feigned a hurt look. "Is he always such a poor loser, Timothy?"

"Usually worse. He's an even more terrible winner. You should see how he gloats when he humiliates me at chess." With that, I took a dollar out of my wallet and handed it to her. "You earned this fair and square, my dear. Use it to buy a bonnet when we get to our destination."

Stomping away in a faux huff, Holmes moved back two seats to read. I wanted to nap, but Violet insisted I play gin rummy with her.

Finally, I said, "I've had enough of cards. I'll see if the porter can find us a backgammon board."

"Fine. I'll beat your pants off."

To my amazement, this porter came back with a board and checkers. At last I was in my element.

On Violet's third roll, Holmes looked over his seat at our game. "Build your three point, my dear."

I would happily have beat him over his head with the board. "No kibitzing allowed. Read your book."

He did, but only for a few rolls. When Violet threw a six-five, he butted in again. "You're way ahead in the count. Run for it."

I stormed to my feet. "That's it. You two play and *I'll* take a nap."

I did, and it lasted until the train stopped at Albany to change engines. Holmes woke me. "Dinner time. I've reserved a table for us."

As the train headed southward, we shared two pheasants under glass with young shoots of asparagus in butter and new potatoes in Béarnaise sauce. Violet offered to buy the non-alcoholic wine with her winnings, but Holmes refused to let her. "Keep your ill-got gains, cutpurse. I would choke on it if you paid for it."

There wasn't much meat on the bird, but the faux wine was good, and Holmes entertained us by making tableware disappear then reappear in strange places. I could duplicate most of his moves, but how he got a spoon into my shirt pocket, I will never know.

At the end of the meal I joined in raising our glasses to the dearly departed Victoria Regina before eating our dessert of sponge cake and wild huckleberries. I would rather have had cherries jubilee, but thanks to people of my dear wife's ilk, alcohol was now illegal.

Holmes paid the tab, and I foolishly offered to pay the tip. Of course he agreed. Three dollars was almost more than what I paid in total tips for a whole month of eating out.

As we walked back, I checked my watch and realized we were only an hour and a half away from our destination. I found a newspaper with an unfinished crossword puzzle lying on an empty seat. Even better, Violet had seated herself next to Holmes, and I had time to work on it without interruption.

I breezed through most of the clues, but twenty minutes later I still couldn't come up with the name of the President of France to finish the puzzle. Much as I hated to, I asked Holmes.

"You don't know that?" he said in a tone that fairly shouted how-much of an idiot I was for having to ask. "Monsieur Gaston Domergue. He just took office this year. For shame, Wiggins."

"It was on the tip of my tongue. What are you two talking about, anyway?"

"Mr. Holmes was telling me all about what happened last night," Violet said in a reproving tone. "I so wished I could have been there."

"Next time, my dear," I said, sitting down in the seat facing them. "I'm far more interested in learning more about Rose Mackenberg. You say she was one of Houdini's employees."

"Indeed. She is a very talented private investigator who worked for Mr. Houdini by attending séances by the various mediums he wanted to expose before he arrived in town. Because she is a master at disguise, she never was detected. Who'd ever suspect an innocent librarian with large round glasses, wearing a plain black dress? Or a simple-minded maid, or a grieving widow, for that matter. She attended armed with the knowledge of all the tricks the mediums used. Then, the first night Houdini was on stage, he would invite the medium to join him. He or she of course would refuse, and Rose would move front stage to explain the tricks. Needless to say, mediums hate her as much as they hated Houdini."

"Are we meeting her in Brooklyn?"

"No, she'll be meeting us at Grand Central station. When she found out we were investigating Mr. Houdini's death, she wanted to meet us as soon as she could. She also is of the opinion he was murdered."

I nodded. "I look forward to meeting her."

"As do I," Houdini said. "Shall we go back to cards or would you rather play chess? I'm sure Violet would enjoy watching us."

"I would," she chirped.

That was the last thing I wanted to do to pass the time. I looked at my watch and realized we were still several hours away from our destination. "Sorry, I still haven't recoverd from my night in the sleeper. If you will excuse me, I'll take another nap."

To my astonishment, I did doze off. For longer than I realized because I wasn't awakened by the voice of the contuctor.

"Next stop, Pennsylvania Station. Be sure to pick up your baggage before you leave."

I moved next to Violet. After Holmes informed us how we would get to Penn Station, she moved next to me and gripped my arm tightly as we headed downward to enter the tunnel beneath the Hudson River.

Though she didn't say so, I knew she was frightened. Even I had my qualms about being buried under tons of water if a sudden earthquake made the concrete give way over our heads. Holmes remained unperturbed, puffing contentedly on his Calabash pipe. After what seemed a very long and dark ride, we slowly pulled to a stop inside an enormous indoor bay. It felt as though we were entering an entirely different world.

Reading my mind, Holmes said, "It is rather overwhelming, right, Wiggins. This is the busiest train terminal in the world. More people pass through here in five hours than a whole day in Victoria Station."

The porter laid our luggage on the platform outside the door and waved off Holmes's offer of a tip.

We were in a tide of moving people. "How shall we find Miss Mackenberg?"

"We don't have to. She's already found us.

CHAPTER 13

A fter greeting Holmes, a tall, slight, middle-aged woman wearing enormous glasses held out her hand to me. "You must be
Wiggins. Welcome to New York."

She squeezed my hand briefly in a firm grip, then reached for Violet's. "And the same to you, Mrs. Wiggins. Mr. Holmes told me about
your help. I suspected Mr. H's death was no accident, but I had no idea
he was poisoned. Excellent insight."

I smiled at her referring to her employer as Mr. H. The tone suggested it was a term of endearment.

"Yet unproved," Holmes said. I was surprised he used his real name,
and even more surprised that Rose used it so freely.

"I had no idea I had uncovered such an important clue," Violet said.
"Had you noticed any hair loss?"

"Yes, but I didn't think anything of it. Men lose hair when they age.
If you'd seen pictures of him when he was young you'd know he had a
full head of curly hair and was very handsome. He still was handsome to
the end. I always thought Bess a lucky woman."

Violet smiled. I had hunch I knew why. Romance was in the air.

"Is there anywhere close where we can talk?" Holmes asked. "I'll be
more than happy to buy you supper if you haven't eaten yet."

"Thank you, but I'm not hungry. You're staying at the Roosevelt
Hotel. It's not very far. We can catch a cab over and talk there."

It wasn't until Holmes and I had gathered up our luggage and started
to follow Rose that I noticed she had a valise in her hand.

Penn Station was an architectural masterpiece whose tall arches of
glass let in maximum light. A queue of taxis awaited us on Seventh Av-

enue, standing on the banks of a river of automobiles. Never had I seen so many vehicles, not even on the Parkway on a Saturday night.

A man in a derby opened the rear door of a yellow cab with a checkered pattern running around its side. Our luggage disappeared into the trunk. Rose sat in the front seat and I got in the back with Violet and Holmes.

With a honk and an authoritative shake of his fist out of the window, the driver swung sharply into the street.

Somehow, like the meshing parts of an enormous machine, the taxi fit into spaces between the pedestrians, and the pedestrians into the spaces between the taxis, and we moved forward. Time and distance were measured by honks of horns, and we stopped within mere inches of the door of our hotel.

Like an automaton, the cabbie opened the trunk and laid the luggage on the ground. Then the next moving part, a man wearing a large coat and top hat, set them on a cart and moved them inside the door of the hotel.

Facing Holmes, the cabbie said, "That'll be fifty cents."

I gave the man three quarters, not wanting Holmes to part with another gold piece. As soon as our feet were on the pavement, the driver opened the back door for three new passengers and left. I imagined an endless succession of cabs and people stretching on forever and without end.

Holmes checked in at the desk and had our luggage sent to our rooms. Then he turned to Rose. "We'll follow you."

"The hotel restaurant's quiet. I used to meet Mr. H. here."

As we walked away I turned briefly and noticed a man in a cap at the check-in pointing in our direction. I assumed it was the cab driver who had driven us to the hotel and wondered if we had left something in his taxi. Before I could react, he turned and left the hotel.

Inside the restaurant, a white-jacketed young man led us to a booth.

"I'll have a Horse's Neck," Rose said. "It's about the only drink on the menu anymore."

Violet ordered tea. I followed suit, but soon wished I hadn't.

The waiter looked at Holmes.

"Tomato juice with a stick of celery, please," he said.

After the waiter left, Rose opened her valise and laid an elongated tablet in front of her. "I understand you wanted Mr. H's itinerary for the month before his death. I have it right here."

Holmes and I traded smiles. This lady was all business.

"He was in Boston from the 24th of September to the 27th. I had investigated two mediums. One in Framingham and one in Lowell. Just a noise-maker and a levitator, and very amateurish at that. Mr. Houdini took the overnight train on the 23rd from Philadelphia after he attended the Tunney-Dempsey fight."

Holmes eyebrows raised. I knew he was a master pugilist, and would have enjoyed seeing the match. I would have, too.

"On the first of October he did his hanging straightjacket escape at the just-completed Hooker Building on Main Street in Hartford—"

"Excuse the interruption," I said, "but I've read that he would put on a free show whenever he arrived in a city where he was going to perform because it was better advertising than putting a notice in the local papers."

"Yes. He'd have the neighborhood police or fire department strap him into a straightjacket and hoist him up by the feet by cable near some building on the main street. Usually it was where the newspaper was located. He'd draw a big crowd, including reporters from the local newspapers, and free himself. When he got back on his feet he'd tell the spectators to attend his show."

"Do you know if he did that in Detroit?"

She looked thoughtful. "As a matter of fact, I don't think he did. He wasn't feeling up to it."

"That must have been quite an important change for him."

"Yes, it was."

"Were you supposed to expose any tricksters in Detroit?"

"Just one. Albert Baker. We were appalled by what he was charging. I was onto his shenanigans in less than five minutes."

I felt a mild jolt of joy. In American slang we had hit the jackpot. Even more appropriate, in British slang it meant putting someone under arrest. "So were we," I said.

"Were you supposed to do the exposure?" Holmes asked.

"No. Mr. H. was very adamant he wanted to do it himself."

"Did he say why?"

"He didn't. But it seemed to be personal. He appeared to be agitated and didn't want to talk about it."

"Were you in the audience on the 30th?"

"Yes. I watched the show and tried to talk to him afterward in his hotel room. Mrs. H. wouldn't let me. I also followed the ambulance to the hospital and asked to see him in his room when he awoke, but, again, she refused."

"That seems a bit strange," Holmes mumbled. "After all, you were a close business associate. Enough of that for now. Please continue with Mr. Houdini's itinerary from the first of October."

"On the second, he performed his escape on the main street in Hartford, at two o'clock in the afternoon."

"The poisoning couldn't have occurred at Hartford," Holmes mused. "That was too far ahead of the onset of the hair loss. Where did Mr. Houdini send you next?"

"To Albany. But Mr. H. went to Providence to meet with Howard Phillips Lovecraft about making a movie of *Under the Pyramid*. They had supper together when he was there."

I felt another jolt, and Holmes and I looked at each other.

"What day was that?"

"The sixth of October. Mr. Lovecraft had ghost-written a supposedly true account of Mr. H's visit to Egypt. Mr. H got trapped inside a pyramid and witnessed ancient rites. Mr. Lovecraft wrote it, even though he didn't believe it was true. Some film producer bought the rights and was going to make a movie out of it, but he went bankrupt. Mr. H and Lovecraft were meeting to see if they could make the movie themselves."

At least the sixth of October fit into the time frame, I mused.

The waiter arrived with refreshments. I had never before seen a longer lemon peel than the one in Rose's glass. Holmes's celery stick took up half his glass, and Violet and I got our tea from bags. Ugh.

"Tell me, Rose," Holmes said, "have you met Lovecraft in person?"

"Only once. Mr. H. brought me along when he met with him at his house in Providence a year ago. Apparently he is a recluse and seldom leaves it. I thought the man very nervous. I didn't know much about him but learned he writes horror stories for some off-beat magazine, and people have compared him to Edgar Allan Poe. Mr. H. apparently thought very highly of him."

Holmes's eyes narrowed. "More importantly, did Mr. Lovecraft think as highly of Mr. Houdini?"

I frowned at what seemed to be a strange question. Rose seemed perplexed, too. "I assume so. Why do you ask?"

"Because it would seem possible someone who had to ghostwrite a popular and successful story under Houdini's name might be resentful."

Rose took a sip of her ginger ale before answering. "I suppose it's possible. Mr. H. told me Mr. Lovecraft had led a very stressful life. Both his mother and father died in insane asylums, and Lovecraft himself suffered a nervous breakdown, though he never was hospitalized. I do very much doubt he would have wanted to poison Mr. H., though. Everything indicated they were friends when I saw them together."

Holmes nodded, but I could see the wheels turning. I foresaw a day at the New York Public Library in the near future. To me, the idea of Lovecraft's involvement seemed a long shot at best.

"Where did Mr. Houdini travel to next?"

"Albany. He did his main street escape on Friday morning, and his show on Friday night. He did his usual matinee on Saturday afternoon, and I did my exposé on Saturday night after his act. Sunday the tenth was a very bad day. Mrs. H. had taken ill, and he hadn't been able to sleep from worry. The Chinese water torture chamber slipped on stage. It landed on his foot. It hurt so much Mr. H. called for a doctor to come on stage. As suspected, the ankle was broken. Amazingly, Mr. H. finished the show. It never even slowed him down, and he kept all his dates until the day he died."

"So he was in Albany on the eighth, ninth and tenth," I said. "I understand he was in Montreal on the 22nd and gave a lecture at McGill University. Did he go directly there from Albany?"

"No. He made a stop at Schenectady first."

"So, Wiggins, we seem to have at least four different cities where the poisoning could have taken place. What can you tell me about Mr. Houdini's eating habits, Rose?"

"He often ordered room service, but he and Mrs. H. regularly ate in restaurants, too. He liked to frequent Kosher delicatessens and order the foods his mother prepared for him. He never had a big appetite."

"Did you eat with him?"

"We would generally get together on his arrival at his venue, and again before he left. He liked to tease me and say I was mere skin and bones. He said he wanted to fatten me up."

"Did he ever complain about the food tasting unusual or it giving him gastric distress?"

Rose squinted. "On the way to Montreal he complained about a loose stomach, but he wasn't terribly concerned about it."

"This would have been *after* he left Schenectady."

"Yes. And he started to have severe stomach pains when he was in Montreal. I know that because I was with him there, giving lectures about spiritualism. The pains got worse, and he really was in agony at the time he got to Detroit. You undoubtedly know about the student, McGill, hitting him in the stomach while he was resting. He said his stomach hurt more after that."

The newspaper accounts of Houdini's death told of his boast that he could withstand any blow to the stomach. The theory was that this boast led J. Gordon Whitehead, a McGill student, to prove Houdini wrong by punching him before he could tighten his stomach muscles. According to theory, the blow ruptured his appendix and caused the peritonitis that claimed his life. Assuming it was actually thallium poisoning, the blow could have sped up the toxic process. We would have to ask Sir Arthur about that.

"Do you know where Mr. Houdini stayed while he was in Schenectady?" Holmes asked.

"The Stockade Inn. The three of us stayed there three days and two nights."

"Did you eat with him while you were there?"

"The second night I joined them in the hotel restaurant. Mrs. H. and I had sauerbraten, and he had German riffle soup. He said he hadn't had it for many years."

Holmes made a note in a notebook he carried in his vest pocket.

"Did he say it had an unusual taste?"

"No. In fact he was delighted he ordered it because it brought back such pleasant memories."

Holmes drained the last of his drink. "You've been most helpful, Miss Mackenberg. I have no more questions. How about you, Wiggins?"

"None, but I did wonder how you became a private investigator, Rose. You certainly are a natural for it."

"I was born in Poland and moved to this country with my husband when I was nineteen. We needed money. I learned to be a private investigator after my second child was born. When I was growing up, my teachers always hated having me in their classes because I always was asking 'Why?' or 'How do you know that?' The headmaster even called my parents in for a conference to try to get me to stop my so-called misbehaviour. No girl—and few boys—ever acted the way I did, and I was in danger of being expelled. I really couldn't help myself. And I've always really hated people who stole from the vulnerable. Mr. H. said mediums are nothing more than circus performers, and no one should ever have to pay more than fifty cents to see their acts. Anything else?"

"I have a question," said Violet. "How did you and Mrs. Houdini get along?"

"I hardly ever saw her. I did think it strange she seemed so overprotective when Mr. H. was taken to the hospital, but she was distraught. I know how much she loved him."

Rose took a final bite of the lemon peel and laid her glass on the table. "Now if you will excuse me, I have some other matters to attend to. I wish you the best of luck in finding out what happened to Mr. H. The years I worked with him were the happiest of my life."

Holmes and I got to our feet. "I will happily pay your cab fare back to your office."

"That's not necessary. I'll take the subway. It's much quicker."

CHAPTER 14

Rose left us at the lobby. As we headed toward the elevator, Violet yanked on my arm and excitedly pointed at a sign above the concierge's desk, a short distance away.

"'The Noose,'" she said, barely able to get the words out. "It's a new play I read about on the train. The article said a wonderful young actress named Barbara Stanwyck is the star. She plays a dancer named Jo, who is the girlfriend of a crook who kills his own father."

"How exciting," I mumbled, fearing what was coming next.

Violet moved closer and continued in a conspiratorial tone. "There's even some gossip in the confession magazines that Miss Stanwyck is playing hanky-panky with the actor who plays the crook."

When I didn't answer, her voice became wheedling. "I really want to see it, dearest. Do you think we can talk Mr. Holmes into going with us?"

"I doubt it, and I'm really sorry to disappoint you. It'll be all right with me if Mr. Holmes takes you, though."

"Stop being a wet blanket! This is New York, for Pete's sake. I want to have some fun while we're here."

"I've had more than enough fun already."

Her expression was breaking my heart, and I relented. "Okay. Find out when it starts. maybe I'll feel more like it after we eat. To tell you the truth, I'd be perfectly happy to get a bite right now."

"Ooh, thank you," Violet said, planting a noisy kill on my left cheek.

The desk beneath the sign was empty, and I stepped over to the check-in desk. "Where is the concierge?"

"He stepped out. I can tell him you want tickets and you can pick them up from me when you leave for the theatre."

"What time does the show start?" I asked.

"Eight o'clock."

"That's only an hour from now. I wanted to get something to eat, and I don't know if we have enough time."

"Just go into the restaurant. The head waiter will get you to your play before the curtain rises."

"Thanks. Will you please ring Dr. Claybrook's room?"

We met Holmes at the elevator. In a jovial tone, he said, "You must be very hungry. I having even had time to open my suitcase yet."

I rolled my eyes. "We've decided to go to a play."

Holmes pulled out his pocket watch and frowned.

"A play. Do you have enough time to eat and arrive in time?"

"The desk clerk says we do."

"Are we dressed all right?" Violet asked, looking around.

"Tails are optional," said Holmes.

I flashed a wan smile.

We were greeted by a formally dressed host at the door. Sounds of polite laughter and tinkling glass filled the air. Tails may have been optional, but I didn't see a single person who wasn't wearing evening wear. I was sure every eye was on my humble black business suit, white shirt, and black tie.

"My friends are attending a play and are concerned they won't have enough time to dine here tonight."

The man handed us a menu that must have been five-feet tall.

"If you order the evening special, I'll put the order in immediately. That should give you just enough time to make it to the theatre."

The special looked very inviting. Oysters on the half shell as a starter, followed by beef consommé and a greens salad, then for the main course, poached salmon with truffles sauce, *pommes de terre au garlique,* and steamed broccoli. It sounded good, and was offered without a price.

I wasn't exactly sure what we would be getting. I certainly knew what oysters, salmon, and broccoli were. I could only guess what *pommes de terre* meant except whatever it was came with garlic. I also knew what oysters were supposed to do for your love life. I hoped this won't shock you, but let us just say that nearly anything would be an improvement in that area.

"We'll take that," Holmes said.

"Very well. Please follow me."

I cringed with each step, certain every eye was on my impoverished dress. In truth, no one seemed to be watching. Violet nodded and smiled to everyone who looked in our direction.

She was in her element. Unfortunately, the posh surroundings only brought back unpleasant memories of my shady past.

The only time I was ever arrested was when I was ten and gainfully employed by Holmes. I tried to lift a gentleman's pocket watch as he waited for his brougham outside of the Savoy in London. A Peeler nabbed me. Mr. Holmes nearly terminated my employment on the spot, and never forgave me. Needless to say, it was my only fall from grace the entire time I knew him. I still don't know why I did it. I was making good money. Maybe I needed to prove to myself I still had the old skills. For whatever reason, I had let myself down as badly as I had Holmes.

"Here we are," the host said. I was happy we were stuck away in a less-crowded corner.

"I talked to Sir Arthur this afternoon," Holmes said. "He's staying at the Boston Park Hotel and will meet us at the train station when we arrive the day after tomorrow. He says he is very excited about the prospect of our meeting Margery. Quite frankly, so am I. Sir Arthur agreed to wait until we could go with him."

"It should be quite an education." I paused. "Please don't take this the wrong way, but I want you to know it isn't necessary to buy us expensive meals every time we eat. Chicken and hamburgers are fine."

I could tell from his expression it wouldn't be fine with him. "Don't trouble yourselves in that regard. I'm enjoying our sojourn immensely, and I want you to experience a little of the better things in life while you can. Everything is well within my budget, dear friends."

"That's very reassuring. Do you think it'd be a good idea to visit Houdini's grave before we leave? We could take the subway to Queens."

"I doubt very much if there would be anything to be learned there for me. However, if you and Violet want to go there while I'm at work in the Public Library tomorrow, please feel free to do so."

I began to suspect Holmes was concerned about keeping Violet entertained.

Totally baseless, of course. She could keep herself busy and would love to find some way to aid in the investigation. I would have to let Holmes know neither of us considered this a vacation.

As if reading my mind, he continued, "Tomorrow will most likely be the last day you'll have for sightseeing. We have a busy schedule ahead for us for the next few days, and I'll need your assistance."

"We're both anxious to help in any way possible," Violet said.

"I know you are. What play are you going to see?"

"*The Noose*," Violet said. I let her explain. The plot sounded a bit implausible to me: a criminal son killing his father so the father couldn't blackmail a senator and thereby put the mother in the middle about what she should do. Nonetheless, Holmes listened with a straight face.

Our meals arrived as she was finishing. The waiter removed the plates from his cart and laid them in front of us.

I looked at my watch and saw we had forty-five minutes to eat and get to the theatre. I quickly regretted we'd have to rush through the wondrous feast. The *pomme de terre* dish was mashed potatoes with garlic and the salmon tasted as though it must have been caught minutes before the kitchen cooked it.

Violet was even more impressed, expressing loud "mmm"s with each bite.

No one spoke another word throughout the meal, and we finished with twenty-five minutes to get to the theatre.

As we got up to leave, Violet shocked me—and probably Holmes, as well—by kissing him on his forehead. I'm sure he must have been caught off-guard or he wouldn't have put up with it. He merely said, "Enjoy the show."

I stopped at the desk to pick up the tickets.

"Will you need any extras?" the clerk asked as he handed them to me.

I had considered asking Holmes to join us, but I hadn't made the inquiry. "No. Why do you ask?"

"Someone called about an hour ago and said he and his wife were from Detroit and recognized you. They asked if there were any more tickets available near you for the show. I told him there were still some left on the top row. They didn't ask me to put them aside, so I assumed they asked you to buy the tickets and meet them at the theatre."

"Did they give you their names?"

"No. I was surprised they didn't."

Perplexed, I slipped the tickets in my pocket and joined Violet. I repeated what the clerk said. "I have no idea who that could be. Do you?"

"I can't imagine! If they recognized us earlier, why didn't they greet us? This is very strange, but I expect we'll find out soon enough."

CHAPTER 15

A cab awaited a fare outside our door and we arrived at the theatre ten minutes later.

I had never been in such a well-dressed mob scene before. All I saw was swallowtail coats and diamonds. Only the lights on the marquee outnumbered the theatre-goers. Someone told me the owners had two employees who did nothing other than replacing them when they burned out.

Surrounded by opulence, I wanted to find our seats as quickly as possible. Fortunately, we didn't have to spend much time in the lobby. The ticket-taker pointed to a staircase at his left. Following the signs, we climbed three flights to find our seats.

A man wearing a red suit and pillbox hat—I always thought of an organ-grinder's monkey when I saw one—looked at the tickets, then pointed to our seats with his flashlight. As suspected, K was at the very top. We had the entire row to ourselves. Despite the location, the view to the stage was surprisingly good, and patrons on the main floor didn't look like overgrown ants in formal wear. I paid a silent compliment to the architects and the late Henry Harris for the excellent design of his theatre.

The house lights dimmed, then came up again.

All smiles, Violet took my arm and snuggled against me. "I'm so glad you decided to come."

I kissed her cheek. "Me, too."

Finally the lights went out completely, leaving the theatre dark. A light zephyr brushed against my cheek as the balcony door opened and the usher stepped out. Below us, the curtains opened on a large desk, and a man in a well-tailored suit sitting behind it. Onstage, the phone rang.

Almost simultaneously, I felt the puff of air against my cheek. Seconds later, a tiny beam of light flashed across our backs. I've always hated latecomers, especially when I paid fifteen dollars for the tickets. I turned my attention back to the stage.

"Governor Lonergan speaking," the actor said.

Whoever came in remained standing in the darkness behind us. I wondered why the usher didn't help him find his seat, then realized the latecomer was standing there alone. My spine tingled. The door hadn't opened again, so the usher couldn't have left. Something was wrong. The inquiry about the tickets was to find out where we would be sitting. My heart skipped a beat when I realized we were silhouetted against the stage.

Long-ago memories of defending my Public House trapline flashed in my mind.

Strike suddenly and unexpectedly.

Violet noticed I wasn't watching the play and elbowed me.

On stage, Governor Lonergan said, "I received your request for a pardon, and I'm considering what to do."

The shadowy figure behind us made a motion toward his jacket pocket.

"Hit the floor!" I shouted, pushing Violet head first. Years disappeared as I turned, made a handspring over the back of my seat and landed my full weight on the interloper.

Something hot chugged next to my left ear, then something heavy dropped to the floor.

The sound of our scuffle caught the balcony audience's attention. I couldn't hold on to my attacker, and he pushed me away. I caught his leg, but he shook me off and, gasping for breath, dashed for the door. I scrambled to my feet to give chase, but the assailant was already out through the balcony door. As I went through I collided with the usher.

"What's going on?" he asked. "I heard a disturbance."

I stepped aside. "No time to explain. Get the police."

I saw him dash through the lobby. By the time I reached it, he had disappeared. Even from behind, I recognized him immediately. Albert Becker was in full flight just a few feet ahead of me.

Rushing feet assaulted the granite floor of the lobby. The door slammed loudly against the frame as I followed Becker onto the street, then came to an abrupt halt. The bugger had disappeared!

"Call the police!" I yelled to the ticket taker. "That man just tried to kill me."

THE PERFORMANCE RESUMED after the police arrived. Each member of the balcony audience was questioned then led to seats on the main floor.

Violet stayed with me.

While the house lights were on, I caught sight of what Becker had dropped. A gun with a long metal tube on the barrel lay on the floor. I had seen such a tube before. It was called a silencer.

After the police cordoned off the balcony, I introduced myself to the one who appeared to be in charge. He was intrigued to learn of my position as crime reporter.

"I'm Sergeant Cooper. What happened?"

I repeated the story, watching as a gloved officer picked up the gun with a pencil in the barrel and dropped it into a silk bag.

"You say you know your attacker?"

"Yes. He's a phony spiritualist from Detroit. My associate and I exposed his fraud just last night. We were concerned he might try to exact some revenge, given his unsavoury background. Ten to one the gun and silencer come from Germany. Mr. Becker is still fighting the war."

"Last night? How did he get here so fast?"

"Most likely the same way we did. By taking the eleven o'clock train from Detroit."

The sergeant nodded. "We'll take his description from you and put out an all-points-bulletin. He'll undoubtedly try to leave the city."

"My wife really doesn't have anything to add. Would it be all right if she found another seat to watch the play?"

"We'll still need a brief statement from her. Otherwise, I can't see any reason why not."

Ten minutes later I joined her.

It was hard to sit and imagine nothing had happened, but we both enjoyed the performance. Highly rated starlet Barbara Stanwyck was beautiful when she came on stage during the second act, and quite believable as the criminal's girlfriend. The governor bristled with authority. The legal action seemed contrived, but plausible—if only barely.

When the play was over, a uniformed officer drove us back to the hotel in his black and white, then escorted us to our room.

The first thing I did when we were inside was to lock and chain the door. The second was to knock on the door connecting to Holmes's room.

He appeared in a robe. "We have to talk," I said.

Holmes stretched out on his bed with his Calabash pipe clenched in his teeth while Violet and I pulled up chairs to be nearer him. He nodded and puffed in deep reflection as I told him what happened.

"You're certain it was Becker?"

"Absolutely. I recognized him the moment I saw him. The officer who took my statement was astonished he'd be here in New York so soon after our skirmish in St. Clair Shores."

"As am I. We could easily have bumped into him."

"And he could have tried to kill us on the train," Violet said with a shiver.

That gave me shivers, too. "Why else would he have been in such a hurry to get to New York if he didn't know we were coming here?"

"Excellent question. He may also have wanted to deal with Rose and accidentally picked up our trail in the process. My guess is she's been followed ever since she crashed Becker's séance."

"Then we obviously must become more circumspect in our movements," I said.

Holmes folded his hands across his chest. "I want to examine this further. Let's assume someone has been following Rose, and he followed her here, and us as well, from Penn Station."

I nodded emphatically. "Yes. I didn't mention it to you before, but I did see someone who I took to be a cab driver at the desk, pointing at us as we entered the restaurant this afternoon."

Holmes's eyes opened wide, and he coughed out a puff of smoke. "Of course. You say he looked like a cab driver? He could say he discovered another one of our bags in his trunk and asked for our room numbers to deliver it. Whatever the answer, we'll have to warn Rose about what happened."

"Yes. She has to know what Herr Becker looks like. I'll try to describe the man I took to be a cab driver, too."

"Absolutely. To continue our reconstruction, after we finished talking to Rose, asking about the theatre tickets. All Becker needed to do was find out where you would be sitting."

I suddenly felt I was back in London making my daily report. "The ruse to find out we were going to the Hudson Theatre tonight was quite clever, though I should have seen through it before our enemy caught up with us. I shudder to think how close we came to death. With the silencer, he could have murdered both of us with nary a sound and blithely walked away. People would just think we had fallen asleep."

Holmes sat up. "I think it would be best if we checked out of the hotel in the morning and immediately moved on to Boston. There's no reason to remain in New York, anyway. I'm sure Sir Arthur will be delighted to see us a day earlier, too. I'll find out the earliest train so we can be on it."

I stood. "Fine with us. Just let us know what time we have to get up."

CHAPTER 16

Violet didn't return to our room with me. She left Holmes's room by the hall doorway. When more than twenty minutes passed and she hadn't reappeared, I began to worry. Finally, I heard a knock.

After a quick look through the fish-eye, I opened the door. Violet came in carrying a brown paper bag.

"Where have you been? I've been worried about you."

Instead of answering, she took a bottle out of the bag and handed it to me with an embarrassed grin.

"Four Roses rye whiskey? Where in the world did you get that?"

"The desk clerk suggested a place I might be able to find it."

I stared at her in amazement. "But you're a member of the Women's Christian Temperance Union. You're going against your own principles."

"My principles never met Mr. Becker's gun before. We probably should have worked on prohibiting the sale of guns while we were getting rid of alcohol. Then the bootleggers and gang members would have to go after each other with baseball bats."

"That'd put me out of a job. Just remember, if we drink this whiskey, we're breaking the law."

"Who's going to tell on us? Mr. Holmes?"

"Maybe we should ask him to join us. Then he'll be party to a conspiracy. Just how much did this cost us?"

"Seven dollars. It's supposed to be a bargain at that."

The alcohol was only two dollars before Prohibition. I went to the bathroom and brought back two glasses. "If we want Mr. Holmes to join us, he'll have to get his own glass."

With that, Violet knocked on the connecting door.

No one answered. "He must be asleep," she said.

"He wouldn't retire without telling us when the train leaves."

I rapped louder. Still no answer. "He must have gone out."

"Then he just doesn't know what he's missing."

"Absolutely, my dear. Tell me. Did you join the WCTU because all the other women in the neighborhood were members?"

"Well, sort of. I really do believe banning alcohol has brought down the crime rate. And just think of all the working men who used to spend all their money on booze. At least their families'll have food on the table now."

"All very true, but you're not a criminal or an alcoholic. You don't think Prohibition was intended to apply to you. Right?"

Unable to look me in the eye, her lips trembled. "I guess not."

"Do you know what you are?"

"A cheat and liar?" she asked in a tiny voice.

"No. You're a Wet Dry, someone who supports the law but still drinks. I'll bet at least half of the women in the neighborhood are, too."

"Oh, stop being so English. Shut up and drink."

Accusing me of being English has always been her favorite last resort in an argument. This time I didn't want to argue. She poured out a couple of fingers of whiskey for each of us, and I took a welcome sip.

"What do we do now?" she asked.

"Find a comfortable place to sit and wait for Holmes to call. I'm very surprised he hasn't already done so."

Sitting in the plush armchair, fatigue hit home. I awoke some time later, startled by the sound of the telephone.

"Holmes?"

"Yes. Get dressed. We have important business to tend to."

"I'm already dressed. I'll meet you in the hallway."

Holmes was dressed in dungarees, a blue mackinaw jacket, and crepe-soled shoes and carrying a black rucksack bag.

"Should I put something else on?" I asked.

"Yes. Wake Violet and tell her not to open the door under any circumstances. You can go back into your room through my door when we get back."

I returned to the room. After giving Violet the room key and passing on Holmes's warning, I quickly changed clothes.

"Where are you going?" she asked, barely able to keep her eyes open.

"Lord only knows. Don't wait up."

A quick kiss goodbye and I was back in the hallway.

"What are we up to now?"

"We're not up to anything. Becker and his associate or associates are definitely up to no good and Rose is in serious peril."

"Where were you after we left you? I called you."

He held up the bag. "I had to retrieve a few things for our mission. These came from housekeeping, but I'll need your skills to open the maintenance room door for the rest."

"Lead on," I said.

"One slight precaution before we go," he said.

Reentering his room, he showed me a small piece of paper with a skull and crossbones drawn on it. He then opened the hall door. Slipping the paper with the drawing aligned horizontally between the door and frame, and with skill perfectly perpendicular, he held it in place with a finger.

"Please pull the door shut, Wiggins."

I did. The slip of paper was stuck firmly out like a pirate ship flag where Holmes had placed it.

"Since our whereabouts has been discovered, I want to be able to find out if anyone has been in my room while we were gone. We obviously will need to exit through your door."

Unlocking his side of the connecting door between our rooms, he rapped.

The door opened and a bleary-eyed Violet appeared.

"We don't have enough time to explain now," Holmes said. "Just keep your doors locked and don't let anyone in for any reason. When we return, I'll knock twice, pause and knock three more times. That way you'll know who's at the door. I suggest you leave your key here, Wiggins, for security reasons."

I handed the key to my worried-looking spouse. "No more Four Roses. Right?"

"I'm too tired to uncork the bottle," she said with a yawn.

"To the maintenance room," said Holmes.

As usual, unlocking the door was easier done than said.

A half-eaten ham sandwich sat on a work table sopping up the oily atmosphere of the room, and tools hung on nails on the walls. Each had its own outline. Taking a look at Holmes's so-called grocery list, I smirked. "This is easier than opening the door."

The hammer and wire-cutting pliers came down from the wall and disappeared into Holmes's mysterious bag A spool of three-mil copper wire rested on the floor at the back of the room. I unrolled a three-foot section. I snipped it, and it disappeared into Holmes' bag.

As we shut the door, Holmes said, "Now we shall need to find a taxicab driver. We can call for one in the lobby."

OUR EARLIER EXPERIENCE had left us edgy. Over the phone, Holmes insisted the driver had to come into the hotel. Seeing him was but a small precaution, but one we felt we had to take, given what had happened earlier that day.

I had always wanted to see the Brooklyn Bridge, but didn't get but a glimpse of it until just before we turned on Center Street to enter the bridge and, again, after we exited at Pearl Street. The lighted towers and pylons filled the sky like the sides of a majestic sloping mountain. Some wag, Mencken most likely, called it the most often-sold piece of real estate in the world. I was almost disappointed no one had a chance to try to sell it to me, considering I looked to be the perfect yokel on vacation and a prime candidate to be the next buyer. I would have liked to meet a realtor just to see how long I could convince him I was a legitimate hot prospect.

We turned onto the parkway leading to Fort Hamilton, passing by single residences and small multiple dwellings. Holmes had given instructions to the driver to stop two blocks away from our destination at 57th Street and Tenth Avenue and wait there until we returned, no matter how long that would be. To insure the driver would stay, we made an advance payment of five two-dollar gold pieces and told him there would be five more when we returned.

"I'll sit here the rest of the night for that," the driver said. Stepping out of the cab, he pointed us in the right direction. "It's just a block away."

A chill wind blew leaves against my legs, and I tightened my collar. "What now?"

"We have to discover how many people are at work. I'm guessing two, but Rose said she only saw one person."

"Becker must be livid by now. I wouldn't be at all surprised if he came here after he fled the theatre."

"Quite so. If that is the case, I'd think there's a very good chance someone's also lurking in the hallway. Herr Becker isn't nearly as smart as Moriarty was, but he shares some of his worst characteristics. He undoubtedly is equally ruthless, if not more so, and his perseverance to complete a job is remarkably similar."

"Characteristics of the German soldier," I said with a sigh. "I think he really considers himself to be one."

"As do I."

The half-moon high in the sky and street light showed we had arrived at Tenth Avenue. A convenient hedge provided me an opportunity to peer around the corner without being seen.

Once again lit by the moon and a nearby street lamp, a man stood in plain view across the street from Rose's apartment. I immediately recognized him as the one I earlier took to be a cabbie. I motioned to point him out.

"Excellent," Holmes whispered. "We shall deal with him shortly. I suspect that the enemy is employing the lion's hunting technique of placing one of the pride in plain sight and hiding the others in the bushes, waiting to attack when the prey bolts. The first thing we have to do is find out if there is anyone in the hallway. Rose's room's on the third floor. I expect there must be more than one stairway. If so, we should be able to catch our human lion in a pincer movement. After he's disposed of, we can go after the one in plain sight with ease."

We circled around to Eleventh Avenue and then to the alleyway behind the building. The back door was unlocked, but to our consternation we discovered only one stairway. It reeked of wood smoke and pine logs, and the boards in the stairway creaked.

"So much for a pincer movement," Holmes grumbled. "I hope we won't be in plain sight when we open the door on the third floor."

We didn't have to hope long. As we started up from the second floor we heard scurrying above us, then a door slamming shut.

"I think we flushed out our lurking lion," Holmes whispered. He reached into his bag and took out a black object. I looked, open-mouthed, at what appeared to be a 45-caliber handgun.

"It's wood," Holmes whispered. "That's the reason I visited a carpenter in Detroit."

We reached the third-floor door. "I'll go out first," he whispered.

Light from the hallway flooded over us as he opened the door. Gesturing for me to follow, he stepped out. I heard a surprised yell, then Holmes's authoritative voice. "Drop the knife."

A long-bladed knife fell to the floor.

"Down on your stomach, hands behind your back," Holmes demanded. Handing me the black bag he said, "Take out the wire and cut it in half."

I did and handed him one of the halves.

"Here's the gun. Don't hesitate to use it if our friend refuses to cooperate."

He wrapped the wire around the man's wrists, then used the pliers to tighten it until our unfortunate trapped lion cried out in pain.

"There. I'll venture even Houdini couldn't have gotten free from this knot."

I noticed a bulge in one of the mark's back pockets. "He has a wallet."

After a brief struggle to free it from the pocket, Holmes read "Jurgen Schmidt, 1211 Kosciusko Street, Schenectady, New York."

I repeated the name and address to send it to my brain file. I have many shortcomings, but I never forget a name, face, or number.

"Schenectady was the second to last stop Harry Houdini made before Detroit. Did you happen to see him there?"

"*Iss scheisse, juden,*" Schmidt said in a growl.

"*Nein, danke.* I'm a Universalist. You're a long ways from home. But so is Herr Becker, *nicht wahr?*"

Schmidt merely hissed in disdain.

"Now I'll need the other piece of wire."

Holmes wrapped it around the man's ankles. Another twist and Schmidt was hog tied.

"Can you breathe?"

The man mumbled something angry.

"I'll take that as an affirmative," Holmes said with a chuckle. "I'm sure this is uncomfortable, but I assure you it won't last long. We'll put in a call to the Brooklyn Police to let them know where to find you. We have no issue with you except for your political views and your choice of friends. Mr. Becker is a very evil and dangerous man."

Holmes got to his feet. After knocking three times on Rose's door, he paused, then rapped twice more. Seconds later Rose opened the door to a darkened apartment. When she saw Holmes, she said, "I'm glad you got here. My husband and daughter are in Baltimore. I'm here alone."

"I'm very pleased you're safe. Have you packed yet?"

"Yes."

"Then I suggest we drag our friend into your apartment so we can lock your door. We want to make sure he can breathe but is unable to move. Please take a look and see if his accomplice is still outside. We'll come back after we've dealth with him."

Dropping to all fours to the window and peered out. "I don't see him."

Holmes shook his head. "This is very bad, Wiggins. He could be anywhere, and I certainly don't want to look for him in the dark. I don't want to give him a chance to become the lion."

"I suggest we call the police and let them handle the situation," I said without hesitation. "The Manhattan police will already have an alert on Becker. Perhaps they can even squeeze some information out of our captive lion."

"Lamentably that may be the best solution, as much as I want to pull Herr Becker's fangs once and for all. Please ring them up, Rose."

She did. "They're sending someone now."

"Did you get a good enough look at the man outside to know if it was Becker?"

"I didn't see his face," Rose said, "but I'm quite sure it's not him. Becker is much heavier."

The police arrived ten minutes later. Rose answered their knock, and they stopped in their tracks when they saw our Mr. Schmidt lying on the floor. One officer, wearing a name plate with the word "Perry" on it, knelt to inspect Schmidt's bonds. Schmidt let out a stream of muffled expletives as he did.

The officer got to his feet. "What's going on here?"

Holmes and Rose looked at each other. With a nod from Holmes, Rose began first. "I got home around four o'clock. When I was entering the building, I happened to notice a man standing across the street smoking. I thought he was waiting for someone and didn't pay much attention to him. I glanced out the window about an hour later. He was still there."

"And half an hour after that, she called me," Holmes said. "I recently hired her to do some investigative work for me. She told me she'd been subjected to harassment before on occasion, and I didn't want her to get hurt. My associate and I found this gentleman lurking in the stairwell. He pulled a knife on me, and my friend and I subdued him."

The officer pursed his lips, then looked at his partner. The second officer shrugged.

Things had gotten off to a bad start, and I realized it was my time to step in. "May I speak to you alone in the hallway?"

"Good idea."

After closing the door, I started in with a forceful voice. "I can see you're confused, but everything we've told you is true. The man lying on the floor and the man who was on the street are working for Albert Becker from Detroit. Becker tried to kill my wife and me while we were at the Hudson Theatre tonight."

"Who's Albert Becker?"

I did my best to give him the revised condensed version of who Becker was and our raid on his mansion. As I spoke, the quizzical look on the officer's face turned into a frown.

When I finished, the officer said, "It sounds to me like Mr. Becker has motive. What does he have to do with the man on the floor?"

I produced Schmidt's wallet. Officer Perry glanced at it.

"I'm certain Schmidt works for Becker. He and the man on the street were trying to kidnap or murder Miss Mackenberg. She's been threatened before."

"How do you know they're working for Becker?"

"Schmidt's associate showed up at our hotel when we arrived this afternoon. He must have followed us from Penn Station. I took him to be a cab driver and didn't pay much attention to him. I'm fairly sure he found out our room number and discovered we were going to attend a play at the Hudson Theatre tonight. Albert Becker showed up and tried to murder us, and the only way he could have found out we were going there was if Schmidt's associate told him."

The words came out in a torrent. With every word I uttered, the less credible the story sounded to me, and I could even see Holmes and I being arrested instead of Schmidt.

Officer Perry was no longer frowning when I showed him my press card. "I believe you, but it may be impossible to charge him with a crime. Everything you told me is circumstantial evidence, and very weak by any standards. You say your friend disarmed Schmidt?"

"Yes."

"I'm confused. Why did Schmidt surrender so easily?"

I'm sure I must have blushed. "My associate has a wooden gun."

The officer rolled his eyes. "Do you have any idea how lucky you are Schmidt didn't call your bluff? From what you've told me so far, I can't see he's committed any provable crime. Owning a knife isn't illegal. Schmidt might have a case to sue you for unlawful detainment."

"Then run a bluff. Tell him you captured Albert Becker, and he confessed to being in a plot involving Schmidt."

"That might work, but I'm afraid we'll most likely have to release him."

"I understand. If that's the case, we don't want to be here when Schmidt is freed. Would you kindly have one of your officers escort us to our cab? He's parked two blocks away, waiting for us."

Five minutes later Holmes, Rose, and I were on our way to the Roosevelt Hotel.

I rapped the code for Violet to open the door. She did and I entered, worried she hadn't kept to her word. I was pleased to find her sober as the proverbial judge.

Holmes went to the connecting door and entered his room. The lights went on and he shouted. "Wiggins, come here immediately!"

He pointed at the hallway door. "You recall I left a slip of paper in the door before we left and where I placed it?"

"Of course."

"Take a look."

The scrap of paper was no longer visible. Holmes opened his hall door and a piece of paper fluttered to the floor. I picked it up and saw the skull and crossbones.

"Someone has been in my room. Whoever it was got the paper back in the door, but he couldn't put it in the right place."

"Will you be able to tell if anything's missing?"

"Of course. I only have some treatises and testing supplies such as litmus paper with me. The most important thing is my diary and notes. I shouldn't like to have Herr Becker know what's in it."

He went to the hautboy and opened the bottom drawer. "Thank heavens it's still here, but I'm sure he must have found it. If so, he knows Boston is our next destination and may pick up our trail once more. At this moment, we're one move ahead of them. Now get hopping and help Violet pack. We have to get to the station to catch our train."

Stowing our belongings took less than fifteen minutes because we hadn't unpacked from our trek from Detroit.

"Is Rose coming with us to Boston?" Violet asked.

"Yes," I said. "We all decided it was too dangerous for her to stay in New York, so Holmes hired her to join us."

We carried our own luggage to the lobby. The driver took them from there.

As we started away, Violet took Rose's hand. It was unexpected, and Rose recoiled. Then she relaxed and returned the squeeze. A sturdy Rose with all its petals in place and a non-shrinking Violet made for a pretty nosegay.

None of us said a word as we rode. At Penn Station we lugged our suitcases to Track 18 to board the 4:00 New York Central train to Boston's South Station.

The porter took our luggage.

"I've booked two sleepers for us," Holmes said, "the only ones available. Rose and Violet, you'll be in D. Wiggins, and I will be next door in E. When we arrive in Boston, the signal to know it's me at your door is two raps, a pause, then three. Otherwise, don't open the door for any reason. Do I make myself clear?"

Rose, looking implacable, nodded. Violet, on the other hand, looked terrified, and I was worried she would need some more nips of the Four Roses to survive the night. We didn't need someone arse-over-tit drunk or suffering divine punishment with us when we arrived in Boston.

"Remember you're an upstanding member of the WCTU, dear."

Violet caught my meaning and flashed a sheepish smile. "Yes, dear."

We followed the porter to our cabin. He opened the door and handed us the key. Holmes was about to dispense another gold piece when I intervened.

Handing the man a silver dollar, I said, "I'll take care of tips from now on. You can repay me at the end of the trip."

The light switch was by the door. After stowing our baggage, I took off my shoes and hung my clothes in the closet. Climbing to the top bunk, I crawled under the bedclothes and fell asleep before Holmes could say another word.

CHAPTER 17

Holmes woke first, and didn't hesitate to wake me.

Giving me a shake, he said, "Rise and shine, Wiggins. We're only two hours from Boston. I trust you had a good sleep."

"Topping." My first normal breath of the day brought me the aroma of Latakia tobacco. "Why did you wake me so damned early? I could have used those two hours. I was dreaming I was at my desk at the Free Press and writing my article. I was almost done, and now I've forgotten everything I wrote."

"Lamentable, but we need to conference. It's rapidly becoming abundantly clear that Becker is somehow involved in Houdini's death. He is extremely dangerous, and whereabouts unknown. I sense a conspiracy, and not just one of angry mediums."

"I agree. The fact that both Becker and Schmidt called you a Jew certainly screams anti-Semitism. And the fact that Becker has at least two men working for him worries me. There could be any number more."

Holmes took another pull on his pipe before answering. "I'm also curious about why Becker's hunting Rose. She was one of Houdini's investigators, but only one of five. Is Becker pursuing them, too?"

"The only way to be sure is to contact them. Do you think Rose might know who the others are?"

"We'll have to ask her. Speaking of Rose, I have no idea how long it takes a woman to get ready in the morning, but there are two of them, and I want to breakfast before the train arrives in Boston. Should I wake them now?"

"I expect they're going to hate you for such a short night, but, judging from my years with Violet, it's going to take them a while to get presentable. Just keep me out of it, and don't tell them what I said. If you do, I'll deny everything."

"I'm a bachelor, and an old one at that. I can be excused for not knowing any better."

"That at least has the ring of plausibility," I said with a yawn. "Don't be surprised if I'm kipping when you get back."

"Indeed? Then don't be surprised when I douse you with cold water to wake you up. We have no time for such luxuries, Wiggins."

I knew he meant it, so I reluctantly climbed out of my berth. I desperately wanted to shower, but felt more than a frisson about leaving the room. If Becker could be anywhere, there was no reason he couldn't be on the same train with us. Maybe even in the shower. I sensed a strange symmetry at work, with Becker balanced against Holmes and me, each mirroring the other's actions. Somehow we were locked together with Becker the way Holmes and Moriarty were at Reichenbach Falls, and I certainly didn't want to be the one to take the plunge.

I looked into the mirror and didn't like what I saw. My grooming bag was in Violet's room. Scowling at myself, I settled on washing my face with cold water and brushing my teeth with my forefinger. The day's growth of beard dappled my cheeks with specks of gray. At least I didn't have to turn my underwear inside out, or wear the same shirt.

I heard the door unlock, and Holmes stepped in. "They told me to come back in an hour. What could possibly take them that long?"

"You can be sure they're both mortified they can't take a shower— and to be honest, I'm with them on that—so they'll take a bath in the sink. After that, they have to disguise their faces with make-up, fix their hair, find the right dress, then press and tug to make sure it looks just right. That all takes time."

"Time that could be put to better use," Holmes grumbled. "What do you make of the fact that Herr Schmidt is from Schenectady?"

"I don't know what to make of it. It could be mere coincidence, but it surely puts him in the geographical area where Houdini may have been poisoned."

Holmes sighed. "Becker's reach seems to grow longer by the hour, doesn't it? I feel I'm playing chess against myself."

"That may be closer to the truth than you realize. It's amazing how we keep crossing paths. I can understand how Moriarty felt with you dogging his heels."

"True, and he was understandably unhappy with my interference. So is Becker, but there's one big difference between Becker and Moriarty. As evil a person Becker is, and how low his motives when bilking his clients, he gave them what they paid for. They left believing there was a life after death, and the belief was comforting. Other than the opium addicts, no one ever left Moriarty happy."

"But why are there so many spiritualists and so many people so easily duped?"

"War, dear fellow. Eight years is not nearly long enough to erase the misery of the nations involved in the Great War. Imagine a whole village of men going off to battle together so they could serve as comrades, and nary a one returning. Now multiply that by the hundreds of villages in Britain. Add in the millions of Frenchmen and Germans who died, as well as the thousands of Americans. The grief must have been transcendent for their survivors. Many literally had to believe a loved one was in a better place after they died to continue on themselves, so they went to the only people who could tell them they were right."

I nodded. "That makes perfect sense."

"There's another aspect, too, that's a sign of our times. Women have been especially susceptible. Many didn't like it that only their husbands could vote, so they changed the law. The same went for their view of religion. They didn't want to be told what and how to believe by a male cleric. They wanted to get to the source on their own terms."

I couldn't help breaking into a grin. "Then along came Houdini proving the bearers of good tidings were liars. I'm sure the mediums weren't the only ones who wanted him dead."

"Very astute, Wiggins. But enough of that. I procured a newspaper whilst I was out. I'll be more than happy to share it with you."

I hadn't read the *Boston Globe* for years. Holmes generously gave me the sports section. Despite finding little to interest me, I was delighted to note that Michigan's basketball team had won its opening game, with star forward Richard Doyle scoring an amazing eighteen points. I wished I had seen it. Everyone was excited about Big Blue's prospects for the year. Otherwise there wasn't very much else for me to read.

After a brief scuffle, I wrested the front section from Holmes.

Before I could read about Belgium's Crown Prince Leopold's wedding to Princess Astrid Bernadotte of Sweden, he got to his feet.

Irritated, he proclaimed, "We've waited long enough. It's time to send some electricity into those feminine circuits."

"It won't do any—" was all I could get out. Holmes had already stomped into the hallway and was rapping on the door to compartment D. This time he rapped three times after four. Ever cautious, he had changed the code again.

A frightened Violet opened the door. "Thank goodness you're here. After you left, someone knocked on the door using the old code."

Holmes turned to me, eyes wide. "This is very serious, Wiggins. Someone, Becker most likely, must have overheard me when I knocked on the door the previous time and tried to gain entry the same way. Worse, he's much closer to us than I could ever have imagined."

"He read your notes when he broke into your room and knew we'd be traveling to Boston tonight. It isn't too surprising to discover we're on the same train."

Holmes put his finger to his mouth and whispered. "Our opponent must be in another compartment within earshot. This is more serious than I imagined."

"What do we do now?" I whispered back.

Holmes's silence spoke volumes. He had no idea, either. Finally he turned to the women and said, "If he knocked on your door, there's no doubt he intended to do you harm. That also indicates he has the means. We have to keep together. Groomed or not, dear ladies, gather up your belongings. We'll bring them to the dining car. I don't know to what lengths Becker's willing to go, but we should be safer there."

Violet sighed and unplugged her curling iron from the outlet. It sizzled as she wrapped it in a wet towel. In what I considered to be remarkable time, both women were packed and ready to leave in ten minutes.

Holmes led the parade carrying Rose's bag, followed by Rose and Violet, with me taking up the rear carrying Violet's luggage. We left ours in the room for the porter to pick up and deliver to us. Violet reached behind her to grasp my right hand, and stretched forward to hold Rose's with the other. The car's constant shifting made it difficult to walk, but our little train within the train soon crossed into the dining car. I was very happy to see that several of the tables were already occupied. It was a form of protection. Or at least I thought it was.

We met a porter in the hallway.

"Good morning," said Holmes, handing him our cabin key. "Would you kindly gather up our bags for us, please."

"Of course, sir."

After we entered the dining car, a white-coated porter led us to a table at the far end of the diner and set menus on the table before us.

"I'm curious why Becker's so intent to find you, Rose. Do you have any idea?"

"I expect it's because I was a threat to expose him, although I understand you've already finished that job for me."

"Then it doesn't sound like he's trying to protect his reputation. It could be revenge if Becker thought you had something to do with our raid." Holmes paused. "Are you Jewish, perchance?"

"Yes. Why do you ask?"

"We suspect anti-Semitism may be his motivation. I'm sure he must have been livid that Houdini should threaten his operation. He would be explosive if he knew you were Jewish, to boot."

"Or Rose may know something she isn't supposed to know," I said," even if she isn't even aware of what it is."

"Excellent point. It could very well be a combination of both." Holmes turned back to Rose. "How long did you work for Mr. Houdini?"

"Four years. I contacted him when I heard about his campaign against spurious mediums. I was as angry about what they were doing as he was. I still am and will do everything I can to carry on the work."

"Do you know how Mr. Houdini began his relationship with Mr. Conan Doyle?"

"When Mr. Houdini first began performing magic on a full-time basis, he knew of Mr. Doyle's interest in spiritualism and the supernatural. That gave him a perfect reason to send him a copy of *The Unmasking of Robert-Houdin*. Mr. H. took on the name for himself and added an 'I' because Houdin was considered to be the greatest magician Europe ever produced. The book also deals with the Davenport brothers. You probably have never heard of them, but they were very well-known and high on Mr. Conan Doyle's list of prominent spiritualists. The book showed their fraud. C.D., as Mr. H. called him, was impressed with the book and Mr. H's interest in spiritualism. They became friends."

"Do you know what caused their break up?"

"It started in 1922. Conan Doyle's wife's a medium, and C.D. wanted to show off her skills."

"I remember reading about that in the *Free Press*," I said. "Doyle and his wife were in Atlantic City to view some new radio transmitting equipment and invited Houdini to meet them there."

"Yes. They had been corresponding for years and Mr. Conan Doyle hoped a séance would convert Mr. H. to Spiritualism. Mr. H. was more than happy to agree and they met on the 17th. That evening Lady Jean put on a séance purportedly to help Mr. H. contact his mother. Cecilia had just recently died, and he really was heartbroken. He never once smiled except when he was on stage for weeks. "

She stopped and cleared her throat. "Lady Jean practiced automatic writing, which meant the spirit communicated by guiding her hand. In the course of the séance, Houdini's mother supposedly wrote notes of condolence and encouragement. Instead of converting Mr. H. to belief, the séance left him doubting C.D.'s competence. The words in the notes were in English, and Cecilia couldn't write anything but Hungarian."

Unable to control myself, I broke out laughing. Violet glared.

"It isn't funny. It eventually brought on a sad ending to their relationship. After that, Houdini's suspicions seemed to grow stronger every time C.D. endorsed another fake. C.D. got angrier at every denunciation. By the end, they were attacking each other as sworn enemies."

"It does seem very sad, doesn't it?" Holmes said. "They both wanted to believe in contact with the dead but came up with different conclusions."

"I discovered I was a lot like Mr. H.," Rose said. "I have always wanted to believe, too. That's why when I travel the country to expose the fakers, I always hope I'll someday find someone who will prove me wrong."

The porter returned. "Are you ready for breakfast now?"

"We've barely glanced at the menu yet," Holmes said. "Please come back in a minute or two."

HOLMES ORDERED THE BOILED partridge eggs, baked Lincolnshire sausage with quince sauce and white toast. I barely noticed Violet's order of French toast, but did hear Rose order breakfast beef with her eggs. I had never heard of that before.

I gave my order last. Instead of eggs and toast, I settled on the medley of raspberries, papaya, and dark cherries; rye toast with whiskey marmalade—undoubtedly illegal—and a cup of espresso. I also ordered freshly squeezed Florida orange juice, which was a rare treat.

"Have you ever been in a situation where you or Houdini were attacked for being Jewish?" asked Holmes.

"Every once in a while, but only once of any significance. Earlier this year we were shouted down on the floor of the United States House of Representatives. We were trying to get a law passed to outlaw the telling of fortunes for pay in Washington, D.C. While we were testifying, spiritualists arrived by the hundreds to heckle us. I testified that the wife of one of the representatives in the House was a Spiritualist, and I had evidence that President Coolidge had attended at least one séance in the White House. All involved denied the charges of course, and our bill never even reached the

House floor. The hecklers furthered my education. I learned some derogatory terms for my religion I had never heard before. Did you know I'm a registered Spiritualist myself?"

We all laughed.

"It's true. I paid my twenty-five dollars to the Christian Spiritual Union and I'm now a registered medium known as Frances Raud. My business cards read F. Raud. Apparently no one in the society ever noticed that until I started passing out the cards to them."

Our laughter was cut short when Holmes suddenly sprang to his feet. "Good morning, Herr Becker. I'm pleased to see you. Did you have a pleasant night?"

Startled, we all turned to look. Becker stood five feet away with open mouth and eyes smouldering in hatred.

"I'd ask you to join us, but the table's too small," Holmes continued.

"Even if you were alone, I would not willingly come within ten yards of a Jew," Becker said in a voice dripping with venom. "You have been lucky so far, but we'll meet again. You have dealt me a blow, but my cause is just, and you cannot escape me. I have a particularly interesting treat waiting for you, Miss Mackenberg."

Rose flashed a wide grin. "That sounds delightful. I can hardly wait."

"You missed a great show when you left the Hudson in such a hurry last night," I said. "You can claim the property you left behind from the Manhattan police. They're very anxious to talk to you."

I cringed as Becker's right hand moved to his jacket pocket. Had we pushed him so far he would shoot at us in front of witnesses?

I mentally sighed in relief to see his hand was empty when he took it out of his pocket. Turning on his heels, he stomped away. Before exiting the dining car, he stopped and glanced over his shoulder. I had never seen a look of such abject hatred before, and it frightened me.

Every eye in the dining car was watching him.

Holmes broke into laughter, and soon nearly everyone joined him.

Becker turned an apoplectic red and left, roaring in indignation.

The porter in white coat came to our table. "Who was that, sir? Did he bother you?"

"Yes," Holmes said. "He's a very dangerous fugitive from the law who tried to murder my friends. You will need to alert security to look for him and tell the rest of the passengers about him, especially the ones in the Pullmans. Tell them not to open their doors until the train reaches the station. He will undoubtedly be one of the first ones to get off and will be gone by the time the authorities have been notified."

"Then I'll alert security now and see you have an escort when you leave the train," the porter said. "Where are you staying?"

Not wanting to be heard, Holmes wrote out "The Boston Park Hotel" at the top of the menu and handed it to the man.

The food arrived. None of us was as hungry as before our run-in with Becker, but I enjoyed the fruit medley, especially the cherries.

Instead of eating, Violet and Rose started a spirited conversation about Houdini's illusions and escapes.

"His shows were always in three parts," Rose said. "He'd start with some of the usual magician's tricks, then he'd do the Chinese Water Torture. After that he'd have me come on stage, and I'd reveal the newest fakers we'd discovered in the area where we were playing."

"I heard he swallowed sewing needles."

Rose laughed. "He certainly did. He'd down a dozen of them, and then swallow a spool of thread. Women actually fainted when he pulled the thread from his mouth with the needles dangling from it."

"How on earth did he do that?"

"He could hide things in his cheeks and knew how to swallow the needles and regurgitate them so they didn't cause any harm. He told me once that he felt a sneeze coming on and was afraid he'd wind up in the hospital or worse. The needles could have killed him."

"How exciting," Violet said.

"One time," Rose said with a big smile, "a man challenged Mr. Houdini to escape from a lock he had worked on for a year. Mr. H. always took a dare. On stage, he performed his act in formal wear with the curtain open to make the escape more exciting. He disappeared from sight into his stand for a moment, then suddenly reappeared on front stage in his shirtsleeves.

He walked to the judge and asked if it was all right to open the lock with his jacket off.

"People started to giggle. When the judge said 'Absolutely not,' the audience broke into loud laughter. 'Very well,' Mr. H. said and went back to lock himself in again. Seconds later he returned to the judge with his jacket on. Everyone got to their feet. I'd never heard such cheering, laughing and clapping before."

Even Holmes laughed. "He knew it was easier to fool someone when you first get them to laugh. No magician wants an audience staring at his every move."

"You understand magic very well," Rose said with a trace of admiration in her voice.

"Is it true he made an elephant and its rider disappear?" I asked.

"Oh, yes. And there even was a huge swimming pool directly beneath the stage. Everyone in the audience gasped. When asked by a reporter how he had done it, Mr. H. said, 'Not even the elephant knows the answer to that.'"

That brought another laugh. Houdini had come up with the perfect answer to the reporter's question, and I felt a greater sense of loss with every new revelation. How could a man who lied with every movement he made on stage be so intent on telling the truth about the Spiritualists?

I took a second look at Rose. Her wan smile, the warmth of her speech and the look in her eyes made me suspect my original thoughts about their relationship was correct. Rose may well have wished Houdini wasn't just her employer.

"He never implied that any of his magic was anything more than an illusion, did he?" Holmes asked.

"No. Only to himself. He forced himself to believe he had supernatural powers so he could perform effectively. On stage he always took great pains to make sure everyone understood that everything he did was an illusion and explainable by natural means. He thought it inconceivable that some people, including Conan Doyle, could be convinced he was actually able to dematerialize himself."

"All very interesting," Holmes said in a stern voice. "Now you two stop your gabbing and eat. We'll be at the station in just a few minutes."

As if to verify Holmes's statement, the train slowed, then stopped.

"Are we in Boston already?" I asked.

"Westchester Station," the porter called. "All ashore who are going ashore."

Holmes and I jumped to our feet and ran across the car to peer out of the window. As suspected, we were just in time to catch sight of Becker running across the platform and ducking into the station.

"Good riddance. Now we can enjoy the rest of our breakfast in peace," Holmes said.

CHAPTER 18

Though I knew Becker had beat a retreat at Westchester, the morning's events had unnerved me so much I was actually hesitant to step off the train at Boston's South Station. If not Becker himself, one of his minions could be hiding in the crowds, just waiting to waylay us.

This time Violet was the brave one in the family; we got out hand in hand with me half a step behind.

I nudged Holmes. "You may want to buy some pipe tobacco while you're here. It's the second largest distribution point in America."

"I never touch American tobacco," he said with a snort. "Mine comes from Turkey."

I'd never used pipe tobacco so I couldn't imagine the difference. The closest I ever came to it occurred when I overheard my ten-year-old son, Cameron, on the telephone asking "Do you have Prince Albert in a can?" After a short pause he said, "Well, let him out," and screeched with laughter before hanging up. I swore I'd tan him until he looked like an Indian if he ever pulled such a prank again.

"What do we do now?" I asked.

"I can see no alternative to catching a cab to downtown Boston and finding Sir Arthur. We're staying in the same hotel with him."

"Becker knows that, too. Do you think it advisable to find another venue?"

"I had forgotten about that. You're quite correct, Wiggins. He knows we'll be visiting Margery also, but we can't merely skulk around like alley cats at St. Paul's Square. I'm very sure the man is a coward. When he strikes, he does so from a distance."

Violet grinned as a muscular young porter appeared with our luggage on a large flatbed cart. "I was told to stay with you while you're in the station. Is anyone meeting you?"

"No," Holmes said. "We would be very grateful if you would lead us to the nearest taxicab."

OUR TAXI MEANDERED along streets that veered off in one direction or another, came to dead ends, and even changed names.

"Forgive me for sounding rude, but isn't there a more direct way to the hotel?"

The driver chuckled. "Nope. It's the way the city was laid out in the beginning to avoid swamps and trees. People ask me about it all the time, thinking I'm trying to squeeze a few more pennies out of the fare."

"Your streets make as much sense as dumping tea into the bay when you were still part of England," Holmes said. "What a shameful waste."

The driver laughed. "Actually, there are people around here who would agree with you. Their ancestors were making a lot of money when we were part of Britain. Not everyone was happy when the War for Independence started."

"It's comforting to know at least some reasonable people lived in this insane country," Holmes muttered. "I understand they wanted to impeach your president when the skirmish of 1812 started. Mr. Madison's War, I believe it was called."

Tall buildings beckoned from afar. The closer we came to them, the greater the number of bicyclists and pedestrians we saw. Detroit's automobile makers had much work to do in this city.

Mostly we saw boats of all kinds, moored and sailing. With a river on one side and an ocean on three others, boats in Boston were as inevitable as poison in bathtub gin. New York Harbor harvested passengers and merchandise; Boston Harbor harvested cod, crabs, and lobsters. All were needed.

Turning onto Atlantic Avenue, we soon arrived at a towering building with miles of windows. A tall-hatted doorman awaited us.

"Here we are," the driver said. "Enjoy your stay."

Leaving the doorman and the driver to tend to the luggage, we passed through gilded doors to be greeted by the violin strains of Mozart's cheerful drinking song from *Don Giovanni*. I know very little about classical music, but Violet had dragged me to see the opera and I'd liked the piece so much, I left the theatre whistling it. Now I had all I could do to keep from joining in with the trio.

I applauded when they finished, drawing stares and strange looks.

"Stop that!" Violet said, cheeks a lovely shade of pink. She led me to a very over-stuffed mauve chair. "Now sit and behave yourself until Mr. Holmes is done."

Sitting and behaving wasn't difficult with the strings starting again. Beethoven with a brisk beat, though I couldn't remember its name. I followed along with a soft whistle until Mr. Holmes showed up.

"Sir Arthur's in his room. He wants us to come up in half an hour."

ON THE ELEVATOR RIDE up to our floor, Rose said she would wait in her room until our meeting with Sir Arthur was over.

"Conan Doyle knows about my connection to Mr. H," she said. "He probably won't want me to be there. I took the photographs exposing Margery's tricks. When they were published, C.D. broke off all relations with us."

Holmes threw her a sharp look. "Don't worry about that. I'm quite sure Sir Arthur isn't going to be pleased with any of us."

"I didn't tell you this," she went on, "but in 1898 Mr. H. himself actually worked as a Spiritualist for several months. This was long before he became a celebrity, and he and Mrs. H. took in more money at seances than he ever made with his magic or his escapes at that time. Then he remembered his promise to his father that he'd never do anything dishonorable, and he quit. Mr. H. always feared Conan Doyle would find out and call him a hypocrite."

"Once again, I'm sure you have nothing to be concerned about," Holmes said. "The way the Spiritualists have been investigating Houdini's past, I'm almost certain Sir Arthur already knows about it."

HOLMES UNLOCKED THE DOOR to our adjoining room, and we stepped inside. Imagine our amazement when we beheld two canopied beds with covers turned down, three dozen roses and a bathtub for four. Holmes took one look and grabbed his forehead. I merely groaned.

"Maybe we can trade rooms with the women," I said. Rapping on the adjoining door, Violet quickly answered.

"May I see your room?" I asked.

"If I can see yours," she said, stepping aside.

I groaned even louder. Their room was a Siamese twin to ours except for the colors of the canopies on the beds. Theirs were maroon and pink while ours were green and baby-blue. Only a whole chorus line of deranged Ziegfeld dancers could have designed such monstrosities. At least both rooms had a shower, and I wasn't going to waste another minute before I used it. Sir Arthur called whilst I toweled myself.

ELEVATORS HAD ALWAYS astounded me. Elisha Otis's invention made possible Louis Sullivan's masterpieces of soaring architecture. Few people had the wind or inclination to climb up and down twelve flights of stairs to get to and from their office. Space in the cities grew almost infinite when buildings became vertical rather than horizontal.

I felt we were being swept to the Maker's Throne as we rocketed upward. I had to hold my breath until we stopped on the eighteenth floor. The door to Room 1808 stood open. A familiar man stepped into the hallway. Always rotund, the years had made him roly-poly. His enormous white mustache hadn't changed, nor had he regrown any hair on his nearly bald pate. His right eyelid, drooping since he was kicked by a horse in Egypt, left him with a permanent, almost rakish wink-to-be. Except for the added weight, he had hardly changed in eight years.

He wasn't smiling.

"Come in, Holmes. I see you've brought your entourage with you. You're all welcome."

The voice seemed breathy and raspy. After a brief handshake with Mr. Holmes, he held out his hand to me. It trembled slightly when I shook it. "Wiggins, isn't it? It's been ages. At least ten years, is it not?"

"Not quite. It was in May of 1919. Just a few months after the war ended. I was visiting Holmes in Sussex. We came to London to see you to try to console you about the death of your son."

He gave my hand a squeeze. "Ah, yes. I remember that quite well. That was very kind of you."

Sir Arthur turned away from me and stared at Rose. "I've never met you, but I recognize you," he said in a cool voice. "You worked for Mr. Houdini, didn't you?"

Not at all intimidated, Rose introduced herself. "Yes, I was one of his investigators. Even though I have been on the opposite side from you on some issues, it's an honor to meet you. I read all your Sherlock Holmes stories that were translated into Polish when I was a young girl. I was astonished as everyone to find out he's a real person."

Without any indication he'd even heard her, Sir Arthur moved on to Violet. "I'm sure I have never met this lovely young woman. I can't believe you'd be associated with a crusty bachelor like Holmes, so I assume you are Mrs. Wiggins."

Violet curtsied. "I'm Violet. I couldn't travel with him in 1919 and always wished I had. I, too, am honored to meet you."

"The honor is mine. You remind me of Touie, my first wife."

Violet blushed deep pink and curtsied again. I could almost hear my beloved's heart pound. I always felt she was born out of her time and should have lived in England when Victoria was but a girl. Would she have been so pleased if she knew poor Louise had spent most of her last years of her life as an invalid, and that Sir Arthur had taken on Jean Leckie as his mistress long before his wife had died?

"Is Lady Jean present?" Holmes asked with a look around.

The skin on the bulbous head wrinkled. Turning red, Doyle looked at the floor. "I sent my wife away on a shopping trip to the apothecary for some of my medicines after you called. I didn't want her here when I talked to you. Or rather, I didn't want any of what we say to get back to Pheneas."

The words were greeted with complete silence.

Finally, I said. "Pheneas?"

"My wife's familiar," Sir Arthur said without looking up. "Her contact with the departed. I love Lady Jean very much and trust her with my life, but I must admit Pheneas frightens me. I feel helpless when he's around, even though he always assures me Jean and I will always be safe in his hands."

"Safe?" Holmes asked.

"Pheneas has been predicting the impending end of the world in the most terrible Biblical terms," Rose said. "All the unbelievers will perish and there'll be a new world order. Houdini's death couldn't wait that long, of course. The sooner that happened the better."

Sir Arthur turned sad eyes in Rose's direction. "I know that's what Pheneas was advocating, but I never wished for Houdini's demise. The press exaggerated the differences between us. He remained respectful to me until the strain became too great for either of us to bear. That's when we both said things we regretted."

"Mr. Houdini never told me what caused the end of your friendship," Rose said.

"It all started after our meeting in Atlantic City. I'm sure he never realized how much he hurt and upset me when he denied my wife's abilities as a medium. Just weeks after our séance with Lady Jean he published a statement that he had never met a true Spiritualist." He stopped. "Please excuse me."

Sir Arthur opened the hall door, looked out, then returned.

Could he have been expecting someone?

"I see I haven't been a very good host. Since we're talking about spirits, I have some I'd like to share with you."

We watched as he disappeared into the bedroom to return carrying a wine bottle showing from the top of a brown sack. "I brought this with me from England. It was wrapped in my pajamas when I went through American customs Fortunately, my celebrity preceded me and no one paid any attention to my luggage. It's a very good Manzanilla sherry. I don't drink it myself, but I don't mind others partaking. I asked the maid to bring us some extra glasses. Please find a place to sit."

Holmes and Rose waved off the offer of wine, but found two heavy chairs. Violet and I, on the other hand, were happy to accept the sherry. Violet especially, it seemed.

"When you wrote to me, you said the police suspected you of being complicit in murder," Holmes said. "Neither Wiggins nor I have ever heard the slightest hint the death was anything but natural. It has been officially ruled as peritonitis. Who is suggesting otherwise?"

"I received a letter from a Lieutenant Dan McGuire with the Detroit police," Sir Arthur said. "He was aware of our feud and said, with all the threats against Houdini's life, he was treating it as a possible murder. I apologize if my letter may have been misleading, Holmes, but I knew with your interest in Spiritualism and magic you'd want to investigate. Lady Jean and Pheneas refuse to tell me if the death was by natural causes or murder. All they say is his death was inevitable."

Holmes rested his face on tented hands, elbows firmly dug into the arms of his chair. "There's something more than luck at work here. Spirits might have been able to cause Mr. Houdini's peritonitis, if that was how he died, but as far as I know, no human could have been able to do that."

"My exact thoughts. It seemed miraculous, if you can call causing such a malady a miracle." Sir Arthur replied. "It just further impressed me with how powerful Lady Jane and Pheneas were. Those involved in the whole Spiritualist movement, in fact."

Holmes smiled wryly. "Wallace Whitehead striking him in the stomach and rupturing his appendix to seal his doom would seem to be just as miraculous, wouldn't you say?"

"Indeed, but I didn't want the power of our religion to be proven that way. I feel very sad about Houdini's death."

"I believe you do, but what if I told you we have strong evidence that it was not a miracle but mere foul play?"

Sir Arthur's eyes opened wide. "What do you mean?"

Mr. Holmes reached into his breast pocket. "This is a photo of Houdini's appendix taken after it was removed. Would you say it has the characteristics of appendicitis?"

Sir Arthur studied the picture, then shook his head. "Not conclusively, at least not in my estimation. Where did you get this?"

"Let's just say it came as a result of an investigation Wiggins and I have been conducting. As a matter of fact, we are finding considerable evidence to suggest Houdini was poisoned. Most likely sometime in October."

Sir Arthur caught his breath and appeared to deflate in front of our eyes. "As much as I want to believe in miracles, I have greatly feared he may have died by human hands. If so, I want his murderer brought to justice. What evidence do you have to support your theory?"

Holmes told him the history of our investigation. Sir Arthur sat up straighter at the mention of thallium poisoning. His once ruddy complexion blanched, and drops of perspiration appeared on his head. "Are you quite sure it is thallium?"

"As sure as we can be without an exhumation and laboratory examination. Why does that surprise you?"

"The man who discovered thallium, Sir William Crookes, had a séance with Margery several years ago."

The words came as a lightning bolt. Crookes's appearance in the narrative certainly could be a coincidence, but somehow it seemed more ominously fateful. My head began to spin. It'd spin even faster.

"Have you ever heard of Albert Baker?"

Sir Arthur turned as white as wallpaper paste and collapsed into a chair, seeming unable to answer.

Holmes and I got to our feet. "Do you need assistance?"

"No," Sir Arthur gasped. "I'm quite fine, thank you. I just wasn't expecting to hear his name in this connection. To answer your question, I know the name well. Margery's husband, Dr. Croydon, has mentioned it many times. How do you know about him?"

"Dr. Croydon?" Violet said.

Rose nodded. "He's a Spiritualist, too, and no fan of Houdini."

"He absolutely hated him," Sir Arthur said. "So did Walter."

Once again his words were greeted with silence. Sir Arthur managed a wan smile. Sitting up in his chair, he said, "I'm sorry. Walter's Margery's familiar. He's her dead brother and despised Houdini even more than my wife and Pheneas did. He called Houdini a son of a bitch after Houdini called Margery a fraud."

"Mr. Houdini was deeply offended by that," Rose said. "He saw it as slander against his mother."

"Houdini's accusations angered me, too," Sir Arthur said. "He besmirched the reputation of one of the finest Spiritualists ever."

With the full cast of characters finally clear, Holmes and I took turns telling Sir Arthur about our encounters with Albert Becker. Our friend listened, often shaking his head. Finally he interrupted in a sad voice, "There's no end to this, is there?"

"So it would seem," Holmes said. "Surely you must know there is a big difference between the true Spiritualist and the charlatan who only believes in the money. Mr. Becker is worst than most, using his income to help rebuild the German war machine. When it moves again, there'll be many thousands more fathers like you who'll lose their sons."

Sir Arthur got to his feet, Holmes's words seeming to put starch back into his spine. "I know, and it worried me at first. But don't you see that even the charlatans further the cause? Because of them, more and more people now believe in the Spiritualist movement. We're far more loving and welcoming than any other religion. Some day, even those who use our cause for their own ends will have to become believers. I don't need Pheneas or Lady Jane to tell me that. Nor did I need Mr. Houdini to try to prove me wrong."

I had never heard "the end justifies the means" put so bluntly. Naïve, but still persuasive, somehow. I knew no one could ever convince Sir Arthur otherwise. The split with Houdini was inevitable.

Mr. Holmes got to his feet and held out his hand to Sir Arthur. "I think we've learned as much as we can. It's probably good we leave before Lady Jane returns. Please don't tell her of our presence."

"You can be assured I won't."

"Very good. Oh yes. Be sure to rinse the glasses and put them away before she gets back."

CHAPTER 19

I fear the poor fellow has slipped terribly," Holmes said, as he put the key into the lock of our room. "I'm amazed at the hold Lady Jean has on him. She was always the meekest of lambs all the time I knew her. That obviously has all changed. Pheneas has him terrified."

"I know. And I don't like what I'm hearing about Margery's husband, Dr. Croydon, either. His connection with Becker sounds very suspicious to me."

"Indeed."

As we stepped into our room, we were overwhelmed by the cloying odor of roses. The sight of the turned covers on the four-poster made me want to go after the bed with an axe. I definitely was not in the mood for satin and lace. Tchaikovsky and Oscar Wilde probably would have been perfectly at home here, but I had never been sprinkled with pixie dust. I had to get away, and fast.

I felt a chilling thought. Maybe I wasn't as different from Becker as I thought or wanted to be. Worse, I didn't even know what I was angry about. I wasn't a close associate of Houdini's, and I hardly knew a thing about the Spiritualists other than what I heard and read about them. Why should I care so much? Was it worth putting Violet's and my life in danger?

I chuckled. Of course it was. It was every reporter's dream.

"What do we do now?" I asked Holmes.

"We look for another hotel. This one isn't safe."

AFTER WARNING THE WOMEN not to leave their rooms and giving them the new knock code, Holmes and I took the elevator to the lobby. The string quartet was gone, and I felt vaguely disappointed. I would have liked to hear a few more strains before we left.

A taxi waited outside the door.

"Good afternoon, my good man," Holmes said. "We're about to check out of our hotel and were wondering if you could recommend another."

"I know just duh place. It's just as nice as dis is and you can get Parker House rolls and Boston Cream Pie while you're there. It ain't too far from here, needer."

"Sounds good to me," I said.

"Youse guys talk diffrunt. You from England or some'in'?"

I wanted to say he talked different too, but didn't. I mentally translated everything else he said. "I was born in London, but I'm an American now. My friend lived there most of his life. Are you from around here?"

"Nah. Brooklyn. Near Ebbets Field. I used to go see the Robins play two, tree times a week. I miss 'em. Ever seen a baseball game?"

"I follow the Detroit Tigers. My son and I go to a game every once in a while."

"I go to Braves Stadium when the Robins come to town. The Robins're gonna win the World Series next year. Just wait 'n' see. What brings yuh to Boston? Is the king stoppin' by or some'in'?"

I smiled at that. "No. We came to have a séance with a woman here. She lives on Lime Street."

"Yeah? Up on Beacon Hill? Lotsa nice houses there."

"You can take us to the hotel a little later," Holmes said. "We'd like to see the house first."

"You got it. 'Tain't far." The driver made a left turn. I didn't try to remember our route, but a short time later he said. "It's in the next block."

He took another left and slowed. We were greeted by a formidable continuous brick wall broken only by doors and windows. The bricks jammed against the narrow sidewalk, seeming pushing unlucky pedestrians into the street. As we moved forward, I saw two men standing and talking on the sidewalk. I didn't recognize one of them, but I certainly did the other. Albert Becker.

We both ducked behind the front seat. "Don't slow up," I said. "You can take us to the hotel now."

Seconds later, I sat up straight and looked back over my shoulder. Becker was still in intense conversation and showed no sign he had seen us.

THE DOORMAN at the Parker House Hotel opened our taxi doors. Two more gold pieces disappeared from Holmes's pocket to pay the driver, and one for the doorman.

Inside we found twin marble columns and a fountain, much like the ones at the Boston Park. But there was one big difference. No musicians. Somehow I thought it should. Every hotel needed them.

Holmes made the reservations, quite sensibly asking to see the room before registering. The bellboy took us to the twelfth floor.

This time we found double beds with oak head and foot boards, plain oak writing desks with Gideon Bibles, a state-of-the-art radio without a coin slot, and numbered prints showing riders, foxes, and hounds. It even had a Kelvinator electric refrigerator stocked with Coca Cola, Dr. Pepper, and Ale-8-One. No Vernor's Ginger Ale, unfortunately, as much as I hoped to find it. Since Prohibition, it had become Michigan's unofficial drink.

"Looks fine to me," I said.

The adjoining room was just as sensible.

"Very good," Holmes said. "We'll take the rooms, and I'll have our baggage sent here."

As he reached into his pocket, I quickly took out a half-dollar and gave it to the bellboy. His eyes lit up. "Thank you very much, sir."

I t took two hours to arrange and complete the move. Violet par-
ticularly was unhappy. "That was such a nice room. We hadn't even
had time to unpack."

I cringed, knowing what was coming next.

Holmes glared at her. "I'm sorry this room isn't as much to your
taste, my dear, but Albert Becker is in Boston, and he knows we were
planning to stay at the Park Hotel. We nearly crossed paths with him less
than an hour ago. I don't want to chance that happening again. I didn't
leave word with the desk where we were going. The less anyone knows of
our whereabouts, the safer we'll be. That includes keeping Sir Arthur in
the dark as well, unfortunately."

Violet said, "I'm sorry. I really don't know what I was thinking. I
feel so sorry for Sir Arthur. I just know his wife's taking advantage of him.
I'm sure she's after his money."

"Most unlikely," Holmes said. "She comes from a wealthy family
and was an uncomplaining mistress for years while Sir Arthur's wife still
was alive. Even if she were a golddigger, no one would be able to convince
him of it. I'm sure he'd happily give her everything he had if he felt she
was advancing the cause of Spiritualism."

"I think we have an even bigger problem," Rose said. "How can you
meet with Margery if Albert Becker might show up?"

"Yes," I said in agreement. "I wondered the same thing. Are you sure
meeting her's really necessary in finding out what happened to Mr. Houdini?"

"Absolutely, Wiggins. She and/or Dr. Croydon is at the crux of the
whole matter. One or the other of them may even know who poisoned

Mr. Houdini. I'm certain we'll never learn anything from Dr. Croydon, and his association with Becker makes contacting him too dangerous to even try. Margery is our only hope."

"You won't be able to talk to Margery without Dr. Croydon present," Rose said. "*Scientific American* offered a ten-thousand-dollar prize to anyone able to prove themselves a genuine spiritualist. Margery insisted on performing her séance at her home, and for some reason, the investigating committee went along with it. Everyone but Mr. H., who wasn't even present, thought she passed. He insisted she be tested under identical conditions but in a different location. She refused. Dr. Croydon wouldn't allow it. He keeps her under lock and key."

"Too bad we don't have Houdini here to free her," Holmes muttered.

"We may have someone as valuable," I said. "We have Sir Arthur."

Holmes's face lit up. "Quite true, Wiggins."

"What about Lady Jean?" Violet asked with a sour look. I could tell she genuinely disliked the woman even though she had never met her.

"Wiggins has found the answer," Holmes said brightly. "We have only to find a way to liberate our caged birds."

NOT WISHING TO RISK being seen in the restaurant, Holmes ordered room service for all of us. Rose and Violet ordered cod, Holmes and I had Atlantic red crab. Each came with Duchess Potatoes and peas, the famed Parker House rolls, and Boston cream pie for dessert. Our order also included a copy for each of us of the two Boston newspapers.

"Our biggest problem seems to be how to free Margery," Holmes said. "What do you know about her, Rose?"

"For one thing, she's very pretty and vivacious. She's also flirtatious, and has given several séances in the nude to prove that ectoplasm actually came from her," she hesitated, "private parts."

I smiled for a moment, knowing she was deliberately being delicate for Violet's sake. I was quite sure if she were talking to Holmes and me alone, she wouldn't hesitate to use the anatomical term.

The look on Violet's face was priceless. "What's ectoplasm?" She asked in a tiny voice. I knew she was fascinated and didn't want to let on.

"It's a fluid that supposed to be inside everyone's body that can be transformed and become visible when a psychic performs a séance. It's reportedly very fragile and would disappear in the presence of light. Mr. H. made it on stage with a mixture of soap, gelatin, and egg white—"

Violet blushed when Rose added, "—and I think you can imagine how it came from inside her."

"I've never heard that part of the story," Holmes said, his voice dry. "Has she ever used her sexuality in other ways?"

"She certainly isn't adverse to kissing her male clients on the lips. Mr. H. was almost certain she was sleeping with Hereward Harrington, one of the members of the evaluating committee for the Scientific American's Prize. Harrington was one of her most ardent supporters. As you can imagine, he and Mr. H. were constantly at odds."

"Wasn't her husband aware of what was happening?"

"I don't see how he could not have been," Rose continued with a cattish smile. "Mr. H. always thought Croydon had some deeper design or purpose for her. Margery never charged for her séances. So it wasn't about money."

"It might have been if she had won the prize," I said.

"A few thousand dollars meant nothing to them. She wanted the prestige of being acknowledged as a true spiritual medium. And she came very close. Houdini was always the one who stood in her way. His reputation suffered because of their fight, too."

"Is there any chance she'll still get the award?" Holmes asked.

"No. The *Scientific American* closed the challenge without a winner."

A knock on the door announced the arrival of the food. The aroma of fish filled the room before the bellhop wheeled in a cart. I had always loved the smell, and the variety of colors on the plate made it an even bigger treat.

This time I didn't watch when Holmes tipped the young man. I was done nursemaiding his finances. The crab was far more interesting.

My unfortunate creature stood stolidly on my plate, waiting to be eaten; I certainly didn't want to make it wait long. We all took time to savour our first bites before resuming our conversation.

"Houdini said Margery was the most talented illusionist he ever met," Holmes said. "What is she like, personally?"

"I don't think she's nearly as mean-spirited as Dr. Croydon or 'Walter.' I've never even been convinced she was the real source of Walter's voice. It could well be Dr. Croydon's work, if he knows ventriloquism. She claims to be a spirit of the Indian tribes who lived in this area, and she never charges anything for her séances."

Holmes squinted. "That *is* the most obvious difference between her and the rest, isn't it?" he mused. "It may even be her greatest claim to legitimacy. Do you think she'd be willing to meet with Sir Arthur alone?"

"I'm sure she'd be delighted. He's probably her most famous supporter."

"Good. From what you've said, getting her out from Dr. Croydon's thumb would seem to be the most difficult task. Sir Arthur, on the other hand, is a world-famous scientist. We should be able to devise a way to send him on a scientific expedition, somewhere where Lady Jean wouldn't be welcome."

"I have just the answer," I said, pointing at an article on the front page of the *Boston News*. "J.P. Morgan is opening a power station in Winchester that's using equipment to regulate the flow of electricity. It's brand new. I'm sure Sir Arthur would be more than interested in seeing it, and Lady Jean wouldn't be invited, so she couldn't complain if he had to go without her."

"Brilliant, Wiggins. Now all we have to do is to find a way to get Margery out of her cage without losing her tail feathers."

We took another break to eat. Doused in butter, my little red beast's claws were delicious. I also knew I could eat what was inside its legs, but wasn't sure what I'd find underneath the mantle when I took it off. Why hadn't it come with instructions?

"Is Dr. Croydon still practicing medicine?" Violet asked.

"As far as I know," Rose said.

"Then why can't we have her meet us sometime when he's gone?"

Rose shook her head. "That isn't as easy as it might seem. She has someone with her at all times. Margery seldom is even allowed out to shop for food."

Holmes, who was tentatively poking at some white mass under the crab's shell, set his plate aside. "If that's the case, we still would have a chance to whisk her away alone. It'll require delicate timing, my friends, but we're more than capable of accomplishing it."

W e spent the rest of the day devising and evaluating our strate-gies. Violet's scheme, involving kidnapping, won my vote in two categories: the most creative, and most impractical. There indeed were windows in Croydon's house, but no obvious back doors. Fur-thermore, though I was still quite athletic for my age, I had never acquired the skills necessary to perform as a human fly.

Rose's idea was to call Margery out on an errand. Far less creative, but more practical. Unfortunately, she had no idea how to distract the bodyguard.

I wasn't surprised when Holmes remained close-mouthed about his stratagem. He began by making a phone call to Boston General to find out if Dr. Croydon would be at the hospital the next day.

His lips pulled into a tight smile as he listened to a somewhat lengthy reply. Then he hung up. "Some very interesting news. Not only will Dr. Croydon be away from Ten Lime Street tomorrow, he's leaving in the morn-ing to attend a conference in New York regarding pathogenic blood diseases. It seems Doctor Croydon was the attending physician when Calvin Coolidge, Jr., son of your president, died in June of 1924. There weren't any medicines strong enough to save him."

"I remember that," I said. "Calvin, Jr., had played tennis without socks and got a blister on his toe. It became infected. He died days later from erysipelas. I've read the president remains heartbroken to this day."

"Is there any chance Margery will be going to New York with the doctor?" Holmes asked.

"I have the answer to that," Violet said. "She's giving a speech to a local Spiritualist society tonight at the Bell in Hand on Union Street. They're holding their meeting there to celebrate Prohibition."

"What time is that?"

"Eight o'clock."

"Then I'm sure Sir Arthur and Lady Jean are already planning to attend," Holmes muttered. "This may be an opportunity in disguise."

"Is there any chance Becker will be staying with Margery while Dr. Croydon's gone?" I asked.

"I doubt it," Rose said, making a sour face. "For one thing, he isn't a very appealing specimen of manhood. For another, there really isn't anything he can do to further her career."

"Even if he's not sleeping with her, I'm sure he's lurking somewhere near," Holmes said with a wry smile. "He knows we'll contact her sooner or later. Put simply, she's bait. All he has to do is bide his time."

"That could work to our advantage," I said. "If he's fishing for us, he won't want anyone else around when we decide to nibble. All we have to do is steal the worm out from under his nose."

"Indeed, Wiggins," Holmes said cheerfully. "Though I doubt Mrs. Croydon would very much like being termed a worm. This is delightful, my friend. Becker knows we know what he's up to. It's playing chess against Moriarty once again. We'll just have to see who is the better chess player. I'm placing my wager on us. Now to work."

FOR THE OPENING MOVE, Holmes had me draw a sketch of Albert Becker. I had not drawn a caricature for several weeks, but, with Holmes's and Rose's assistance, we came up with a good likeness.

"Now we need to turn this drawing into fifty copies," Holmes said. "I understand a miraculous new printing process will do just that."

"It's called mimeography," I said. "It's not that new, nor is it all that miraculous. The hotel will know where to find printers that use it."

"Then I'll call room service and have them take care of it. How would you like to be in charge of recruiting the Lime Street Irregulars?"

"Me?"

"Yes. I'm far too old for such matters. You'll need a costume, of course. I should have kept the cap with earflaps you bought for me. That and a scarf around your face would make a good disguise."

"Ha ha," I said in a mirthless voice.

"I recommend you find an older boy to be your sergeant to gather and pass on intelligence to you. He'll help you do the recruiting, too. I'll be the paymaster, of course. Will fifty cents apiece per day to our agents be enough, do you think?"

"You can buy almost any boy in Boston for a week for fifty cents." I said. Years melted away and all the pleasures of my London boyhood returned in strength. "The Croydons live in a pretty exclusive neighborhood. It may not be easy for our Irregulars to get information."

"Boys are still as cunning as they were when I needed them in your day, Wiggins. You never let me down."

"This'll take time. What if Dr. Croydon returns before we're done?"

"The hospital said he won't be back until the end of the week. That gives us four days."

A BELL TINKLED A MERRY warning as I opened the door to the nameless basement level grocery on River Street. A large display case filled with a king's ransom of sweets at the front of the store was the first thing that caught my eye. It meant there were children in the neighborhood. I eyed the liquorice pipes with especial interest. I fancied them myself.

The man behind the front counter noticed. "Afternoon. Anything I can get you?"

"Give me a dime's worth of the pipes. My grandson really likes them."

He dropped ten into a paper bag. "Anything else?"

"Not now, thanks. Actually, I'm looking for a young man to help me move some boards onto my trailer. You know anyone who might want to earn a dollar for a few minute's work?"

"Heck, even I'd work for that."

"I'm afraid you're too old for the job, but I appreciate the offer."

"Sam Albright's twelve, so he should be big enough to be able to help you. He lives just down the block."

"Would you mind calling his mother to see if he'd be interested."

"Got a nickel?"

I handed him one, grinning.

A large rectangular wooden box with sizable pieces of metal bursting out of it hung on the wall next to counter. The grocer cranked the handle. "Hi, Bernice. Andrew eight two three four."

I bit off the handle of one of my liquorice pipes. I never chewed them. They were just the right size to suck.

"Hi. Is that you, Sam? Your mother around?"

I stood on one foot and then the other. I always hated to have to listen in on a conversation.

"She's not? Well, that's okay. I wanted to talk to you anyway. There's a man here who needs help loading some lumber. He says he'll pay you a buck. You interested?"

The grocer nodded at me. "He'll be right over."

WE MET NEAR the schoolyard two blocks away from Lime Street. The day was still warm, and just a thin wisp of smoke seeped out from the building's smokestack. Seagulls hovered like oddly angled marshmallows against the cold gray sky.

Sam seemed surprised I had neither a car nor lumber but didn't really care. All he wanted to know was what he had to do to get his dollar.

I took a copy of the sketch from my bag and showed it to him. "Have you ever seen this man?"

"No. Who is he?"

"His name's Alfred Becker. I think he's staying with Dr. Croydon. Do you know Dr. Croydon?"

"Of course . Everyone does."

"Good. Do you know those fellows playing football?"

Seven boys—nine or ten year olds, I guessed—were tossing a football around. One even wore a leather helmet and a blue jersey, the others, grass-stained denim and sweatshirts.

"Yeah. I know 'em."

"Have them come over. We'll want to ask them, too."

Sam trotted over to them, and they eagerly followed him back. They all looked interested to find out what I wanted. I passed out copies of the drawing.

None had seen Becker.

I reached into my pocket and passed a nickel to each of them. "Bring the picture home with you and ask your Mom and Dad if they've seen him. Your friends and brothers and sisters, too. Do any of you know Dr. Croydon?"

Four of them nodded.

"I think he knows the man in the picture."

"I don't like Dr. Croydon," the boy in the helmet said in a quiet voice.

"Why?"

"His son Mitchell was my friend. He came from England and talked like you. The doctor had adopted him and had him sent here. Mitchell played baseball and football with us, and came over to my house after school just about every day. Mom really liked him. One day he told me he was afraid of the doctor and wanted to run away. After that, he just disappeared and no one knew what happened to him. My mom asked the doctor, and the doctor said he had sent Mitchell back to England, but he wouldn't give her his new address. She says she's going to tell the police."

"I think she should. Does anybody else know anything about Mitchell or Dr. Croydon?"

A red-haired boy in a large gray woolen shirt raised his hand. "Mitchell told me he thought there were other boys who had lived in the doctor's house. He found clothes that weren't his, and a boy's ring with a 'T' on it. The doctor got real mad when he saw Mitchell wearing the ring, and almost tore Mitchell's finger off to get it."

"Dr. Croydon sounds as if he may not be a very nice person, but the man in the picture is even worse. If you see him, or find out anything about him, tell Sam. Don't go anywhere near him. I'll see you get a quarter."

They all ooed at the mention of the king's ransom.

A third boy, teeth wrapped in braces asked, "You gonna to tell my ma if you give me a quarter?"

I strongly suspected he would make a quick, illicit visit to the candy store when paid, but I decided to play along. "I bet you're saving your money to get her a present, aren't you? I won't tell her. It'll be our secret."

The sun had set and a much colder wind began to blow. The seagulls had departed for a warmer clime. The boys waved at me. "Bye, mister. We gotta go home."

I gave Sam his dollar. I also gave him a card with our phone number at the Parker House. "Be sure to call me when you learn anything. I have a lot more dollars in my pocket and will be happy to spend them. Oh, and by the way, don't tell anyone how much I'm paying you. If anyone comes to me and asks for more money, our agreement is off."

CHAPTER 22

Mr. Holmes wasn't in the room when I got back. Neither Rose nor Violet knew where he had gone, only that he had left a few minutes after I did and hadn't returned.

"Darn," I said, snapping my fingers. "I have news for him."

Violet straightened a small pile she had torn out of the local newspapers. "I hate feeling useless," she said. "I wish Mr. Holmes had given me something to do."

"You seem to be keeping busy on your own. What are all the paper bits about?"

"Everything I can find about the Croydons and the Spiritualists. I didn't realize the Spiritualists actually had churches."

"That's just what they call their meeting places," Rose said. "I held my gatherings in my living room. The Baptists and the Methodists really hate the Spiritualists because they think they're stealing their members."

"Good to know," I said. "Anyone want a liquorice pipe?"

I got no takers. I fished one out of the bag and stuck the stem into my mouth. "Does this remind you of anyone you know?"

I was a little disappointed when neither of them scarcely looked at me. I decided it was because Holmes hadn't smoked his pipe very much on the trip.

Rose was excited to hear my information about Dr. Croydon's son.

"One of Mr. H's investigators got wind of Mitchell's disappearance months ago," she said. "Mr. H. followed up, and the Boston police promised to make an inquiry. Months went by, and nothing happened. The British police said they were baffled. Mr. H. said he was sure they were being paid off."

"Maybe I can talk Mr. Holmes into investigating when he gets back home."

"That may be the only way to get any results. I'm sure Mr. Houdini never heard about the ring Dr. Croydon's son found. It could be important, but you can be sure the Boston police won't want to cause trouble for a member of such an important family on a child's say-so. Even if they found the ring, it wouldn't prove anything illegal had happened."

I heard a scratching at the hall door, a rattle. Then the handle turned, and Mr. Holmes walked in. In fine fettle, I might add. "Good evening, everyone. I'm glad to see we're all here. Did you have a successful recruiting trip, Wiggins?"

"Yes. Where have you been?"

"At the library. I needed to do some research I deemed important enough to be worth the risk of being discovered."

"From your jaunty mood, it looks like you were successful," I said.

"Quite. For one thing, Dr. Croydon wrote a book, *Surgical After-Treatment,* in 1905. It's mostly concerned with techniques to prevent infections in hospitals after surgeries. Not being able to prevent President Coolidge's son from developing erysipelas must have been a severe blow to the doctor's ego and reputation, even if it wasn't his fault. His wife's fame as a Spiritualist could have been seen as a way to regain some of the family's status. He's the one who insisted she had extra-normal abilities and pushed her into performing séances."

"Why?" I asked.

"I really don't know, yet. Dr. Croydon is Margery's second husband. Her first was a grocer here in Boston. She had a son, John, with him. She met the doctor when he performed surgery on her. When she divorced, John came with her."

"Did you also know they adopted a boy from England who mysteriously disappeared when they sent him back?" I asked. "That's my big discovery of the day."

"I didn't. Very good. I see you've already made some progress."

I told him the details I learned. Holmes seemed especially interested in Mitchell's discovery of a boy's ring.

"I expect Sir Arthur may be able to give us a few more details," Holmes said. "Another interesting tie-in to our investigation is that Dr. Croydon is very active in the American Eugenics Society."

"What's that?"

"It's part of a world-wide organization that claims to promote the overall betterment of the human race by the elimination of inferior races and individuals. Many of the richest people in the world are ardent supporters. Even your Oliver Wendell Holmes backed a Tennessee law that would have allowed the sterilization of a family with a history of feeble-mindedness, though the majority of the Supreme Court disagreed. Dr. Croydon's a very close friend of one of the society's founders, Andrew Preston of the American Fruit Company."

"Preston!" I sputtered. "He's got a worldwide reputation for mistreating everyone who works for him."

Holmes shrugged. "Working them to death is one of the ways to eliminate inferior races, you know. Getting back to Dr. Croydon—he seemed to be particularly unhappy that Houdini, the man attacking his wife, was Jewish. Margery's dead brother especially enjoyed referring to Mr. Houdini as 'the dirty kike,' the vulgar term for 'copulating Jew.'"

I whistled. "It does sound as if he's reading from the same script as Albert Becker."

The conversation ended with the ring of our telephone. Holmes answered, then held out the receiver toward me.

"Wiggins."

"Sniggiw, it's Mas."

I cringed. Why had I agreed to using backward names as codewords, as much as Sam had insisted on it? Then I remembered I had been a boy myself, very much like him, once upon a time.

"I have something to report," Sam said. "My mother told me a little boy named Tom once lived with Dr. Croydon. She said she used to find him crying on the curb by the doctor's house, and she would bring him a cookie to make him feel better. Then she just never saw him again. She was always afraid to ask if something had happened to him." He paused to take a breath. "Do I get my dollar?"

"You certainly do. Meet me by the school tomorrow afternoon and I'll give it to you. Have you heard from any of the other boys?"

"Not yet. If I do, I'll call you. Otherwise, I'll see you tomorrow."

Holmes eyed me expectantly.

"Nothing new about Becker," I said, "but apparently Dr. Croydon did have other wards. The ring young Mitchell found probably belonged to a boy named Tom."

"If we weren't so involved in our inquiry regarding Houdini's death, I'd very much like to learn more about Dr. Croydon's history with children. Right now, I'd like to know more about his relationship with Margery and Albert Becker."

"I can't tell you anything about the Croydons' private life," Rose said, "but I do know the doctor always sits at Margery's right when she conducts a séance. Mr. H. was sure that was how she was able to perform some of her tricks."

"Perhaps you should become Margery and put on a séance for us," Holmes said. "You undoubtedly know more about her than all the rest of us combined."

"That'd take too much time and work, and you wouldn't learn much from it, anyway. The fact that Dr. Croydon is absent and Conan Doyle will only be around for a short while may work to our advantage. Margery might be persuaded to put on a séance without her husband."

Mr. Holmes's eyes lit. "Very good, my dear. She wouldn't be alone against a hostile audience. Lady Jean probably would be happy to take the doctor's place."

Violet got up from her table. "And don't even think of not taking me with you this time. I'm still mad you left me at home when you confronted Albert Becker."

"Have no fear, dear lady. You're essential to the proceedings. It's Rose I'm concerned about. Margery and Lady Jean may consider her too hostile."

Rose jumped in immediately. "I agree. I'll spend the time contacting the other investigators. They may have information we don't know about. Unfortunately I may have to run up a large long-distance bill if I do."

"Don't hesitate to do whatever you find necessary. We have myriads of intriguing possibilities in our investigation, but little hard evidence. Anything you find out could be vital."

"It may not be too hard to get Sir Arthur and Margery together as it might seem," Violet said. "She's lecturing tonight, and I wouldn't be surprised if Sir Arthur was intending to attend."

Holmes rubbed his hands together. "Excellent, dear lady. I'll give him a call and find out. What time does the lecture start?"

"Eight o'clock."

"It's only five-thirty now. We should have more than enough time to make our arrangements."

The phone rang and Holmes answered. "It's for you," he said with a nod in my direction. "It sounds like a youngster."

"Hello."

"Mr. Wiggins, this is Terry Fields. I was one of the boys you talked to earlier. The one with the braces."

"I remember you, Terry. I suggested you pass on your findings to Sam, but I'm happy to talk to you, too."

"Sam told me to call you because it's important."

My ears pricked. "Did you see the man in the drawing?"

"Yes. I went back by Dr. Croydon's house after I left the schoolyard. Dr. Croydon and this man were talking. The man in the picture is staying at the Milner Hotel."

My heart started to pound. "Great job. I've got a whole dollar for you when we meet tomorrow."

"Wow! That's great. Remember, don't tell my mother."

"THE MILNAH HOTEL?" the driver parked outside the hotel asked. "That's by the Leatha District and China Town. It's not the Parka House, but it's a nice clean place to stay. It's ova on Cholls Street. You want me to take you theah?"

"Not exactly," Holmes said. "We'd like you to drive by it. A friend is staying there, and we want to see what the hotel is like."

"Get in."

We did, and were greeted by the essence of pastrami. The driver must have just finished his supper. There had to be a delicatessen nearby, and I was dying to sink my teeth into an old-fashioned Reuben sandwich. Almost anything, actually. The expensive fare Holmes kept forcing on us was fine, but even chop suey or chow mein from China Town would be just as welcome.

Once again the insane illogic of Boston's streets played out for our amusement. I had never before heard of moving west by going northeast and doubted I ever would again. Finally, we turned onto a street with traffic. Atlantic Highway quickly took us where we wanted to go.

A canopy with the words "Hotel Milner" rigidly guarded the sidewalk to the hotel. Trees in boxes stood like tiny sentinels along the carpet to the door. In nice weather, guests would sit out on their balconies above the street. Now, the windows were shut snugly, and the flowerboxes stood empty except for the occasional dismal bit of wilted green.

"Stop," Holmes said.

The driver put on his brakes, then moved up against the curb to park behind a black Pierce-Arrow 33 motor car.

Holmes got out. I followed. The Arrow, one of the legendary "three P" automobiles, had always been my favorite car. The Packard and Peerless were beautiful, too, but I liked the Arrow's canvas roof and the silver archer on the front of the hood. I could never understand why they had two tires strapped to the trunk. Did they really run the risk of a double blow-out? Or were they of such poor quality they could never be trusted at all?

Having had my fix of arrow-envy, I got back into the cab.

"How do you like Bas-ston?" the driver asked.

Under the circumstances, I wasn't much in the mood for small talk. "It's very scenic. I'm from Detroit, so it's entirely different."

"I s'pose it is. You know why we ah called Bean Town?"

Though I didn't really care, I said, "No. Why?"

"The colonists liked to bake beans in molasses. The name stuck. There's another interesting story about molasses, too. Did you ever hear about the big molasses flood of 1919?"

I snapped to attention. That intrigued me, even though I had to translate every other word he said. "No. What happened?"

"Some company turned molasses into alcohol up the north end of town, right on the sea. They stored the molasses in a huge tank. One day in mid-January they had more'n two million gallons waitin' to be converted. It had been cold overnight, but the next day it warmed up. People say they heard what sounded like machine-guns firin', and then all of a sudden, everything around was flooded with molasses. Men driving wagons in the streets had their horses drowned. Anybody walkin' on the street either got sucked under or swept away for blocks to get up and walk away unharmed. The company had to pay a million dollars in fines. The tank wasn't strong enough to hold that much molasses. I can still smell it sometimes on a hot summer night."

"That's really interesting," I said, hoping Holmes would get back soon.

He did—ten minutes later. He was scowling when he got into the seat next to me. "Please return to the Parker House."

CHAPTER 23

s was his wont, Holmes kept his silence on the ride back to the hotel. While we rode, he wrote in his notebook, his mouth working as if he were adding sums before shaking his head and starting anew.

At the hotel, he let me pay the taxi driver and the door man, barely looking at them as he passed. I followed behind, puzzled. I had never seen his thought processes so close to the surface before.

Finally, he bent close to my ear and said, "Your intelligence report was correct. Albert Becker is staying at the hotel, but he isn't in his room. I called the Boston Police. They said they'll contact the New York police to verify the attempted murder charges before they try to arrest him. Even if they succeed, which I very much doubt, we still have to contend with Schmidt and his accomplice."

"We have to assume Becker is still on the loose. I'm certain he knows about our intent to meet with Margery and the three of them are waiting for us to make the first move."

"Lamentable, but quite true," Holmes said.

I broke into a broad smile. "But what they may not know is that we've already met with Sir Arthur. I expect we moved too quickly for that."

Holmes eyebrows raised. After a moment of silence, he said, "Brilliant, dear fellow. I'm amazed I didn't realize that myself. Sir Arthur probably is the only one who can contact Margery safely. What we told him about Becker would allow him to help us without having to switch sides. What time is it?"

"Nearly six-thirty."

"That should give us just enough time to get to Margery's speech."

WE STOPPED AT THE FRONT desk to learn Mr. Holmes had a message. Holmes read it aloud when we got back to our room. "Sir Arthur wants you to know he'll indeed be in attendance at the lecture, and he'll be delighted to see you. He'll get you invitations. The lecture isn't open to the general public."

Rose, who had been sitting reading a newspaper, got to her feet. "Since I won't be going with you, this'll be a good time to start making my calls. Anyone need to use the phone before I start?"

Finding no takers, she lifted her briefcase from the floor, set it on a chair and moved it next to the phone.

"I wish you could come with us, Rose," Violet said in an excited voice. "I'll wear what I was wearing at the play. I've already pressed it so it doesn't even look as if it's been worn. Doesn't that sound like a good idea to you, Timothy?"

She already knew the answer. She always looked dazzling in whatever she wore, and I could never understand why she asked for my opinion so often. Some deep-seated insecurity women seem to have, I suppose. I found it flattering, and never had to say anything more than mere truth. "You always look a vision, my dear."

She certainly outshone me. My serge business suit had gone limp, so I solved the problem by wearing a cardigan sweater and tie with the pants. I did send my shoes down to be shined, putting a rush on the job, but I knew my attire didn't measure up to Boston standards by any means. I really didn't care. Except for the Fords and the Durants and the other automobile manufacturers, and maybe the mayor of Detroit and the governor of Michigan, my city didn't go in for such snobbery. Holmes, on the other hand, could wear the same tweeds he wore when he hired me to be an Irregular, and he'd look as gentlemanly as ever.

With a knock on the door, my shoes returned. They charged me a whole dollar for the rush job and a half-dollar tip. Outrageous, of course, but I have to admit they did an excellent job of polishing them. I could see my reflection when I looked at my feet.

"Let us be on our way," Mr. Holmes said.

Violet took my arm as we waited for the elevator.

We stepped out of the hotel into a beautiful late fall evening with a light, refreshing breeze. I took a deep breath. Our cab was waiting, idling. The Bell in Hand was just a few blocks away. I hesitated before opening the door.

"Come along, Wiggins," Holmes said. "I'd like to walk, too, but it's far too dangerous."

Suddenly I felt like Dr. Watson. "But how . . . ?"

"You are transparent, dear fellow. You were looking longingly up the street and determining how far it would be to our destination. I don't fault you one bit for wanting to walk. I haven't been getting my constitutionals lately, either."

This time we didn't engage a chatty cab driver. He dropped us off on Union Street in front of a red brick building, allegedly the longest continuously operating pub in Boston. Or at least it had been until Prohibition.

A small crowd already was waiting outside on the sidewalk. As a Midwesterner, I hadn't realized the popularity of ankle-length dresses with the cream-of-society woman, or the appeal of bowler hats to their husbands. They gathered in a tight group outside the pub. Though the tones of their conversation were subdued, the gay laughter wasn't.

With a huge smile, Violet said hello to a woman in a taffeta dress. The Brahmin worthy gave her a sidelong glance before turning away. My heart fell as Violet's smile disappeared.

Mr. Holmes opened the door to the pub.

"Do you suppose we could stay out here for a moment?" I asked.

"It isn't that warm," Holmes said. "You certainly may, if you wish."

Violet turned and joined me. "Save us a seat," I said.

The odors of cigar smoke, mingled with what probably was expensive perfume, wafted towards us, but we barely noticed it. I could see Violet trying to eavesdrop on the Bostonians' conversation, but she quickly gave up.

I was about to suggest we go inside when a cab pulled up. The driver opened the rear door and Sir Arthur and Lady Jean got out.

One of the men in the group waved at him. "Good evening, Sir Arthur. I'm glad you came to the lecture. Please join us."

Though Lady Jean smiled and waved back, Sir Arthur absently nodded at him before turning his attention to us. "Wiggins and Miss Violet. I'm so happy to see you. I'm sure Mrs. Croydon will do a good job of convincing you of the truth of Spiritualism."

"I have an open mind," I said.

"Excuse me," Lady Jean said, turning to me and speaking in a not especially friendly tone, "Just who are you?"

"I invited them," Sir Arthur said. "They're friends of Doctor Trevor Claybrook." He turned to me. "Is he inside?"

"Waiting for us. He's saving our seats."

"Then we'll join you. How do you like Boston?"

"We haven't seen much of it," Violet said.

"Yoohoo. Lady Jean," one of the Bostonian women called.

Lady Jean broke into a wide smile. "Louise! I thought you might be here tonight. We'll join you inside."

Sir Arthur stiffened. "But my dear, I want to sit with Doctor Claybrook and his friends."

"Absolutely not." With that, Lady Jean pulled on her husband's arm and tried to drag him to the other group.

Sir Arthur stood firm. "Sit where you will, my dear. I'll sit with Mr. Holmes and join you after the lecture is done."

The look of shock on Lady Jean's face was a sight to behold. I could barely believe Sir Arthur would flaunt social custom in public, but he clearly wanted to talk to Holmes.

I held my breath. Lady Jean's eyes blazed at Violet and me. She opened her mouth, ready to return a verbal volley, then shut it.

Would she relent and sit with us? I prayed she wouldn't.

Turning with exaggerated delicacy and sporting a big smile, she said, "Very well, my dear. Go sit with Dr. Claybrook and his friends." After another glare in our direction, she contemptuously turned her back to us and walked toward Louise. "How are you, darling? It's so wonderful to see you again."

I blew out a big breath as I opened the door for Sir Arthur and Violet, though I could still feel Lady Jean's eyes burning into the back of my neck.

We stepped into a different era. Huge timbers and exposed joists outlining the interior stood bravely, now deeply cured from years of wood and tobacco smoke. The booths along the wall opposite the bar were obviously added in a different century. Holmes, who had taken a seat in the second row, stood and gestured to us.

We walked past bare shelves under huge mirrors behind the long bar. The area where owners once stored barrels stood empty. It seemed ironic that a watering hole where George Washington and John Adams met to quaff an ale on a winter's evening had to serve near-beer, sarsaparilla, and ginger ale. Somehow, they didn't quite have the same panache.

Mr. Holmes stood, and Sir Arthur seized him in a hug. The gesture was so uncharacteristic, I could see the look of embarrassment on Holmes's face. He didn't return the embrace, but, by his faint smile, I could tell he was delighted to find Sir Arthur alone.

Was his uncharacteristic show of affection another effect of embracing Spiritualism? I really wondered.

Sir Arthur turned to look back toward the entrance. "I'm glad to be able to speak to you alone," he said in a low voice. "There's more I need to tell you, and there won't be enough time tonight."

"Then you need to go on a scientific expedition," Holmes said with a twinkle in his eye. "The local power plant has just installed some important new equipment. I'll have J.P. Morgan call you tomorrow morning and invite you to view it."

Sir Arthur looked startled for a second. "Morgan? Oh, yes I see. Of course. I'll be delighted to take a look. Lady Jean will be pleased, also. It'll give her more time to spend with her friends."

"Excellent." Holmes's voice lowered to a near whisper. "Tell me. I know you are very fond of Margery. What do you think of her husband?"

Sir Arthur faced away from me, but I could see his back stiffen. "He's done a great service to the cause. Without him, most people would consider Mrs. Croydon to be nothing more than a skillful magician."

"I understand there's been some question about the whereabouts of a young man the Croydons adopted. Dr. Croydon says he returned to boy to England, but no one seems to know where he is."

Sir Arthur stiffened again. "The doctor actually asked my assistance in the matter. I have no real influence with the sheriff or the local constabulary, so I haven't been able to do much on his behalf. He's asked how to go about adopting other boys, too."

We turned at the sound of footsteps and quiet talk behind us. The seats began to fill. I gathered that the custom in Boston was to socialize somewhere other than in the lecture hall, and then come in just before the event. Lady Jean and her friends sat several rows behind and on the opposite side of the aisle from us. She noticed my glance and returned it, hurling several sharp daggers in my direction. I threw her an open-handed innocent look in return. I wanted her to know it wasn't my fault.

Soon every seat was taken, and I took a deep breath.

CHAPTER 24

The audience applauded as a matronly woman wearing a hat with a pigeon roosting on its brim suddenly appeared at the podium. After a flowery and longer-than-necessary introduction, Margery stood to enthusiastic applause. Her easy smile told me she was used to public speaking. She was tall and attractive; her chaste gingham dress and low-heeled shoes belied her high social standing. She also was very pretty without makeup.

I was impressed.

I jumped when Violet jammed her elbow into my side.

After acknowledging the applause, Margery began. "Good evening. It's a great pleasure to see so many friends. Especially Sir Arthur Conan Doyle, our greatest friend in the cause."

Sir Arthur stood and bowed to even louder applause.

"Would you like to introduce your guests?"

Sir Arthur gestured for us to stand. I wondered how he would introduce us. "Of course." He put a hand on Holmes's shoulder. "This is my very old friend Doctor Trevor Claybrook. I've known him since my days in medical school."

I nodded to myself in triumph. I loved the irony. He didn't introduce him as Holmes. His real name now had become the name Holmes used in public.

"My newer friends are Timothy and Violet Wiggins. They're long-time friends of Dr. Claybrook and have come all the way from Detroit to meet you."

We stood, turned and smiled, nodding to the polite applause. I noticed that Lady Jean didn't join in.

156

We sat and Margery continued. "I bring you greetings from my husband, Dr. Croydon, who can't be with us tonight because he's in New York for a medical conference. I also have had recent word from my late brother, Walter. He sends his greetings and wants you to know everything's up to date in hell. They switched from coal to oil heat a week ago."

Like most of the audience, I laughed at that. Perhaps a bit louder than the rest. It won me another poke in the ribs from Violet. Despite my suspicions about her, I found myself liking Margery. Other than the cab drivers, she seemed to be the nicest person I had encountered since coming to Boston.

"All of you by now know about the death of Harry Houdini. Much has been made about my so-called feud with him. As strange as it may sound, I actually liked and respected him. He was honest and forthright. I still don't believe the charges that he cheated when trying to discredit me before the Scientific American committee. I have no idea where the rubber eraser or yardstick found inside my cabinet came from, though my husband and Walter are convinced they were placed there by Houdini to try to prevent me from conducting my séance. I always thought it sad to realize he could have become the greatest Spiritualist the world his ever known. Instead he followed the dictates of his conscience."

She paused. "And made millions of dollars *that* way."

That brought loud laughs and enthusiastic applause.

I liked the gentle irony. Her attitude toward Houdini wasn't what I expected. Holmes's raised eyebrows suggested he felt the same way.

"I have some exciting news for my followers and the entire Spiritualist community. My husband LeRoi and I have been invited to meet with the prime minister of Canada, Mr. Thomas Glendenning Hamilton, to put on a demonstration in Winnipeg next February. Mr. Hamilton is an enthusiastic Spiritualist, and I know our visit will spread our message in our neighbor to the north. He has also volunteered to extend our Spiritualist custom of sharing living quarters with fellow members. I've never been a guest with a high government official before."

She was greeted with polite applause. For the first time I turned to take a look at the rest of the audience.

And wished I hadn't. I caught my breath, gasping loud enough to cause Violet to grab my arm. Even Margery stopped speaking and threw me a worried look.

"Sorry. Gas pain," I mumbled. "I'm fine."

Mr. Holmes stared into my face, and I made a small head gesture over my shoulder.

After Margery resumed her speech, Holmes surreptitiously turned his head to look behind him. He turned back, shrugged and gave me a puzzled look.

Steeling myself, I made another glacially slow turn. The rear aisle chair behind us now stood empty.

Albert Becker had left the premises.

I found it impossible to follow the rest of her lecture. I did understand Margery to say she never knew she had psychic powers until her husband brought a specially made séance table into the large room on the fourth floor. Almost as a party joke, the doctor suggested she conduct a mock séance, since séances were all the rage at the time. To everyone's surprise the table lifted off the floor and hung midair. After that, she made regular invitations to those who wanted to see her. She also said she didn't charge for her services because she and her husband felt her contribution to Spiritualism wasn't based on money.

"If anyone is inclined to donate financially, they can do so to the Spiritualist Church of their choice."

The more she spoke, the more confused I became. This was no mere charlatan advertising for customers. I could detect not even a whit of deception. Her words, expression, and voice all bespoke sincerity.

Perhaps I was too confused by fear to be able to judge her adequately. My heart still beat so violently from seeing Becker I could feel blood rushing through the veins in my temples. Violet kept looking at me with a worried expression, and even Holmes sat forward to study me from time to time.

At last, the lecture was over and everyone stood to give her an enthusiastic hand. Could she be a true medium? I couldn't tell. I was sure I missed the tell-tale clues to her possible deception. I could only hope Holmes and Violet could see through her.

"What on earth is wrong with you, Wiggins?" Holmes asked.

"Albert Becker was sitting in the back row." I said in a whisper. "I spotted him, and he nodded at me with a frightful look. He must have left seconds later. I'm sure he went to fetch his shorts."

Smiling, Margery got down from the stage and approached Sir Arthur. His face lit up brightly, then he blushed, clearly pleased, as she threw her arms around him.

Remembering what Rose had said, I half expected her to kiss him. Or him to kiss her.

Lady Jean appeared. In a half-scolding voice she said, "Arthur, behave yourself."

"Sorry. I couldn't help myself. This is the greatest woman who has ever lived." Then he caught the expression on his wife's face. "After you, of course, my dear."

"I have something important to tell you," Holmes said in a firm voice. "Albert Becker, who you know as Albert Baker, was in the audience earlier tonight. He'd tried to murder Mr. and Mrs. Wiggins at a theatre in New York. Now he's here in Boston, undoubtedly lurking about somewhere to make another attempt."

"Albert Baker?" Margery said in what sounded to me like total disbelief. "He's a good friend of my husband and a well-known Spiritualist. Why would he want to kill your friends?"

"Vengeance," Holmes said. "Wiggins and I exposed him as a fraud, and he thinks we're Jewish. As a radical anti-Semite, that's something he couldn't abide."

A young woman wearing a short coat and knitted scarf and cap appeared. She barely looked in our direction. "Is something wrong, Mrs. Croydon?"

"No, Lucille. Just wait for me by the door. I'll be out shortly."

"I'm totally at a loss what to do," Sir Arthur said. "I certainly cannot allow you to be murdered."

"Nor can I," Margery said. "I can scarcely believe it's true. Mr. Baker's been friends with my husband for years."

"How long?" Holmes asked.

"Sometime before the war. LeRoi was a surgeon with the US Army. How they met, I can't say. I do know Mr. Baker and he both were very interested in eugenics and belonged to the Eugenics Society together."

"Has your husband ever said anything about the war?"

"Only that he regrets America decided to side against the Germans. He admires them very much. He says they're the greatest scientists and surgeons in the world."

"Enough about Dr. Croydon," Sir Arthur said. "We have to come up with a way for everyone to leave safely. Perhaps I should find a phone and contact the police."

"That isn't necessary, Sir Arthur," Margery said. "I'll have my chauffeur take your friends to their hotel. There won't be room for all of us, so Lucille and I will wait here. I'd welcome a chance to converse with you and Lady Jean, anyway, if you're willing to stay. Much has happened since our last correspondence."

"We'd be delighted," Lady Jean said, and Sir Arthur nodded an enthusiastic assent.

"Lucille," Margery called. "Would you please have Simon come in?"

"Of course."

I felt a twinge of suspicion. Could my impression of her be wrong? Was she looking for a way to deliver us into Becker's hands? But then, even if that were true, how could he have known we would be attending tonight, or that we would feel threatened and seek protection?

"We appreciate your kindness very much," Holmes said. "I hope this won't be an inconvenience to you."

"Not in the least. Any friend of Sir Arthur is automatically a friend of mine."

A swarthy young man wearing a tight navy-blue double-breasted coat and chauffeur's cap approached us. "Yes, Miss?"

I could smell garlic on his breath.

"Simon, I want you to drive my friends to their hotel. Where are you staying?"

I let Holmes answer. "The Park Hotel, the same as Sir Arthur."

Sir Arthur was about to say something, then quickly shut his mouth. I didn't need to be Sherlock Holmes to realize he'd almost blurted out something about our earlier visit in front of Lady Jean.

"Yes, Miss," Simon said. "I'll be back in ten minutes."

After brief handshakes with Sir Arthur, Lady Jean, and Margery, we fell in behind Simon. Light snow was falling, clinging to our clothes and our hair as we stepped outside. I felt a moment's panic. Would Becker be bold enough to attack us as we came out? Holmes said the man was a coward and would wait until we were alone to strike.

Even so, I could only hope his henchmen were equally cautious.

Simon opened the back door of a black limousine. Violet entered first, followed by Holmes.

I took a long look at the incredibly lengthy snout of the Croydon's limousine and caught my breath.

"My God. It's a brand new Studebaker Commander. I've seen pictures of them, but this is the first one I've actually laid eyes on."

"Yes, sir. The doctor bought it. How did you know that what it is?"

"It's an automobile. I know all the makes and models of all the cars. I have to."

That brought a puzzled look. "Very good, sir."

I stood dumbfounded inspecting the vehicle. A six-thousand-dollar hunk of metal boggled my mind.

"Get in here, Timothy!" Violet said, nervous, as she tugged at my coat. "Don't stand out in the street."

Then I remembered Becker and scrabbled inside.

As we started away, Holmes took his pipe from his jacket pocket and put it in his mouth. There was no tobacco in the bowl, and he made no movement to fill it. I'd seen him do it before many times when I was a boy. Since conquering his drug addictions, his pipe had been his dummy, as necessary to him as a rubber nipple was to a baby. "Well, Wiggins, what do you make of Margery?"

"I was too distracted by Becker's presence to listen or watch her too closely. I was surprised how likable and honest she seemed. To be truthful, I was counting on your observations."

"I think we should hear Violet's appraisal before I give mine. What did you think of her, dear lady?"

"She's an interesting woman. She's not from an upper-class background, so she works very hard on her speaking and demeanor to be accepted. And she likes to make eye contact with her audience—doesn't she, darling?"

"I didn't notice," I lied.

"Yes, you did," Violet said firmly.

I blanched.

"I don't think she liked Harry Houdini nearly as much as she claimed," she continued, "but otherwise, I think she was being honest."

"Bravo!" Holmes said. "You indeed have keen powers of observation. Almost exactly the same conclusions I came to, myself. I'm also convinced she doesn't know everything about her husband, or she doesn't want to know some things. One of them is her husband's relationship to Albert Becker."

His sentence ended in an explosion. We slammed against each other as the vehicle caromed to the left. Wheels squealed, and we stopped abruptly as an oncoming vehicle slammed into the front bumper.

"Sorry," Simon's hollow voice said from a speaker behind my right ear. "Is every one all right?"

We untangled. "No injuries, it seems," Holmes said. "What happened?"

"One of the tires blew out. I'll talk to the other driver and put on the spare. We'll be on our way in a jiffy."

"Which tire?" Holmes demanded sharply.

"Rear passenger. Just be patient. It won't take me long."

I bent forward to look out the passenger-side window and saw a dark alleyway across the street. My heart pounded as I caught movement. Someone had backed against a wall to get out of sight.

"Down on the floor!" I shouted.

I flattened against the seat. Holmes and Violet dove to the floor.

"What is it, Timothy?"

"That wasn't a blowout. We're being ambushed."

Though this seemed a very gangster-like attack, it wasn't Al Capone watching us from the alley. It was Albert Becker, or one of his henchman.

I had no idea what he had planned, but I wasn't going to stay around to find out. Lying on the seat, I crawled forward to open the door opposite the alleyway. My age fought me, making me gasp for breath as I slid to the end of the seat and out the door. I dropped my feet to the pavement and landed in a crouch.

I saw Simon with his back to me, talking to another man. One glance was all it took to recognize who he was talking to. Schmidt, standing next to an expensive automobile.

Luckily he hadn't seen me, though whoever was in the alley could have seen my door open.

I understood Becker's plan in an instant. It was a kidnapping.

If I tried to run, I'd be in full sight. I'd never escape.

I had only one chance.

Using my bare fingers and the toes of my shoes, I push-pulled my way under the limousine.

Gasping in a breath, I turned my head to the side and saw two men's shoes appear. Then I heard a car door open and a loud voice say, "Get out."

Two more men's shoes appeared, and then two with high heels.

"Where's the second man?" said a voice I didn't recognize.

"The other door's open. He must have got out that way."

"Oof," Schmidt cried.

Mr. Holmes had not forgotten his boxing skills.

I heard a thud, and saw Holmes fall to the ground. A pair of hands grabbed him under his arm pits. Still conscious, Holmes was being bull-dogged away dragging his heels.

Luckily for me, automobiles were parked along the whole side of the street, and I saw an alleyway no more than ten feet away.

"Find the other one. We have to get out of here."

"He has to be around here somewhere," said Schmidt.

I saw feet scurry as one of them made a hasty search, then I heard the sound of a distant siren that steadily got louder.

The cavalry was coming.

"Get them into our car. We have to get out of here."

Violet lost a shoe as she was whisked away. "Take your hands off of me," Holmes threatened, "or I'll thrash you again."

Doors slammed, and I heard a powerful automobile engine start up and the machine screech away.

Then silence.

Exhausted, and terrified for Violet and Holmes, I collapsed and waited to catch my breath and for my heart to slow down.

Then the siren stopped.

CHAPTER 25

The police were examining the damaged front bumper and looking for the driver of the limousine when I squirmed out from under it. A man in the gathering crowd helped me to my feet.

I dashed toward the police, waving my hands. "There's been a kidnapping. They just left. You may still be able to catch them!"

One of the officers loped toward the patrol car with me right behind him. "Who? What happened?"

"The kidnappers took my wife and our travel companion. They must have taken Dr. Croydon's chauffeur also. I was hiding under the doctor's limousine or they would have taken me, too."

The patrol car's engine ground, coughed, then started. "Which way did they go?"

"Straight ahead." I pointed just to make sure.

The street appeared deserted, but in the distance, a single small pinpoint of red light shone through the falling snow. The officer floored the accelerator and turned on his siren. A Rio roadster that had started to nose out into the street immediately reversed into its parking space to let us by. The red light ahead got smaller with the sound of the siren.

"It looks like they're running," I said. "That must be them."

As I said it, the red dot disappeared.

"They turned," the officer said. "Did you see which way?"

"No."

"If they turned left they'll be heading toward the harbor. They'd have more road ahead of them by turning right."

He turned off his siren. The blocks were long, so we had a fairly accurate idea where the Essex had turned.

Nothing moved on the street in either direction when the patrol car stopped in the middle of the street. The snow had turned heavier. Reaching into the glove compartment, he took out a flashlight.

I watched as he scanned the surface of the street looking for fresh tracks. Nothing had disturbed the snow. "Let's backtrack and look in the other direction."

We passed through the intersection and the officer once again got out, leaving the engine running. Shining the flashlight on the street surface, we could see fresh tire tracks quickly filling with snow.

"The snow's coming down harder. I don't know how much longer we'll be able to see the tracks."

We started forward at a crawl, headlights centered on the driver's side track. What seemed like bare seconds later, the tracks began to disappear from view.

"Is there anything down this way?" I asked.

"Warehouses and office buildings. I don't see any lights."

At the news, I realized how hard my heart was pounding. The two most important people in my life were captive, and I had no idea how to find them. Almost no idea, anyway. "We know they're not on this street. What do you say we drive up to the nearest intersection and look there. We may get lucky."

With that, he floored the accelerator. Slewing to a stop, we arrived at the next intersection mere seconds later.

He carefully got out. Bending low, he searched the rapidly accumulating snow for tire tracks. Then he straightened up and shook his head at me.

"Sorry," he said. "I can't find them."

"Let me use your flashlight."

"Sure."

Walking to the middle of the intersection, I dropped to my back. Holding the flashlight next to the surface, I slowly rotated myself with my feet. I stopped and got to my knees before standing. I knew that raised ridges left on the edges of the tire tracks cause noticeable irregularities in the surface of the snow. It showed the direction the auto had taken.

"They turned left."

To my dismay, the wind picked up. Snow flew at the windshield as I slid back into my seat. The street had become a snow-lit, silent corridor offering hardly any visibility. I caught a glimpse at the officer's name plate. Grover O'Neal. Undoubtedly named after President Cleveland. Officer O'Neal turned and sped forward, still hoping to catch sight of the tail-light. My heart fell when he finally slowed.

"It's no use. They've gotten away. Can you tell me anything about the car they're driving?"

"It's a 1926 Hudson Super-Six Essex. It's a very expensive car."

"How do you know that?"

"It's part of my job to know everything about automobiles that's worth knowing. I've actually been able to assist the Detroit police identify them on occasion. I helped them put Manny Epstein of the Purple Gang in jail. They caught him in a car I identified. It was full of rye whiskey from Canada."

"I'm impressed. I'll put out an all-points for the men to be on the look-out for an Hudson Essex with a damaged fender, but that's about all we can do. Do you want us to put you under protective custody?"

"No. Earlier, my friend made a call to the police to report that Alfred Becker was staying at the Milner Hotel. He's an escaped suspected felon wanted in New York. Did you send anyone there?"

"Yes. The room was empty, though Becker hadn't checked out. I'll make a call to get someone to go back."

"He won't be there," I mumbled.

"Any other ideas?" O'Neal asked.

"Yes. Let's go to the Park Hotel. The kidnappers may have tried to contact me."

CHAPTER 26

At nearly eleven o'clock, the Park Hotel lobby teemed with young women in short skirts sitting at the tables smoking or giggling with their friends. Their dates sat near, reading newspapers or leering at them lasciviously.

Officer O'Neal watched their antics as I approached the desk.

"Good evening, sir," a smiling young man said. "How may I help you?"

"My name's Timothy Wiggins. I was a guest here earlier today. Have there been any messages for me?"

"One minute, please. I'll find out."

Boom! Boom! Boom! My pulse pounded in my ears as I watched him shuffle through a pile of yellow papers.

"Sorry, sir. No messages."

I turned to O'Neal and shook my head. He stepped to the desk, flashed his badge and picked up the phone on the desk. "Please connect me with Sir Conan Doyle's room. This is official police business."

"Y-yes, sir."

The young man no longer was smiling as he pushed a metal connector into one of the holes in the beehive of openings behind the desk. Then he nodded.

He introduced himself and asked to speak with Sir Arthur.

"Can't this wait?" came Lady Jean's worried voice. "He's sleeping."

"I'm sorry, but this is extremely important."

O'Neal handed the receiver to me as Sir Arthur answered with a yawn.

"Sir Arthur, this is Timothy Wiggins."

"Good heavens, Wiggins. It's past eleven o'clock. What happened?"

"Mr. Holmes and Violet were abducted on the way back from the lecture. I nearly was, too." Dead silence. "Are you there, Sir Arthur?"

"Sorry. Yes, I'm here. I merely didn't know what to say. Do you have any idea of who committed this atrocious deed?"

"The man who calls himself Albert Baker and two of the men who work for him. I'm in the hotel lobby with the Boston police, and we need to speak to Margery tonight. Do you have her phone number?"

"Somewhere," Sir Arthur replied, voice trailing off. "Find Margery's number for me, love."

I handed the phone to O'Neal. who was standing next to me with an open notebook on the desk, pencil in hand.

"Andrew 4228? Yes I know it's an unlisted number. Thank you."

The desk clerk had arranged for me to be able to listen in on a lobby phone, and I had to bite my tongue to keep from speaking out as O'Neal and Margery conversed. She indeed had heard what had happened. Another officer had contacted her about the kidnapping and the damage to the limousine soon after the attack. "I don't want to leave the house, but you are welcome to come here if you think I may know something that will help you find them. I won't be able to sleep, anyway."

"Thank you," O'Neal said. "I have Mr. Wiggins with me. He was the third person in the limousine. Luckily, he escaped and can give you a better account of what happened. We'll be there in ten minutes."

SNOW WAS FALLING more heavily as we arrived at Ten Lime Street. At home, Violet and I often sat for hours watching it fall, and I knew she would like the fluffy flakes drifting down in the now windless night. Nearly all the other houses on either side were dark, but the lights in Margery's house shone brightly.

O'Neal lifted the hammer of the knocker on the heavy oaken door and let it fall once.

Margery answered immediately. "Officer O'Neal? Mr. Wiggins? Please come in, but take off your shoes in the hallway. I promise they won't walk away while you're here."

Considering the circumstances, I wasn't in the mood for humor. But, given her occupation and reputation, I had to smile in spite of myself.

A wood fire at the far end of a large room crackled behind an iron screen. Antique furniture rested on an enormous Persian rug. Oil paintings, mostly of stern-faced men scowled at each other from the wood-paneled walls. I knew very little about antiquities, but had seen pictures of some similar pieces in the *Free Press*. The exorbitant prices Federal Period furniture brought in auction astonished me. If I weren't so worried about Violet and Mr. Holmes, I'd be afraid to take a step.

Margery pointed us toward a spindly davenport. "Please sit. I'm very glad you're safe, Mr. Wiggins. I'm terribly worried about your wife and friend."

"I can't even tell you how worried I am."

"I'd ask Walter to find out for you, but we don't have enough energy to call him. We need at least six people."

"I appreciate the thought," I said, half-believing he could tell us.

"I've made some tea. I'll have Lucille serve it."

"Thanks, but we won't have the time," O'Neal said. "Mr. Wiggins tells us that someone well-known to your family, Albert Baker, is the person behind the kidnapping. Mr. Wiggins also says he saw the same Mr. Baker on the sidewalk in front of your house earlier today."

"Yes. He told us he had just arrived in town and wanted to stop by to talk to my husband. At the end of the lecture, I was shocked when Sir Arthur's friend accused Mr. Baker of trying to murder the Wigginses in a theatre in New York. I still can't believe he would do such a thing."

"Why?"

"Because LeRoi would never knowingly associate with a criminal. My husband is the most honest man I have ever known."

I had to break into the conversation. "He's a wonderful parent, too, isn't he? There were Tom and Mitchell and lots of other boys, too."

That brought the first frown to her face. "He is. Unfortunately some of the boys he adopted didn't work out. LeRoi was as sad when he had to give them up as the boys were themselves."

"What was wrong with them?"

"They were lazy, or disobedient, or didn't try very hard in school. LeRoi has strict rules, and they didn't follow them."

My eyes flashed. Before I could say more, O'Neal headed me off.

"Let's get back to your husband's relationship with Albert Baker. How often did they meet?"

Margery closed her eyes, then answered. "At least once or twice a month. They were involved in developing some kind of a educational program."

"About Spiritualism or eugenics?" I asked.

"Neither. Aryanism. H.G. Wells wrote about how great the Aryans were. Groups in England and Germany are devoted to learning about them. Both Mr. Baker and my husband have already spent a great deal of money on the project."

"And your husband thinks Jewish people are inferior or evil, doesn't he?" I said. "I know Albert Baker does."

Margery shook her head. "Oh, no. LeRoi doesn't think that at all. That's Walter. He says most of the people he meets in hell are Jewish, and that he's sure there'll be many more coming."

My skin crawled. Could she actually be as naïve as she was acting? "Has Walter ever met Albert Baker?"

"Many times. He always looks forward to their get-togethers."

That didn't surprise me at all.

"Has Mr. Baker ever stayed here with you and your husband?" O'Neal asked.

"On occasion. Although he's always welcome to stay here, he doesn't like to intrude, so he usually stays in a hotel downtown."

O'Neal's voice became sharper. "Do you have any idea where Mr. Baker might be now?"

"No. Of course not. If I did, I would tell you."

"Would your husband have any idea?"

"I don't know," Margery said, voice faltering.

"Then please call him. This is very important."

"I already talked to him," she said, averting her eyes. "He's leaving the conference and coming home tomorrow morning."

"We can't wait that long," O'Neal said. "Your husband may be the only person who can help us find Baker before he does harm to his hostages."

Though obviously reluctant, Margery took a piece of paper down from the mantel of the fireplace. Handing it to O'Neal, she said, "Use our phone."

I tried to listen in, but gave up. I could tell from the officer's facial expressions that he wasn't getting any new information. He ended with, "Thank you. I'll call you when you get back if I have any other questions."

He hung up. "I appreciate the use of your telephone, Mrs. Croydon. I don't think we need to take up any more of your time." He handed her his card. "I expect you'll call me if you hear from Mr. Baker. His real name is Becker. See if you can find out where he is."

"Of course. But I'm sure he wouldn't contact me."

"I have a last question," I said. "Your lecture was by invitation only. How did Becker get invited?"

"LeRoi told me to make sure he could attend. I left word with the church to expect him."

She showed us to the hallway, and as promised, our shoes were still there.

Outside, the snow had stopped and a bright moon now lit up the landscape. Dead silence lay atop the newly fallen snow. Inside, a vise circled my chest, and my gut churned noisily.

O'Neal opened the door for me. When he settled into the driver's door, I couldn't control myself any longer. "Well? What did the good doctor have to say?"

"Essentially, nothing. The doctor has the same opinion as Mrs. Croydon. He refuses to believe Becker could be involved in a kidnapping or anything else illegal. Croydon claims the last he heard, Becker was staying at the Milner Hotel, otherwise he has no idea where else he might be. The estimable doctor was very concerned about his auto and chauffeur. He didn't say a word about your wife or friend."

"About what I expected," I said. "There were a lot of other questions I would've liked to ask him, but they wouldn't've helped us find my wife. Do you want to talk to Sir Arthur tonight?"

"Is there some reason not to?"

"Yes, but it doesn't have anything to do with the kidnapping. I know he'd tell us if he had any idea where Becker might be. He told us some things in confidence, things he wouldn't want his wife to know he told us."

"Then I'll trust your judgment. We can talk to him tomorrow."

CHAPTER 27

Rose was on the couch in our room, waiting for me when I got back. She had become worried when we didn't return. I spent the next half hour relating everything that had happened. She caught her breath loudly several times before I was done.

"How terrible," she said. "I'm so sorry. I can't even imagine what you're going through."

"Thank you. You're absolutely right. Has anyone called?"

"No, but I've been on the telephone almost the entire time. I learned a few things, but it isn't the right time to discuss them."

"Not unless you have some idea where Violet and Mr. Holmes might be."

A knock. We both looked toward the door.

I carefully moved closer. "Yes."

"Mr. Wiggins?" a voice said in a gasp.

"Who are you?"

"Simon Bertolini . . . the Croydons' chauffeur."

I threw caution to the winds and opened the door. A battered young man stood in the hallway.

"Come in," I said, grabbing his arm and gently pulling him inside. "What happened to you?"

"I . . ." he said, obviously in great pain.

"Don't talk," Rose said, disappearing into the bathroom. Water ran. She came back with a wet towel. Without a word she gently laid it against his face.

Seconds later he pulled it away. "Thank you. That felt good." Bertolini's voice came out in a whistle because one of his front teeth was broken off and the words emerged over the edge of a badly swollen upper lip. His coat was missing two buttons, and he had a livid-looking knot in the center of his forehead.

With effort, he said, "I'm supposed to tell you your companions are well and safe, and that you will get instructions about what to do to get them back."

"Can you identify the kidnappers?"

"I only saw one of them, and he told me to deliver the message or he'd kill me. Then he threw me out of the car. I'm sure they had to be going thirty miles an hour. I must have hit my head when I landed and passed out."

"You're lucky to still be alive."

I took O'Neal's card out of my pocket. "This officer is working with me. I'll give him a call for you. He'll want to talk to you, too."

Officer O'Neal arrived twenty minutes later and escorted the ill-treated chauffeur from the room in a wheelchair. "I'll talk to you first thing in the morning," the officer said as he left.

Rose and I stood watching until the elevator arrived and the two men disappeared.

"I have something to give to you," Rose said. "Mr. H. gave it to me and I want you to have it. You may need it."

She left the room through the adjoining door and quickly came back carrying something her hand nearly covered. When she opened it, I recoiled at the sight of what appeared to be a human finger. "Wha-a-a-t?"

"It's not real. It's one of Mr. H's escape kits."

She pointed to a barely visible line in the middle of the right side. Using a finger nail, she separated the grim object into two pieces.

A piece of coiled wire with teeth came out first. "This is what's called a gigli saw," she said. "It can cut through steel bars."

I took it from her to examine it. Even its appearance frightened me. If it could cut through steel, it could as easily cut through nearly anything else.

"You already know what these are," she said, taking out two small lock picks. "Mr. H. said these two working together would be capable of opening just about any lock in the world."

"Very ingenious. Did he ever use the contents of the finger?"

"Many times. The most important was when he escaped from a Siberian Wagon in Russia. They were supposed to be escape-proof and were used to transport prisoners. No one had ever even tried to escape. Mr. H. cut through the floor of the wagon with the saw and walked to the nearest town. The secret police were absolutely furious. I think some of them are still convinced he had an accomplice."

"Why did he give the false finger to you?"

"He was worried I might need it if one of the mediums got angry enough to want to do me harm. I've carried it with me ever since."

"Thank you," I said, putting the two pieces back together. "I'm sure it'll come in handy."

"I'm so sorry about your wife and Mr. Holmes. You know how much I hope they are all right."

"Absolutely. Mr. Holmes can take care of himself, and I'd be very surprised if he isn't planning some escape this very minute. Violet must be terribly frightened, and I'm very worried about her. But she's much stronger than she might appear at first glance."

"I gathered that. Actually, I don't think Becker will want to harm either of them yet. He wants to punish us, too."

"I agree, but I know how angry Becker was with Mr. Holmes. He might very well be trying to torture him right now. It won't do any good, though. Mr. Holmes has studied eastern religions and knows how to suppress feeling pain. Violet isn't as lucky."

"There's nothing we can do until we hear from them."

UNABLE TO SLEEP, I sat up on the sofa until sheer exhaustion took over. I awoke with a start to the sound of the telephone.

"Hello!"

Instead of an answer I heard the click of a telephone hanging up, and a dial tone.

Becker or an underling. Undoubtedly calling from the lobby to see if we were in our rooms. I glanced at my watch. Seven o'clock.

"We have to get out of here," I said, taking Rose by the arm. "Leave everything."

I swallowed hard and put the false finger and picks into my left pocket, but kept the saw wrapped in bathroom tissue in my right.

Where could we go? Down the stairway? I was sure our foe would be smart enough to make certain we couldn't leave that way, and felt certain someone was already on the way up by elevator.

My blood ran cold. Becker knew he couldn't force us out of the hotel at gunpoint, so this would have to be a tidy execution. Fortunately for us, he didn't realize I'd have a weapon.

Certain the stairway up would still be safe, we climbed three flights. Even so, I still opened the door to the hallway with caution.

No one about. Now the elevator seemed our best escape route. Pulse racing and short of breath, I tiptoed to the tightly closed double doors. "Against the wall," I whispered.

With finger shaking, I pushed the summons button.

One of the pairs of elevator doors opened. Anyone within ten feet should have been able to hear my heart pound.

Rose started to take a step forward, but I restrained her. The elevator door began to close, and I jumped out to catch it.

Schmidt, dressed as a gentleman and wide-eyed in surprise, stood inside holding a gun. I ducked back and heard a hollow "*chuk*." A vase of flowers sitting in an alcove shattered as the elevator door closed. Rose and I fled willy-nilly back toward the fire escape. We would have bare seconds before the door reopened and he'd be on our backs.

In a flash I knew what to do.

I pulled out the picks and headed for the nearest hotel room door. With a prayer, I set them in place. Houdini was right about them. A few movements, and the tumblers moved. I turned the knob and the door opened.

"Go to the fire escape and hold the door open until you see him coming from the hallway. Then duck into the fire escape."

She threw me a questioning look, but did as directed. I opened the hotel room door far enough to slip inside, leaving the door open a crack.

Almost immediately I heard the sound of rushing footsteps.

I took out the saw and grasped it tightly, listening for him to pass the door. When he did, I opened it and ducked into the hallway, two steps behind him. He heard me and tried to turn, but I was directly behind him and wrapped the gigli saw around his neck.

"Drop the gun or I'll cut your head off."

When he hesitated, I gave the saw a tiny pull to show I meant business. He screamed in pain, and the gun dropped to the floor.

Rose reappeared. I motioned at the gun with my foot. She picked it up.

With a twitch of the saw, I said, "Open the fire escape door."

Quivering, Schmidt did as instructed.

"What's your friend's name?"

"Max Hahn," Schmidt choked out.

"Call him and tell him we're dead and he should come up. If you say anything else, or if he doesn't come, your head will end up in the basement."

"I understand!" he gasped.

I eased the pressure enough to let him take a normal breath.

"Komst, Max," Schmidt called in a normal voice. *"Ils sind todt."*

Doublecross! I started to pull the gigli tighter, intent to carry out my threat.

Before I could, a voice from a lower level called back. *"Sehr gut, Kamerade. Ich bin gleich da sein."*

It was just then I realized how close I had come to being hoisted by my own petard. It never occurred to me the assassins would speak to each other in German. Poor Schmidt had been so frightened he summoned his partner-in-crime as I told him to do. There was no telling what Max would do if he heard English.

I pulled Schmidt back and closed the door. *"Bitte, bitte,"* he gibbered. Rose stood beside the fire escape door, back against the wall, waiting.

The door opened. A man, taller than Schmidt but similarly dressed in suit and tie, came through. Catching sight of Schmidt and me, he turned on his heels.

Rose stepped out. "Don't move."

He stopped short and raised his hands.

"Is Becker with you?" I asked.

"*Nein!*" Schmidt cried.

"Are you sure?" I shouted, giving the saw another twitch.

An unmistakable outhouse odor filled the air. Poor Schmidt was almost foaming at the mouth. *"Mein Gott, Max! Sagst ihm!"*

"Herr Becker is at the farm," Max said.

"Farm?"

"Yes. He's waiting for us to bring you back."

"Are the hostages with him?"

"*Ja!*" Schmidt blurted.

"Are they still alive?"

"*Ja!!*"

"Has Herr Becker hurt them?"

"Not yet. They don't even know he's there. He wanted to wait until he had all of you."

The words surprised me. I had been certain they were on an assassination mission. "How did he expect you to get us out of the hotel without a struggle?"

Neither said a word. Then it occurred to me. "Check Max's pockets."

"Take your jacket off and lay it on the floor," Rose said.

Max did. Holding the gun on him, she knelt and felt inside the side pockets. She held up a small black case in triumph.

"What do you suppose is in there?" I asked.

Rose handed it to Max. "Open it."

When he did, I knew what their plan had been. It was a hypodermic syringe with needle in place nestled inside the case.

"Only one?" I said in a suspicious voice. "I bet you have one, too, don't you, Herr Schmidt?"

Before he could answer, I said, "I think we'd better move back into the hotel room where we can sort this out."

Rose marched Max, and I followed with Schmidt walking on eggs in front of me.

We entered the room. I shut the door behind us. "We seem to have a slight problem. We're understaffed. I need both of my hands, and Rose can't do everything one-handed and keep our friend Max under control. However, if what I suspect is in that hypodermic, we may have a solution. Do you have any idea what it is, Herr Schmidt?"

As I said it, I twitched the saw.

"Phenobarbital," Schmidt gasped.

"Then I suggest Max inject you. You were planning to do the same to us, right, so turnabout is fair play."

Max didn't move.

"If Rose shoots you, we won't have a problem."

Max reluctantly took the hypo out of the case.

"Hold out your left arm, Herr Schmidt. It's unfortunate, but we'll have to inject you through your jacket."

"*Nein,*" Schmidt blubbered. "*Bitte nein.*"

Max seemed to realize he had no choice. Schmidt let out a cry of pain as the needle struck home. I bulldogged him to the bed and took the saw from his throat. The hapless man collapsed face down.

I nearly did, too. The tension had left me exhausted, and my hands shook from the nervous strain. Free of my burden, I walked to the desk and took out an envelope. With a sigh of relief, I dropped the saw inside it. Then I returned to Schmidt, unconscious or too frightened to move. His head lolled to the side when I rolled him over on his back and went through his pockets. I found the twin to Max's black case in a jacket pocket.

I took the gun from Rose. "Get two pillow cases and tie his hands to the bedstead," I said.

She removed the bed cover and dumped the pillows out of their cases. "Be a good boy, now, Jurgen, and slide back. I don't want to have to shoot you."

He did, though he could barely move. Rose folded the pillowcases in half and wrapped one half around a wrist, and the other around the post at the end of the headboard. I doubted she had ever had to be quite as active in an investigation, but she quickly had the nearly unconscious German with his arms stretched wide apart and lashed to the bedstead.

"Mr. H. would escape in in a second," Rose said, "but I think it will hold Herr Schmidt just fine."

"Now take the sheets and tie his ankles."

Minutes later, Schmidt was spread-eagled on the bed. He lay without struggling.

"Now for you, Max. Take off your coat."

As I said it, I opened the second kit and took out the unused hypodermic. When I held it up, Max cried out. "No. Don't. You want to rescue your friends, don't you? You'll never find the farm without me."

"Where is it?"

"Just a few miles from here. Near Framingham."

CHAPTER 28

The kidnappers' 1925 Pontiac hummed nicely on six cylinders as we motored along over Route 9. The snow of the preceding night lay melting on the roadway, water standing in the centers of slushy auto tracks. What ice there had been had melted to slush, so our breakneck fifty-mile-per-hour speed presented no hazard of driving off the road.

Mr. Holmes would be pleased with my plan.

"Turn left at the next road," Max said. He had sat quietly next to Rose the entire trip. I didn't doubt he was giving me good directions.

I reluctantly slowed. I loved the power of the six-cylinders. No other passenger car had more cylinders than the Pontiac. The difference in the ride compared to our four-cylinder Chevrolet amazed me.

I made the turn and immediately wished I'd been going slower. We hit a water-filled rut and bounced. I barely missed banging my head on the ceiling.

"Are you all right, Rose?"

"I'm fine. Do drive slower. No one's going anywhere at the farm."

"Sorry." The automobile pulled to the right as I put on the brakes. "How much farther is it?"

"The next farmhouse on the left."

In the distance I saw a stone wall, typical of New England farmsteads. My heart beat faster as we approached the breach in the wall. What would we find? Max swore Mr. Holmes and Rose were unharmed when he and Schmidt had left for Boston three hours before.

I slowed to a crawl, then stopped. Narrow tracks, undoubtedly from the Essex, led into the yard.

"What do we do now?" Rose asked.

Instead of answering, I got out and moved next to stone fence. When I got to the driveway, I peeked around.

The two-story wooden farmhouse, resting on the same type of stone used in the walls surrounding the farm, stood eerily quiet. The Essex, if anywhere around, was out of sight. A thin wisp of maple-scented smoke trickled out of the chimney.

One thought filled my mind. *Was Becker waiting in the house?*

I turned and stared Max in the eye. "Is anyone here?"

"Herr Becker was here when we left."

"Was the Essex here, too?"

"Yes. It was parked beside the house."

Taking another peek around the edge, I tip-toed inside the wall. Three large pine trees provided a modicum of cover, and I used them to scurry to the edge of the house. I pressed my ear against the side of the building and listened.

Nothing but the wind.

I followed the wall to the other end of the house. The Essex was nowhere to be seen.

Had Becker flown the coop?

I allowed my tension to ease and cautiously made my way to the door. Laying an ear against it, I listened for sounds of movement inside.

Silence.

Taking a deep breath, I fished the picks out my pocket and inserted them into the lock. The mechanism was rusty and wouldn't move. But I knew how to fix that. I returned to the car and lifted the hood. I knew where to look for the oil cap and unscrewed it.

I opened the rear door next to Rose. "Do you have a handkerchief?"

She handed her purse to me, and I quickly found what I was looking for. Dipping it into the well, I covered the end with motor oil.

I set the purse next to her and headed for the house. Wiping each pick with oil, then daubing the rest into the mechanism through the keyhole, I went to work on the lock once more. The tumblers fought me valiantly, but the picks finally prevailed.

I cautiously opened the door. The house was dark, lit only by the light through the windows. Nothing stirred.

About to call out, I thought better of it. Someone could be lurking in the shadows.

Taking three soundless steps forward brought me into a kitchen. I paused. Suddenly, out of the corner of my eye, I saw an upraised fireplace iron ready to crash into my skull.

I dropped to the floor and rolled to my back to kick.

"Wiggins?"

"Holmes! For God's sake, what are you doing?"

Mr. Holmes bent over me. "I do apologize. I had no idea it was you."

He gave me a hand to help me to my feet.

"How did you get free?" I asked.

"Herr Schmidt didn't tie the ropes tight enough. You didn't actually believe I'd calmly submit to my captors, did you?"

I got my first look at him. Even in the dim light I could see blood had congealed on the right side of his face, staining his collar and cheek a darker color, and leaving his pompadour plastered against the side of his head. And he was sporting what is popularly called a shiner. "Did Becker do that to you?"

"No. The one called Hahn did. I haven't seen Herr Becker. My head's a bit sore, but I don't think anything's scrambled inside. Otherwise, I'm in fine fettle, if a bit short of breath. I'm very pleased to see you escaped unscathed."

"I am too. How is Violet?"

"Frightened, but otherwise unharmed."

"Where is she?"

"In the bedroom. This way."

Violet lay face down and gently snoring, her arms tied behind her back and her feet lashed together.

Near tears, I bent down, giving her shoulder a gentle shake as I kissed her neck.

She sighed, then her eyelids fluttered. Turning her head, her eyes opened wide. "Timothy? Is it really you?"

"Yes, my love. It's me. Are you all right?"

"Yes, but my arms and shoulders are sore, and my feet are numb."

Holmes handed me a long-bladed knife. It wasn't sharp, but with some strenuous work I cut through the rope and freed her arms. She rolled to her back, reached up to encircle my head and pulled, nearly breaking my neck. "I knew you'd come to rescue me."

"I could think of nothing else. Now let me untie your feet."

"I'll do that, Wiggins. Contact the Framingham police."

"Good idea. Neither of you saw Becker?"

"No," Holmes said. "I thought I heard his voice. He must have left while I was sleeping."

The phone was the old-fashioned wooden-box-and-crank type hanging on a wall near the kitchen. Most of them had been replaced with the modern rotor dial models, but this was the second one I had seen in two days. I hadn't seen any in Detroit for years, but I still remembered how to use one. Holding the receiver against my ear, I turned the crank.

"Operator," a female voice squawked.

"Good morning. Please connect me with the Middlesex police."

"Who are you? You're not Isaac Bradford."

"You're right. This is an emergency."

"I'll get Sheriff Pibbidy for you."

The sheriff answered on the second ring.

"Someone's calling from Isaac's house," the operator said. "He says it's an emergency."

"Who is this, and what are you doing in Isaac Bradford's house? He's in England."

"It's too hard to explain over the phone. How does kidnapping sound to you."

"I'll be right over. You can hang up now, Bernice."

I heard a second click as I replaced the receiver. I was immediately attacked by a sobbing Violet, who threw her arms around me and squeezed for dear life. I gave her a hug and a proper kiss, but she wouldn't let go. I felt her blond hair, her most prized possession, hanging in sweaty strings against my face. It never looked or smelled more beautiful to me.

"Rose is still in the auto," I said, untangling myself from my beloved's grasp. "Why don't you get her? She must be freezing."

WITH MAX SAFELY LASHED to a chair, the rest of us were warming ourselves around the well-stoked wood stove when the sheriff arrived.

I unlocked the door for him, and he shuffled in.

I guessed my summons had interrupted his breakfast, because his salt and pepper mustache had bits of egg yolk stuck to it. The zipper of his puffy red coat was open, and his buckle galoshes dripped water on the bare floor. "Good morning. I'm Sheriff Peabody. What's this about a kidnapping?"

"This is Max Hahn," I said, pointing. "He's one of the two who kidnapped my wife and my friend out of a limousine in Boston. His partner is out cold in a room at the Park Hotel."

"I saw the bulletin about a kidnapping in Boston when I went into the office this morning. I just figured it was the work of Frankie Wallace."

I knew Frank Wallace was the head of the Gustin Gang, Boston's version of the Purple Gang. Both were ethnic groups. The Purple Gang was Jewish, Wallace and company Irish. From what I had read, the Gustins were more interested in hijacking trucks and running rum than kidnapping, but I was sure they were capable of snatching someone off the street, if properly motivated.

"You made a reasonable assumption, but Frank Wallace isn't involved. Albert Becker, a phony medium from Detroit, is the ringleader. We exposed him, and now he wants revenge. Who owns this house?"

"Isaac Bradford. This is one of the original Danforth Farms Thomas Danforth sold in 1660. One of Isaac's ancestors was on the Mayflower."

What would he have to do with Albert Becker? I couldn't even imagine. "I think you said he was in England."

"With his girlfriend," the sheriff said, nostrils flaring. "She goes around in public in dresses halfway up her thighs and necklines so low they barely cover her nipples. More makeup than a Ringling Brothers clown. Isaac just bought a new flivver to please her, and now he's spending all the rest of his savings on an expensive trip. She has to be at least forty years younger than he is. Everybody tells him she's just a golddigger, but he won't listen. Says he loves her and she loves him. She says it was in the stars they'd finally meet."

I smiled. "Of course. Do you know where they met?"

The sheriff brushed his chin with a hand. "Not around here, that's for sure. From what I hear it was at a séance in Boston. Isaac's wife, Rachel, died about ten years ago. Isaac said he kept getting a strong feeling she was trying to contact him. He went to see some woman in Boston who people say talks to the dead. That's where he met Junie. After that, Isaac, Junie, the woman who put on the séance, and the woman's husband got to be pretty tight."

"You mentioned he just bought a new motorcar," Holmes said. "Do you know what make?"

"No, but it's brand new. Black. I'm surprised it isn't here."

"I think I know what happened to it," I said. "Was the woman who put on the séance named Margery?"

"Dunno. I never heard her name."

"One of the kidnappers is a friend of her husband. Do you have any idea why Isaac would have let the kidnappers use his house?"

"I'm not sure even Isaac knows the answer to that. He isn't thinking very straight anymore, but I wouldn't be a bit surprised if he doesn't know anything about it." The sheriff squinted. "Tell me. How'd you get into the house? The front door has a deadbolt."

"One of the windows wasn't locked," I said. Too quickly, I'm sure.

The squint turned into a scowl. "You let me in through the door. Someone had to have unlocked it."

Suddenly, everything right had gone terribly wrong. Like a Tigers' game I saw with my son last summer. Ahead of the Yankees by four runs in the top of the ninth, a couple of walks, a swing of the bat by Gehrig and another one by Ruth and we lost six to five.

The sheriff's scowl got deeper. "Well?"

"Okay, I picked the lock. I'm a crime reporter with the *Detroit Free Press,* and the police taught me how to do it. Albert Becker tried to kill my wife and me at a theatre in New York. Then he kidnapped my wife and friend on the street in Boston. Fortunately, I got away."

He didn't look any happier. "Is that so?"

I fumbled for my wallet and took out my press card. The sheriff glanced at it without changing expression."

"Call the New York police. Better still, call the Boston police. They'll have to come to pick up Max, anyway. They'll confirm my story. I know I should have called you first, but I was nearly crazy worrying about my wife. I just saved you having to knock the door down or break a window to get in."

The silence became unbearable. I half expected him to arrest me.

Instead, he nodded. "Okay. I'll have someone come and lock up. I really should confiscate those picks. You may try to use them again."

I could imagine the explaining I'd have to do when I pulled Houdini's false finger out of my pocket.

The sheriff sighed. "Tell you what. I'll save the county some money. I'll let you lock the door when we leave."

CHAPTER
29

Sheriff Peabody marched Max to the door. "I'll be back to drive you to Boston after I've put Mr. Hahn behind bars. In the meantime, make yourselves at home. I'm sure Isaac won't mind."

We intended to do just that.

Holmes, Rose, and I found places around the pot-bellied stove and soaked in the warmth while Violet puttered in the kitchen, going through the ancient pantry. Lost in thought, Holmes sat a short distance away with unlit pipe in mouth, and Rose next to him paging through her notes from her phone calls.

"Your impromptu meeting with Mrs. Croydon sounds very interesting," Holmes said in a desultory tone. "Her offer of a séance is just the opening we need. Maybe Walter can tell us where Albert Becker's hiding."

I snorted. "Why don't we just ask him who poisoned Harry Houdini while we're at it?"

His eyebrows raised, puzzled. "Why not? That's an excellent idea."

"You're serious, aren't you? The only real benefit I can see in a séance is that it'll give us a chance to meet Doctor Croydon." I squinted at what he said next. "I'm surprised you have such a limited imagination. That's not the Wiggins I remember patrolling the London streets. Certainly you must see it'll also give us an opportunity to find out about Dr. Crookes's visit. That's the only direct link we have to Thallium so far."

"That's true," I said with a scowl, deciding to be angry rather than embarrassed. Holmes certainly had his nerve. "Anything else?"

"A séance will loosen tongues that aren't usually speaking at all. Imagine the benefits we can glean from that."

"Sorry, I don't have any idea what you're talking about."

"Come, Wiggins. All you have to do is think."

Obviously noticing my expression, he gave me a hearty pat on my shoulder. "Be of good cheer, my friend. You're the man of the hour for foiling the kidnappers. I couldn't have done better myself."

"I know," I said dryly. "Everything's hunky-dory. Mr. Holmes was asleep when Becker left this morning. Do you have any idea where he went, Violet?"

"I didn't hear a thing. All I know is he didn't stoke the fire before he left. I woke up freezing in the middle of the night."

"That's interesting," I said. Happy to gain the upper hand. I pressed the attack. "That means he left before daylight. Unless there's another vehicle we don't know about, he obviously drove the Essex. I know we didn't pass him on our way here, so it must have been much earlier than when we left the hotel."

Holmes took the unlit pipe from his mouth. "Excellent reasoning, Wiggins. I take back everything I said about you."

Grr. Even that sounded like a left-handed compliment.

"Leaving aside how Becker and company got use of the farm," Holmes said with a noisy suck on the pipe, "the question of the various automobiles is intriguing. How did you get here this morning?"

"On six cylinders," I said. "A Pontiac motorcar, which must belong to Max or Jurgen Schmidt. The owner will need to hire a good lawyer. I'd love to take the Pontiac off his hands to help him pay for it."

"Don't be silly," Violet said. "What would we do with two cars?"

"I don't know. I'm sure I could come up with some logical reason."

"You don't need any more toys. You're a big boy now."

I flashed a mock smile.

"Be that as it may, you raise an important point, Wiggins," Holmes said. "What about the vehicle the kidnappers drove?"

"From what the sheriff said, it most likely belongs to the man who owns this farm."

"What happened to the Croydon's chauffeur worries me," Holmes said. "I never saw him again after we were forced into the escape machine."

"He's no longer of any concern. He came to our hotel room with a message from Becker. They damned near killed him by throwing him out of a speeding car."

"*C'est la guerre,* Wiggins. Warfare always slaughters the innocent." Getting to his feet, he took his pipe out of his mouth. "What bothers me the most is that the scope of the conspiracy seems to grow by the day. I doubt very much Isaac Bradford is knowingly involved, but even assuming a logical explanation for how the kidnappers got the use of the farm, why did Becker have a hotel room in Boston? And how did he get to Framinghamn?"

"I think I have the answer to the last question," I said. "He must have driven the Pontiac."

"Whichever car he drove," Rose said, "he obviously had a reason for taking a room in Boston. Otherwise he would have stayed here with his friends."

"Very good, m' lady," Holmes said. "He may have stayed in town just to be able to hear Margery's lecture. He couldn't have known we'd be there, too, so he had to cobble together a plan at the last minute."

"I have another good question," I said. "Schmidt and Max had hypos filled with phenobarbital. I don't know much about it, but I do know you can't find it on a drug store shelf. Where did they get it?"

Holmes nodded with enthusiasm. "Another excellent question. Either some doctor prescribed it for them, or they blagged some pharmacy. Most likely the former."

"Somehow I don't think they robbed a drug store. But a doctor, hmm, I wonder who that could be? Either way, the police should be able to trace the source. I'll have to say Becker's gotten very sloppy."

"Don't be so modest," Holmes said. "They didn't have much choice. You threw the spanner into all their plans."

"Give the credit to Houdini. We never would have gotten away from the goons at the hotel if Rose hadn't given me his false finger. That gigli saw is horrific."

Holmes turned. "Rose, we've been neglecting you. What did you learn from your telephone queries?"

"For one thing, many of the Spiritualists were following Mr. H's movements closely by the time of his death. Several of them even predicted the exact date to impress their clients."

"Wishful thinking, undoubtedly," Holmes said. "It's next to impossible they all played a role in Houdini's poisoning. Did your sources have any idea where these predictions came from?"

"Mostly from Pheneas and Walter. Somehow they've become the leaders of the movement rather than Sir Arthur and Margery themselves."

Holmes nodded. With a tight smile he said, "Not at all surprising, as strange as that may sound. They are the strongest voices, and the ones with the message the faithful most want to hear. I should think it would almost have become inevitable."

Conversation ended with the aroma of fine coffee.

Violet, while rifling through the cabinets, found a two-pound can of Timur brand arabica. I recognized the tin sitting on the counter because I have one in my basement where I keep my nuts and bolts. Violet occasionally bought the brand, probably because of the beautiful blue and multi-color lithograph of the horseman and stallion on the front. If Isaac Bradford had questionable taste in women, he knew good coffee. An enormous pot steamed away atop the Franklin Stove. The aroma also reminded me how hungry I was. None of us had eaten since last night. "I don't like the idea of raiding Mr. Bradford's larder, but is there anything to eat around here?"

"There's nothing in the ice box, but I did see a few cans of sardines in one of the cupboards," Violet said. "I think I saw some hardtack, too."

"A feast fit for the gods," Holmes said. "I'll leave a few coins as payment."

"One will be more than enough," I said. "Make it two for the sleeping accommodations. I have a feeling Isaac is going to need every penny he can come up with before too long."

We found only two plates and one coffee cup in the cupboards. Holmes grumbled about the absence of cream and sugar, but he forced the brew down, making only one or two pained expressions while he swigged from the cup. The rest of us drank our coffee from water tumblers. The sardines and hardtack quickly disappeared, and we bravely pretended we weren't still hungry. Violet and Rose were just putting away the dishes when Sheriff Peabody arrived.

"Officer O'Neal just picked up Mr. Hahn. He wants you to call him when you get back to Boston. He's very anxious to talk to Mr. Conan Doyle. Everybody ready to go?"

Sheriff Peabody reminded me of my promise to lock the house. "Pretty handy," he said as he watched. "I still think I should take those picks away from you."

I saw he was smiling.

"Officer O'Neal tells me you like automobiles. I think you'll like mine."

A large auto with the word "SHERIFF" and a seven-pointed star on the front door waited beside the house. The sheriff laid an affectionate hand on the hood. "You know what this is?"

"Of course. It's a Lincoln Police Flyer. Detroit has been buying them to upgrade the fleet for a couple of years. Bullet-proof glass?"

"The works. Four-wheel brakes. You can see all the way to Boston when I turn the spotlights on. It even has an ashtray, but I'm not going to start smoking just to try it out. I'll leave that to the youngsters."

"That's quite a car," I said. "Middlesex County must really appreciate your work."

"They better. There hasn't been a serious crime hereabouts since I took office. Who's riding in the back?"

Violet and Rose immediately climbed in. Holmes and I traded glances, then he settled in between them. After leading such an ascetic life, I think he rather liked being between two women.

"Looks like you got shotgun," Peabody said.

"Shotgun?"

"You're riding up front with me. Haven't you ever seen a stagecoach? The man sitting next to the driver carried a shotgun."

"It never even occurred to me. I'll have to remember that. My police friends would get a kick out of it. What's going to happen to the Pontiac?"

"One of the deputies is driving it back to town. We'll impound it until we get everything sorted out."

"Does Max want to turn state's evidence on Becker?" I asked.

"No. In fact he claims he never even heard of him. He says he and his friend were innocently visiting someone at the Parker House Hotel, and you and your wife attacked them for no reason whatsoever. Says he has no idea how your friends ended up in Isaac's house, where the phenobarbital came from—though he thinks you planted it on him—or why everyone should make the same mistake identifying him as a kidnapper."

Holmes's head and shoulders loomed over the front seat. "If a prisoner made a statement like that in the Old Bailey, he'd wind up with a rope around his neck before he even finished the sentence."

"It'd be better for him if he cooperated," I said. "Maybe Officer O'Neal will have better luck with Herr Schmidt."

"Could be. But don't give up on Hahn. At least not yet. One of the lieutenants in the Boston police has gone to a special interrogation school course at the Federal Bureau. He took a class in psychology from them, so he may be able to get one of them to talk."

I had to smile. Psychology? Freud knew mothers had been using it on their children from the beginning of time. German police had been using it for centuries. Talk, or I'll kill you. The Russians used a different approach. Talk or I'll kill your mother. Only the constabulary was naive enough to think it was something new. "I sure hope so."

"So do I. By the way, I called the New York police. There weren't any fingerprints on the gun this Becker was supposed to have used. It's his word against yours if he ever gets caught."

"Somehow, I knew that'd be the case," I mumbled.

Conversation ended, and we arrived at the Parker House fifteen minutes later, dumbfounding the doorman. With the poor man obviously unsure what to do, the sheriff opened the doors for us. We parted company with a quick handshake.

My heart skipped a beat to find the door to our room open. Holmes and the women stood back as I peered around the corner. A maid's cart stood in the kitchen area. A petite young lass with red hair peeking beneath a bandana emerged from the bathroom, saw me looking in and let out a cry.

She held her chest as she caught her breath. "Oh, hello, sir. Forgive me. I'll be leavin' in a trice. I made the beds, but I didn't change the Turkish towels in the bathroom because they looked like they haven't been used."

I loved her Gaelic brogue and her bird-like twitter. "I can see you've done a wonderful job. Thank you."

"Have you been out sight-seein'? Today's Armistice Day, you know. There'll be a big parade downtown."

"No. But thanks for reminding me. I forgot."

She pointed toward the sofa. "There's newspapers for you, and chocolates on the beds. The paper says there's going to be a big parade in Chicago. The mayor will cut a ribbon to open a new road that runs to California. Route 66. It's called the Will Rogers Highway."

Fearing she would run out of breath and collapse, I reached into my pocket and took out a half-dollar and handed it to her. She curtsied. "Oh, thank you, sir."

"You have other rooms to clean. Ours looks just fine."

She curtsied again before hurrying to her cart, her face redder than her hair. "Thank you, sir," she called over her shoulder.

After she left, Holmes turned to Violet. "I suggest you and Rose check your belongings," he said flatly. "That woman obviously feels guilty about something."

"I don't think she's been up to any mischief," I said. "We just surprised her."

"You're far too trusting, Wiggins."

"Maybe. Actually, I'm glad she reminded me today's a holiday. Our young friends, the Irregulars, will be off school, and I think I have a way to put them to good use."

SAM, AS WELL AS SIX of the seven Irregulars, waited eagerly at the schoolyard when Holmes and I arrived twenty minutes later. Holmes was grumbling. I'd just as happily have left him at the hotel to rest. But I needed help transporting the troops. I knew why he was crotchety. He liked my idea but didn't want to admit it because he hadn't come up with it himself.

We hired two taxicabs, and they stood along the curb. The gulls were back, gyrating in the cloudless sky. All traces of snow had disappeared, and the only moisture was dew in the shadows that hadn't yet fled from the morning sun.

The boys were lined up with eager faces. "Did you bring the money?" Sam asked when I got within ten feet. Not a good morning, or a nice day. This young man was all business.

"We sure did. Who's missing?"

"Mike. He had to go fishing with his parents. He wants me to collect his money for him."

We had it. Before we left the hotel, Holmes had stopped at the front desk at the hotel and turned a few of his gold pieces into shiny new quarters.

"Do you think you could find someone to take Mike's place? I'm going to need all eight of you today."

"I can get my brother. Why do you need him?"

"I have a special job for you. Are you all sure you want your money?"

They all responded with cries of "Yes."

"Line up," Sam said.

They did. Each in turn inspected his quarter as if it were a foreign object. I almost expected at least one of them to bite it to see if it would bend. Sam and I stood at the back of the line. When all the backs were turned, I surreptitiously slipped him his dollar.

All the young soldiers were paid in a matter of minutes. "What's up?" Sam asked.

"As I said, I have an important job for you. This may be a bit boring, so I'm raising all your wages to a dollar for today."

I was greeted with a chorus of Ooos. Some of their fathers didn't make that much.

"You're probably too young to know that there are four newsstands in Boston that sell German newspapers. You all know what Mr. Becker looks like. He may already have left town, but he may still be here. He has a lot of friends in Germany, and I'm sure he wants to know what's happening there. If he buys a paper at one of those stands, we may be able to catch him. You all told your parents you would be playing outside all day so they won't miss you. Right?"

They looked at each other and nodded.

"Good. You'll work in teams of two at each of the newsstands. If he should show up, one will stay to watch him, the other will find a policeman. Trade off when you start to get cold. Whatever else happens, don't ever get anywhere close to him. He won't hesitate to hurt you. Do you understand?"

Wide eyes and quick nods.

"My friend and I will take you where you need to go. Someone will have to sit in someone else's lap when we get in the cab."

As expected, I was greeted by a chorus of "Uh uh. Not me."

"We'll meet back here at four o'clock. My friend or I will pick you up before then. That's a long time to be standing around, so I'm giving you each another quarter so you can buy a candy bar or a soda pop. Is everyone ready to go?"

"Yeah," they shouted, taking off on the run toward the cabs.

C H A P T E R

S am won the race to the taxis and staked out the one parked in front. "My brother can sit on my lap," he said.

I thanked him for his generosity. No one else volunteered to double up to ride in Holmes's taxi. We also didn't want any whining about who'd be riding with whom in the taxis. Holmes came up with his own solution. Reaching into his jacket pocket, he took out a box of lucifers and removed two. He broke one of the matches in the middle, and the second so one end was decidedly shorter than the other.

"You, you, you and you are riding with me," he said, pointing at four of the boys at random. "I have four match sticks. The short one will sit in the long one's lap."

We heard mutters as he held out his right hand. "Each of you take one." The boy named Eric was the loser, with Charlie getting the short match. The other two enjoyed a good laugh at their expense.

"Now that's settled, we have to decide who goes where," I said. "Two of the teams will ride in each cab. Three of the sellers are downtown, the fourth is at Harvard Square."

Holmes cut me short. "I want the venue at Harvard. I've never visited that educational citadel, and I doubt I'll ever have another chance. I'll take any of the remaining three."

The words brought a stab of sadness. Even the great Sherlock Holmes knew he was mortal. I showed Sam the list of addresses. "Which one would be easiest to get to from Harvard?"

After a quick look he pointed at the one at 284 Tremont Street.

"That'll be Mr. Andelman," I told Holmes. "I talked to Officer O'Neal. The vendors all know what we're planning. I'll meet you there."

Just as Holmes's contingent was about to get into the cab, I took out my bag of liquorice pipes, giving each of them one from my precious stash. "I don't need to tell you to be careful."

Sam lived three blocks away and jumped out as soon as the driver stopped. Bare seconds later, he came back with a slightly shorter, sandy-haired boy in tow. "This is Vince. He doesn't know what Mr. Becker looks like, so he'll be the one to fetch the cop. You're giving him a dollar, too, aren't you?"

"Absolutely."

Sam elbowed his brother. "See? I told you I wasn't kidding."

As we neared downtown Boston, traffic got heavier. People sought out places to sit or stand along Downtown Crossing to watch the parade. Despite the delays, it only took ten minutes before we arrived at 520 Broylston Street where Ada Twombley offered a worldwide selection of papers. Sam and Vince got out first. I followed them into the shop.

The tiny store was unenclosed, with papers clipped to tall stands covered from bottom to top with newspapers from presses in Europe and Asia, as well as an enormous selection of local papers. Ada, diminutive with black hair streaked with splashes of gray, bent forward and held a hand next to her mouth. "Are you the boys working with the police?" she asked in a stage whisper.

They both nodded with enthusiasm.

"This is exciting. I hope I'm here if he comes in. Do either of you like cookies?" The boys beamed. "Yeah." Neither noticed when I stepped back to return to the cab.

Art and Patrick got the last post at Court Street at Corner Square. This shop had a front door with a large sign reading "Non giornate Italiano," in red letters. Stepping in, I didn't see as many papers as the other shop, but Tom Flanagan sold tobacco, cigars, and cigarettes as well as candy bars to supplement his wares. A sharp-featured man in a flannel shirt came forward with a jaunty step.

"Top of the morning to you, boys. I'm pleased to meet you. I always like to help the police. Since you're working for them as special agents, you're welcome to buy a Baby Ruth bar or a Coca Cola for a penny. But let me warn you. Don't let me catch you trying to steal cigarettes. If I do, I'll send you to the pokey for a week, special agents or not. Do we understand each other?"

Eyes the size of dinner plates, they nodded vigorously.

Has anyone been in to buy a German language newspaper recently?" I asked.

"Just old Gerhardt Schultz. He buys a copy of *Frankfurter Zeitung* every week. No one else I can think of."

"Any chance you have a copy of the *Detroit Free Press*?"

"Sorry. I'm sold out. I have the *Dearborn Independent.*"

My teeth gritted. Even the mention of the rag made me furious. "Thanks, but I wouldn't even light my stove with it. If I'm not mistaken, you don't carry Italian papers."

Flanagan shrugged. "You're right. I don't want any dirty W.O.P. coming into my store looking for them."

I wanted to say I was willing to bet his parents probably didn't have papers when they came to America, either. "Why? Are they trying to buy them with Lira?"

He frowned. Before he could say any more, I turned my attention to my young minions.

"Good luck, men, Here's a pipe for each of you. Just don't try to put tobacco in them."

They eagerly snatched the last of my liquorice from my hands, then immediately began to argue about who looked older with a pipe stuck in his mouth. They were still at it when I left.

With the parade only half an hour away, it took us more than fifteen minutes to get to 284 Tremont. I paid the dollar fare and added another dollar for a tip. "I may quit early today," the driver said without irony. "Thanks."

The door to the shop stood open. Instead of hangers, shallow shelves bulged from floor to ceiling with newspapers of all sizes. A short ladder on wheels allowed customers to reach the upper levels. Across from them,

Terry Fields stood on tiptoes rummaging through the candies. He saw me and showed off his braces with a grin. With customers in the shop, I put a finger to my mouth to prevent him from greeting me aloud.

Mr. Adelman emerged from the back of the store. "Good morning. Can I help you find something?"

"If you've got a copy of the *Detroit Free Press*, I'll buy one."

"It's a day old. Today's edition hasn't come in yet."

"Yesterday's is fine."

He knew exactly where it was. With an apologetic look, he said, "Six cents. I have to charge extra because it has to come by train."

I had six cents in coppers. Folding the paper under my arm, I passed Terry on the way to the door. "Good job," I whispered.

Terry's partner waved at me from across the street. Pedestrians ignored the traffic light and crossed in a steady stream. Certain I wouldn't be noticed, I joined them and ducked into the doorway of a dry cleaning shop. My young irregular joined me.

"No luck yet?"

"Nope. This is getting kinda boring."

"That's the way these things work. I don't know your name."

"Neil Tully. I just moved here from Cleveland three years ago."

The conversation ended immediately as a familiar-looking black automobile stopped in front of the news stand. I knew in an instant it was an Essex.

I dashed across the street to get a better view of the auto. My heart pumped faster when I noticed the dented fender. Out of breath, I darted back to where Neil was standing watching me with a puzzled expression.

"Get the policeman! The man we're looking for just went into the shop!"

CHAPTER 32

My heart pounded.

I stood frozen in place. Instead of joy, all I could think of was what could go wrong. *What if Neil couldn't find a policeman before Becker returned to the auto and drove away? What if Becker somehow recognized Terry Fields and abducted him from the shop? What if the villain saw me?*

The last, at least, was something I could control. I backed into the doorway of the jewelry store behind me and took out my pocket watch.

Seconds ticked by, and nothing changed. Neil was nowhere in sight, and I became more and more certain Becker would reappear at any moment. I was bound and determined he wouldn't get away again.

My suspicions were confirmed. Becker stepped out carrying a newspaper. Just as he was about to get into the auto, I sprang from my hiding place. "Stop! Thief!"

Seeing me flying willy-nilly in his direction, he turned tail and headed toward the ever-growing crowd. The auto was of no use to him. The steady stream of traffic prevented his driving off.

"Stop thief!" I shouted again.

That brought plenty of stares, but no one tried to stop him.

It never even occurred to me he could have had a weapon. I forged onward in hot pursuit.

"Stop that man," I called as he dodged forward at full speed, elbowing and pushing aside everyone in his path. "He's a wanted criminal."

I should have known what would happen. Far from offering assistance, frightened-looking people stood aside to make way for him.

A toddler girl suddenly appeared in my path, escaping from the grip of a terrified mother. If I were twenty years younger, I would have hurtled over her, but I had no choice but to put on the brakes. Becker disappeared as the crowd closed. By the time I skirted the terrified tiny obstacle, I'd lost sight of him.

I forged ahead a few more yards, then gave up. As I struggled to catch my breath, I realized Becker had defeated me again. The only consolation was that he had been forced to leave the stolen automobile on the street.

I returned to it. After taking a look around to be sure no one was watching, I casually peered through the passenger side window to see if the scoundrel had left anything behind.

My heart skipped a beat. A hat, coat and briefcase lay invitingly just a few inches away.

I took another look. No one was even looking in my direction.

Heart banging wildly, I opened the door and lifted the briefcase from the seat. It took all of my will power, but I casually nudged the door shut. Everyone from blocks around could hear me and know I was up to no good.

What now?

Terry Fields stood a foot away. "Take this," I said, thrusting the valise toward him. "Go down the street to the drug store and wait there for me. If anyone asks you, tell them you're waiting for your dad to come and take you to his office. Got that?"

With a dubious look, he nodded and took the briefcase from me. He turned and started to run for his destination.

"Walk. Don't run. I'll be down to pick you up as soon as I can. Here," I said, reaching into my pocket for a fifty-cent piece. "Buy yourself a chocolate soda while you're waiting."

Despite my warning, he took off at a trot.

Bare seconds later, Neil showed up, out of breath, with a police officer following. "I'm sorry," he gasped. "I couldn't find the policeman. He was helping an old lady get to an automobile. She had fallen."

"It looks like I'm too late," the officer said. He could have been a stock character from a vaudeville play, with a gargantuan stomach assaulting the buttons on the front of his uniform, and an enormous rose, lovingly nourished by years of strong spirits, hanging between his eyes.

"He—he was getting into the auto," I stammered. "I didn't want him to escape. I chased him into the crowd."

"You should have waited," the officer said. "He wouldn't have gotten very far with the traffic the way it is."

I felt my face turning red. I hadn't even thought of that. Not knowing he was in danger, Becker would probably have sat waiting until he could find a break in the traffic. "I just wanted to make sure he couldn't just drive off."

The officer pursed his lips and nodded. "Well, he's on foot now, so he can't get very far. Is this the car he stole?"

"Yes. You can see the dent in the front bumper."

The officer peered into the auto and spied the hat and coat. "He's going to be plenty chilly. It's supposed to get close to zero this afternoon."

"Maybe he left something in the overcoat," I said, envisioning what I would find in the valise.

"That's possible. I'll get someone to tow the auto and bring the clothes into the evidence room. Too bad we couldn't catch him red-handed."

"It is," I replied, forcing a sad face. "Maybe we'll have better luck next time."

WITH THE PARADE less than half an hour away, nearly all street traffic had come to a standstill. Neil Tully and I waited for Holmes beside the Essex. I could hardly wait for the great detective to appear. In our friendly but intense game of one-upmanship, I had pulled ahead by a mile.

He arrived ten minutes later, immediately catching my expression. "What makes you look so smug, Wiggins? Did you capture Mr. Becker?"

"No. But he did show up. I tried to chase him, but he got away in the crowd."

"That hardly sounds like a victory to me."

Vowing not to be offended, I patted the Essex's fender. "Does this look familiar to you?"

He gave the auto a cursory sidelong glance. "No, but judging from the dent in the fender and the fact that Becker appeared here, I assume it's the carriage used in the abduction last night."

206 / Who Done Houdini?

Once again his attitude annoyed me. "Indeed. Our foe knew he couldn't drive away, so he left the auto behind. Some of his belongings as well."

This time Holmes couldn't hide his interest. I didn't wait for a response.

"He left his hat and coat on the seat . . ."

Holmes glared at me. "Stop being silly, Wiggins. We don't have time for nonsense. Get to the crux of the matter."

Damn! "He left his briefcase. One of the Irregulars is waiting for us down the street with it."

TERRY FIELDS SAT at the drug store's counter with the foamy remains of an ice cream soda before him. When he saw us, he took a noisy last slurp, snatched up his change and slid off the stool to his feet. With a big smile, he lofted the valise. "Here's your briefcase, Dad."

Luckily, no one else but the soda jerk, a morose male teen who obviously wasn't listening, was around to hear.

"Thanks—son," I mumbled.

Remaining in character, Terry took my hand as we left the pharmacy. Wraithlike, Neil followed without a word. I had to believe the poor fellow was low-man on the neighborhood totem pole.

"Where to now?" Holmes asked. "We certainly aren't going to find a cab anywhere around here, and we have the rest of the Irregulars to retrieve."

"Do you have a nickel?" Terry chirped.

"I just gave you half a dollar ten minutes ago."

"All I have is dimes."

Grumbling, I handed him a nickel. "What do you want it for?"

"I'll call my dad and have him pick us up."

AFTER PAYING our young charges their wages at the Parker House, and giving Michael Fields a dollar for his assistance, we still had forty-five minutes until the end of the parade when we could pick up the rest of the Irregulars.

In our room, Holmes, Rose, and Violet hovered over me like vultures as I pried open the valise with a sturdy table knife. As suspected, it was stuffed full of papers of all sizes and shapes. I dumped the contents on our table and divvied them up.

My pile included used train tickets from Detroit to New York, and New York to Boston. "Interesting. Becker bought a return ticket to Detroit for tomorrow. I'll tell O'Neal. Our foe may still be planning to leave on that train."

Violet opened a bulging file of newspaper clippings showing drawings and diagrams.

"I know what they are," Rose said. "Mr. Houdini published articles for months explaining the tricks the mediums used to gull their clients. Whenever one of us discovered a new one, we drew it or photographed it and sent it to the newspapers. Mr. Becker must have been collecting them for years."

"He probably was looking for new material," Holmes said in a laconic tone. He laid a similar folder in front of him. "Apparently Hitler has been recruiting heavily from the veterans groups for his private militia. In fact, that's where much of his money's being used."

I shook my head.

"Hitler's Brownshirts patrol the streets beating people up and looking for ways to extort money. The local police forces can't control them. Weimar doesn't even try. I suspect President Hindenburg may even sympathize with them."

"Our Mr. Becker must be quite a scholar," I said. "He's been tracking Mr. H's movements for years."

I flipped through the clippings again. This time I noticed a *Detroit News* cut with a circle around the date of Houdini's visit in May of 1923.

My heart beat faster. "This may be important," I said, dealing out four piles. "See if any of the other clippings have circled dates."

After a quick search, Violet found two. Rose and Holmes, one each. All were announcements of Houdini's upcoming performances.

We arranged them by date on the tabletop. The earliest was a December 1924 blurb in the *Minneapolis Times,* and the latest, October 15, 1926, in the Schenectady *Daily Gazette.* The date was circled in red.

I looked at Rose. "You said Mr. H. played in Schenectady just before he went to Montreal, didn't you?"

"Yes. It was a stop I wished we hadn't made. I told you Mrs. H. got sick and had to go the hospital, and Mr. H. broke an ankle on stage."

"Bess was hospitalized?" Holmes asked in excitement. "I forgot about that. Do you know why?"

"Severe nausea and stomach pain. The doctors thought it was food poisoning and pumped out her stomach. She was still sick when we arrived in Montreal."

Violet gasped.

"Yes, dear lady," Holmes said in a serious tone. "I was thinking the same thing. But Mrs. Houdini and Rose had different meals as Mr. H. Nonetheless, Becker's newspaper articles provide a strong chain of circumstances that suggest he was the force behind Harry Houdini's poisoning, and the fatal dose was administered in Schenectady. The circled dates may indicate other, unsuccessful attempts. It's quite possible the magician developed something of an immunity from insufficient doses. I wish we could find out if Bess became sick at the same time."

"She was often in poor health," Rose said. "Poor Mr. H. was always tending to her needs and trying to console her."

Once again, the words and tone made me wonder about Rose's feelings for her employer. My musings ended with a look at my pocket watch. "This is all very exciting, but we have to collect the rest of our Irregulars. I suggest you pick up the ones in Cambridge, Holmes. I'll get the ones downtown. If you ladies will order dinner from room service and have them deliver in an hour, we'll all get something to eat."

CHAPTER 33

Rose had splurged and ordered lobster for us, paying for it from her own pocket. It was our first real meal of the day, and a bit rich for my taste, but it certainly couldn't have been more delicious. Unfortunately, my wife's efforts to force temperance on our nation had been all too successful. A nice chilled sauterne would have been the perfect complement, immoral and illegal as it may have been.

"One thing bothers me," I said, picking at the bread pudding that came for dessert. "I simply can't imagine Albert Becker would use thallium to poison Houdini. I doubt he even heard of it. Why didn't he use something more common, like arsenic?"

"Too easy to detect, Wiggins," Mr. Holmes mumbled. "Houdini could have suspected its use himself. Thallium's far rarer and, therefore, more insidious. But you bring up an important point. There must be another, even higher, echelon at work. A Moriarty to Colonel Moran, as it were."

The telephone rang. I put down my spoon and got to my feet.

"Good afternoon, Mr. Wiggins," said a cheery voice. "Conan Doyle speaking. Officer O'Neal will be interviewing me in my room at the hotel, and I thought you and Mr. Holmes might want to be present. Your wife is welcome, too."

"What time is he coming?"

"Two o'clock."

"That's only twenty minutes from now. Thank you for the invitation. We'll see you then."

AFTER VIOLET FRESHENED up a bit and I changed my clothes, we met Holmes and took the elevator to the lobby. To our delight, we stepped out

209

into bright sunshine. I caught Holmes looking wistfully in the direction of the Park Hotel. My turn to play mind reader. "It is sad, isn't it?"

To my dismay, Holmes paid no attention to my newfound skill. "Quite. My calves are castigating me for lack of use."

"Do you get the feeling Becker's still watching us?"

"No. He's been dealt another serious blow. He's definitely on the defensive. He no longer has his henchmen, and he'll have to buy himself another chesterfield, but I can assure you, we haven't seen the last of him. He would love nothing better than to catch us in an unguarded moment. Ah well . . ." With a pensive look, Holmes opened the back door of the waiting taxicab and gestured for Violet and me to get in.

"To the Park Hotel, please," he said, climbing in after us.

I settled into the plush seat. "Do you think Lady Jean'll be there?"

"I'm sure Sir Arthur would insist on it. She'd be quite furious if she isn't allowed to stay." With a mischievous chuckle he said, "Do you know Sir Arthur's pet name for her?"

"I can't even imagine."

"Lady Sunshine."

BY CHANCE, WE MET Officer O'Neal in the lobby of the Park Hotel, and the four of us took the elevator to the Eighteenth Floor. Sir Arthur stood waiting outside his door with an expression that reminded me of a worried walrus. I smiled as he greeted Holmes with an unwelcome hug, whilst Lady Jean stood by, pretending to be a statue.

When Sir Arthur turned his affections to Violet, his enthusiasm aroused the lady's attention, and she became Pygmalion with a loud clearing of her throat.

"Please come in. I've set chairs for everyone," Sir Arthur said.

I felt a tingle of expectation as I did.

O'Neal remained on his feet, and was the first to speak. "When I called you last night, Sir Arthur, I was hoping to get information about where the kidnappers had taken their victims. Fortunately, that's no longer an issue. Thanks to Mr. Wiggins, everyone is safe and sound."

Sir Arthur applauded. "Thank heavens for that. I barely slept all night."

"Nor did I," Lady Jean grumbled.

"I can understand why. Actually, because of Mr. Wiggins's heroics, I only have a few questions," O'Neal took a notebook from his pocket. "Two of the kidnappers have been captured. The third, Albert Becker, also known as Baker, is still at large. What do you know about him?"

Sir Arthur's smile faded. "I've never met the man, but I do know he's a close associate with Dr. Croydon, and important to the Spiritualist movement. Our religion is barely known in Germany, and Mr. Baker has been working very hard to promote it there. I contributed more than a thousand pounds to the cause, and I know the Croydons and others in this country have made similar donations."

O'Neal jotted a note. "Do you know why Mrs. Croydon invited him to the lecture last night?"

"She told me she invited him so he could announce a fund-raiser he would be holding in Boston next month. Dr. Croydon thought we could raise at least twenty-five thousand dollars. I planned to donate a thousand pounds myself."

A good start. That amounted to nearly twenty-five hundred dollars. O'Neal jotted another note. "Go on."

"Margery told me she was surprised Mr. Baker left before she could introduce him. She was absolutely dumbfounded to learn of his alleged involvement in the kidnapping."

O'Neal responded. "The kidnappers took the victims to a house in Framinghamn that belongs to an Isaac Bradford. Mr. Bradford is in England. Do you have any idea how they got use of his house?"

Sir Arthur smiled wistfully. "The Spiritualists *I* know are happy to share food and lodging with other members. In that way, we are a lot like the Masons. I don't know if Mr. Bradford is a participant, but if he is, he may have given Mr. Becker the keys as a gesture of his trust and respect."

O'Neal's lips pursed. "Do you have any other information that might help us find Becker?"

"Unfortunately, no."

"Mrs. Croydon offered to put on a séance to help us. Would you mind arranging it?"

Sir Arthur beamed. "Not at all. In fact I'd be delighted to show off her abilities. Walter undoubtedly will have many interesting things to say. From what I've heard, he and Mr. Baker were very friendly."

I responded to O'Neal's puzzled look. "Walter is Margery's familiar. He's her dead brother."

"I see," the officer said with a shrug. I could tell he was having a hard time keeping from smiling. "If tonight isn't too short a time to prepare, I'd really like to meet them. The Wigginses and Mr. Holmes would be welcome, too."

I scarcely could believe my ears.

"Thank you," O'Neal said. "I have an appointment and will have to leave shortly. I'll be happy to give you a call when I'm finished and meet you at her house. I've heard a great deal about Mina Croydon. Do you know where she got her medium name?"

"I heard she was told to take the name of one of her great aunts who had spiritualist talents. You'll have to ask her yourself."

"I certainly will. I don't have any more questions at this time, so I'll be leaving. We'll meet again shortly."

Sir Arthur followed the officer to the door. When the rest of us remained in place, Lady Jean seemed surprised, but remained silent.

"That was a quick interview," Sir Arthur said as he returned. "Now that the constabulary is gone, can I offer anyone some sherry?"

His smile faded when there were no takers.

"Thanks for the offer," Holmes said, "but I have a few questions for you that aren't directly connected with Becker or the kidnapping. I understand Dr. William Crookes visited the Croydons. Do you know when this was?"

Sir Arthur looked thoughtful. "Sometime in 1919, just a few months before he died. Why do you ask?"

"His meeting with the Croydons is the only direct connection to our investigation of Mr. Houdini's death by thallium poisoning."

"Investigation?" Lady Jean said. "Why should you be investigating? He died of appendicitis."

"Is that what Pheneas told you?"

Her eyes widened. "I-I don't think I ever asked him. It never occurred to me it was anything other than what the daily journals said."

Sir Arthur quickly stepped in. "Don't be concerned, love. I'm happy to answer Mr. Holmes's question. Dr. Crookes and I were longtime friends. He had an interest in our religion and wanted to visit the people who knew the most about it. I offered to contact the Croydons for him."

"How did you know Mrs. Croydon at that time?" Holmes asked.

"I became aware of Margery's extraordinary gifts soon after Dr. Croydon married her in 1918. The doctor recognized her talents and quickly helped her put them to use. Overnight, she became one of the most important leaders of our religion."

"I see." I could tell from Holmes's expression he was lost in thought. "What happened then?"

"Dr. Crookes was coming to America for a scientific conference in '19, and the Croydons were anxious to meet him. From what Dr. Crookes told me, he was very impressed with Margery, though I'm not certain he converted. It seems Walter was very intrigued and wanted to know all about thallium and its uses. The others at the séance weren't that interested, so Dr. Crookes didn't go into much detail."

I wasn't surprised to learn it was Walter who had the most interest in the new element. If he had been there, Houdini probably would have been interested in it, too. He might have realized why his hair started to fall out. "Was Albert Becker in attendance when Dr. Crookes was here?"

"He could have been. I never heard."

Holmes's voice became gentle. "We know Mr. Becker has been raising money to aid Adolf Hitler in building a new political party that intends to restore the German empire by any means possible. Becker and Dr. Croydon also are propagating eugenics and anti-Semitism in the form of Aryan superiority theory. From what you just said, don't you think it's possible some of the money Mr. Becker purportedly collected for the

Spiritualist movement may have been given to Hitler and his National Socialist party?"

Sir Arthur didn't respond immediately. "It never occurred to me before, but yes, of course it's possible. I doubt it. No one would even think of questioning the legitimacy of someone Dr. Croydon endorsed."

"If you don't mind, Lady Jean, I have a question for you."

Her eyes opened wide. "For me?"

"Yes. Who is Pheneas, please?"

"Why, he's a soul I contacted during a séance in Windlesham, an Arabian seer from ancient Ur who lived before the time of Abraham."

"I fear he may have misinformed you," Holmes said quietly. "There weren't any Arabians before the time of Abraham. They were all part of the area we now know as Palestine."

Sir Arthur cut in. "You misunderstood, my dear. Pheneas was merely trying to describe the area where he lived in terms you would have recognized."

Obviously anxious to shield Lady Jean from further questions, he quickly continued. "I can tell you about our first encounter with Pheneas. It was in 1912, and our whole family was present at the time. All the children and I got to talk to him. He told us some very bad things were about to happen, but that we shouldn't be afraid because none of us would be hurt. When everything was done, the world would be a better place."

Sir Arthur paused and took his wife's hand. A faint smile appeared on his face. "I thought the children might be afraid, but they seemed to think he was funny."

"I see," Holmes said. "Did you believe him?"

"Of course," Sir Arthur sputtered." Why should I have doubted? I hadn't been aware my wife's spiritual gifts were so powerful, but I immediately knew Pheneas was a genuine spirit. Now he's like a member of the family. He's been with us for more than fifteen years."

"Could you invoke other spirits if you wanted to, Lady Jean?" Holmes asked.

"I don't know," she said in an offended voice. "I've never tried. Pheneas chose me to be his contact with the spirit world, and I have no reason to even attempt to summon anyone else."

"Can you call him now?"

"I don't call him, and he never appears. I automatically write what he wants to communicate. He won't visit me in the presence of non-believers."

"I'm not a non-believer," Holmes said, "merely an agnostic. I'm not yet convinced, but I certainly haven't made up my mind that he doesn't exist. I expect Wiggins feels the same way."

He barely had the words out of his mouth when I blurted, "Absolutely. I couldn't have put it better myself."

"I believe in him, too," Violet chimed.

Lady Jean still looked suspicious. "What did you want to ask him?"

Holmes paused a moment. "I'd like to know If Harry Houdini died a natural death, or if he had been poisoned. And if he were poisoned, who administered it to him. I think your husband wants to know that, too."

Lady Jean glanced at her husband with a deadpan expression. "I'll ask Pheneas after you've left."

"It may not be necessary," Holmes said. "Walter may tell me in the meantime."

CHAPTER

We were all lost in thought as we rode the elevator to the lobby. The doors opened to the strains of violins. The string ensemble had returned and was stroking out a jaunty tune. I didn't remember the name, but I remember the lyrics. "Oh, we sailed the ocean blue . . ."

Holmes stopped in his tracks. "Ah, wonderful Wiggins. *The H.M.S. Pinafore.* I haven't heard that for years. I took you to see it at the Adelphi just before you left for America. Do you remember?"

"Just the melody. Seems to me I remember a busty lady named Buttercup."

"You would remember that," Violet scolded.

Holmes wagged a finger in time with the beat. "Our dear Gilbert and Sullivan. Can you imagine they hated each other so much, they sat back to back when they had to work in the same room? Mycroft always wondered what they would have come up with if they got along."

"Probably 'She's Only a Bird in a Gilded Cage,'" Violet said, giving my arm a tug.

Holmes actually laughed. "Very good, my dear. I can't imagine anything more silly."

Stepping out, we were surprised to discover snow had again begun to fall. For once we found no taxi waiting, and Holmes didn't seem to care.

"A very productive day so far, Wiggins. I can hardly wait to attend Mrs. Croydon's séance."

"Indeed."

"I can't, either," Violet squealed.

"Did either of you observe anything unusual about Sir Arthur's relationship with Lady Jean?"

"He seemed protective, if that is what you mean."

"Precisely, Wiggins. Though she's the one who tends the gate when we talk to him, Sir Arthur seems to be aware of the inconsistencies in her version of Spiritualism and is quick to explain them away."

"They're protecting each other," Violet said in a firm voice. "It's almost as if she doesn't really believe in it herself. I think she understands how much Sir Arthur has declined because of his beliefs, and she wants to shield him from ridicule."

Thunderbolt!

Holmes, as excited as I had ever seen him, seized her by her arms and squeezed. "You are the wisest of us all, dear lady. Of course you're right. It explains her truculence toward us to perfection."

While Violet beamed, I held my breath in amazement. This was probably the closest Holmes had ever come to embracing any woman, and I expect he was more impressed by her insight than anything Dr. Watson or I came up with.

"Bravo, my dear," I said, with a quick peck on her cheek. "But just to let you know my deductive faculties haven't been asleep for the last two days, I've noticed some interesting inconsistencies between what Sir Arthur says and what Margery told me when Officer O'Neal and I visited her last night. I asked her directly why she invited the man she knows as Baker to her lecture. She said it was because her husband asked her to. And now Sir Arthur says she told him she wanted to give Becker an opportunity to announce his fund-raising event. It appears she lied to someone, and for no good reason I can come up with."

Holmes nodded with a thoughtful look. "She's being guarded, at the very least."

"More than guarded, I'd venture. Sir Arthur seems to relate all of Becker's motives and actions to his supposed desire to promote Spiritualism in Germany. Margery, on the other hand, told Officer O'Neal and me the friendship between Becker and her husband was based on shared affection for Germany and a common interest in eugenics and Aryanism. Knowing Becker, I tend to believe she was being truthful with us."

"I concur, Wiggins."

Violet flashed an angry look. "I don't know Mr. Becker at all, but I certainly hope you don't think everyone who's involved in Spiritualism has bad motives."

"Of course not," Holmes said. "I never said any such thing."

"I just wanted to let you know there's a woman down the block from us who reads tarot and has a crystal ball. She puts on séances for us every once in a while, and hardly charges anything for her services. What she does take in provides a little more money for her husband to play the stock market. She calls herself a Spiritualist, and she's probably contributed to the national organization. I'm sure she must know Albert Becker, but I'm equally sure she has no idea of where his money is going. Most of all, she certainly isn't a bad person."

"Absolutely not," Holmes said. "At worst, she's a petty thief. Not even that, if people consider her to be an entertainer only. I would guess she's like nearly everyone else in the profession. Harmless and, essentially, a good person."

"Exactly."

"I expect nearly everyone in Detroit admires Henry Ford, too."

Caught off guard, Violet frowned. "I've heard that some business leaders are angry because he pays his workers so well, but, at least as far as I know, everyone else considers him to be a good man."

I never regretted not telling Violet about my friendship with Mo before. Now I wished I had.

"And in most ways, he undoubtedly is." Holmes continued. "But he hates Jews, and he's one of Adolf Hitler's biggest supporters. At best, he's misguided. At worst, he's extremely dangerous. With his wealth and influence, he has almost unlimited power to put his unfortunate beliefs to work."

"Maybe so, but I never even heard of Hitler until Timothy mentioned his name."

"Right now, that's one of his greatest strengths. He's just the leader of one of the scores of political parties and causes in Germany thriving on the poverty caused by uncontrollable inflation."

"It's almost unimaginable," I said. "People had to carry their money around in wheelbarrows, and spend it as quickly as they got it. Otherwise it became worthless in a matter of hours. Some think Germany will still become the next Russia because the Socialists are so popular and want to confiscate the wealth of the rich. It's led to open warfare between Left and Right. What makes matters even more complicated, many of the communist leaders are Jewish."

Violet yawned. "I've had enough of politics. Let's get back to the room so I can finish my bread pudding."

ROSE MET US at the door, bubbling with excitement. "I've found the name of a scholar Becker's been corresponding with. He's very well-known."

"Indeed," Holmes said. "Who would that be?"

"Madison Grant."

"The naturalist?" I blurted in surprise "He's a close friend of Theodore Roosevelt."

"And John Muir as well. He's visited Muir at Yosemite on more than one occasion. Grant's been concerned about the decline of the moose population because of disappearing habitat, and he's been trying to keep it from becoming worse."

"Many Progressives are worried about declining species," I said.

"Very true, but Grant also has extended his concerns to humans, especially the Nordic race. He says it's being taken over by hordes of inferior stocks from Africa and the Mediterranean who reproduce at a much higher rate."

Mr. Holmes stroked his cheek. "Why does he think the Nordics are superior?"

"He claims the cold northern climate has winnowed out the weaker members, leaving only the hardiest behind. This has also meant they are a smaller population and vastly outnumbered by the other races, and will have to battle for their survival."

"I see," said Holmes. "I expect Mr. Grant is arguing that the Nordics either have to remove the intruders from their land, or expand into other places."

"He recommends both. It's all in his book, *Passage of the Great Race*. According to him, the same thing is occurring in this country. He says there are far too many inferior peoples. He wants sterilization of mental defectives, to begin with—if there are still too many, he has a much more drastic solution."

"I'm afraid to ask," I mumbled.

"He wants them euthanized."

"Euthanized?" Violet shouted. "*Murdered*, you mean. What a perfectly horrible thought. This is by a noted scholar?"

"Absolutely. And it is horrible. Apparently Becker's convinced it's a splendid idea. He sent a copy of Grant's book to Hitler's secretary."

"Although I'm sure the great leader was already familiar with it," Holmes said dryly. "Mr. Grant's ideas couldn't have fallen on more dangerous ears."

"It gets worse. Hitler wrote a personal letter to Becker thanking him for the gift. He says the book has become his Bible. I get the impression that isn't the first or only correspondence. Hitler considers Becker to be one of his most loyal and important supporters, and a tireless worker for the cause."

The words made me shudder.

CHAPTER 35

I had been dreaming Violet and I were sunbathing in the Bahamas when I awoke at Holmes's rough shake of my shoulder. "On your feet, Wiggins. It's four-thirty, and Sir Arthur just called. We have been summoned to 10 Lime Street."

I jumped from my chair. The only time I ever came to quicker was when the nurse at the waiting room at Grace Hospital in Detroit awoke me to announce the birth of Cameron. "Is Violet ready to go?"

"Hours ago. She must have asked Rose or me about every dress she brought with her at least twice, and I doubt there's a hair on her had that hasn't been finger-curled and patted into place at least a dozen times. I would have thought she was awaiting a call from Buckingham Palace."

"That," I said, smoothing out the wrinkles on my trousers and stretching into my somewhat limp suit jacket, "would very likely be fatal. She would never be ready."

"I'll pass the word to Mycroft. Good King George would never forgive himself if that happened."

I had to chuckle in spite of myself.

"Just to fill you in on what I have been doing while you were napping, Rose enlightened me about all the tricks Margery uses. To prove she was a fraud, Houdini constructed a box for her to sit in so she couldn't move her feet or hands without his knowing. She still nearly escaped detection, but her foot brushed his ankle. He says she was the most skilled contortionist he had ever met. He also couldn't detect if Walter's voice was coming from her or her husband."

I stifled a yawn. "All very interesting. Forgive me if I sound rude, but I don't care whether she's undeniably genuine or the most blatant fraud in the world. I just want to get some insight about the Croydons' relationship with Becker and their possible involvement in Houdini's murder."

The words brought a fleeting look of admiration. "I see I taught you well, Wiggins. Those should have been my words. And you are absolutely correct. That indeed is all that matters. For my own part, however, I'll continue to keep a watchful eye on Mrs. Croydon's activities during the séance. I'm quite sure I shall learn something new about her. Perhaps even something to help me talk some sense into poor Sir Arthur's addled brain."

"I wish Rose were coming with us," Violet said with a sad look in her friend's direction. "She shouldn't be left behind all the time."

Holmes nodded. "I wish she were coming, also. But in light of her history with the Croydons, it would merely add unnecessary stress to an already tense situation."

"Don't fret about me," Rose said in a cheerful voice. "I'm just as happy to stay here. Mr. Becker's briefcase is a totally new world for me. I never know what I'll discover next. I've also come across new names to investigate. The work of exposing frauds must continue even though Mr. H. is gone."

Violet still looked unhappy when she waved goodbye.

She fidgeted as the cab made its way down Beacon Street. I knew the cause of her discomfort, but I couldn't account for mine. I expect it probably came from having to meet the Croydons on their home turf. Officer O'Neal would be in charge of queries, though I had a dozen or so questions I wanted to ask, myself, and I was certain Holmes had at least as many. He sat next to Violet lost in thought, unlit pipe in his mouth.

Listening to his occasional pull, I wished I hadn't given all my liquorice away. I needed something to suck on, too.

Not that it would be a long ride. The lights of Boston Garden and the Commons already glowed in the gathering twilight. Lime Street was just north three blocks. Beacon Hill was still thought by some—most of the residents, of course—to be the hill referred to in the Biblical quotation from the Sermon on the Mount: "You are the light of the world. A city that is set on a hill cannot be hidden."

Be that as it may, we were about to visit the home of two of the most important figures of Boston society, living on just that hill. I think Violet must have realized that because she shivered and snuggled closer to me. I knew it couldn't have been because the taxi was cold. Heat from the engine eddied around our feet and worked its way upward. Of all the advances in automotives in the past few years, heated enclosed carriages was the one I appreciated the most. I hardly ever drove in winter before we bought our Chevrolet with its circulating heat system.

Violet snuggled even closer to me. "I'm scared," she said in a small voice. "What if Margery really can talk to the dead?"

"Then you'll get a chance to ask your mother where she hid the silverware she promised to leave to you."

She turned towards me with a smile and punched my arm. "You never take anything seriously, do you?"

"The jury is still out on whether I believe in spirits," I said, "but I certainly believe that Albert Becker is responsible for the death of Harry Houdini. If it turns out the Croydons were also involved, the story is going to appear in the *Free Press*, no matter how much weight the family wields in Boston society."

Violet gave my wrist a sharp pinch. "You're not going to be unpleasant, are you?"

"Of course not. But I'm not going to be charmed into losing my objectivity. Even if she performs in the nude."

"You can't tell me you wouldn't like that," she said with a low laugh. "We're not that old yet."

"Maybe not, but if she does, I'll just have to shut my eyes."

"You'll peek."

Holmes cleared his throat. Loudly. "If you two adolescents can stop cooing, we have to decide on a strategy to get the information we need. From what I have heard and read, we'll be faced with many distractions.

Noises come from all over the house. Objects fly through the air. Most of all, Walter will be devious. If he gets angry, he'll stop answering questions. Rose told me he once screamed at Houdini, 'Either you go, or I will.'"

I threw him a questioning look. "You talk as if you believe he's real."

"It doesn't matter if he is or isn't, does it? Whatever he is, we'll have to deal with him on his own terms. We must get him to answer our questions about his encounter with Dr. Crookes."

"What if he doesn't cooperate?"

"Then we press Margery or Dr. Croydon. I'm sure they'll be surprised by our questions about thallium. If either is in collusion with Albert Becker, they'll most certainly try to hide it. We may even find an ally in Sir Arthur, who seems to have a remarkably clear remembrance of what happened."

We passed the historic Bull and Finch Pub, light twinkling through the shutters of the ancient windows even though alcohol could no longer be served there, and the cab turned right.

As the cab slowed, Violet squeezed my hand. Even though I squeezed back, my heart began to beat faster.

CHAPTER 36

Holmes got out first and offered a hand to Violet. The front light in the house beamed out a cheery welcome, even though we all knew what lay beyond might be anything but.

Margery, wrapped in a white silk robe that barely missed swishing on the floor, answered the door with a radiant smile. She covered my hand with hers as we shook, then greeted Violet with a hug. I could tell at a glance I'd be the only one in the family to battle our hostess.

Holmes gallantly kissed her hand.

The taxi remained in place, its headlamps glowing brightly. I guessed it was the driver's way to make sure we were safely at our destination and appreciated the courtesy after what he had been through in the last twenty-four hours.

"Come in, come in," Margery bubbled, "but please remove your shoes before entering the living room."

When I knelt to take them off, I noticed a pair of plain back brogans already on the floor. "Is Officer O'Neal here?"

"Yes. He came about ten minutes ago. He's in the séance room talking to LeRoi. Sir Arthur and Lady Doyle will be arriving any minute. This should be an exciting evening."

Little do you know how exciting, I thought with a smile. "Will Walter be in attendance?"

"It wouldn't be a séance without him. I do want to warn you, I never know what he'll say. A lot will depend on whether he likes you or not. He'll be pleased to see Sir Arthur and Lady Jean again."

"I'm anxious to see the séance room," Holmes said as he finished aligning the heels and toes of his Oxfords beside mine.

"It's right this way."

I took a deep breath and looked around the living room once again. I liked the bare wood floor. Tawny oak, burnished to look like amber, stretched for at least forty feet from the entry room to the opposite wall. Violet oohed and aahed at the furniture, which I thought looked uncomfortable. Besides family portraits, the Croydons liked large canvases, two at least ten feet long and nearly reaching to the ceiling. One showed a hunter with his dogs, all mere insects between soaring mountains and violently rushing water. No way would that be me. The other depicted Jesus, standing with Pontius Pilate and the Pharisees on a balcony, and a roaring crowd beneath. All I knew about it was it was Italian, and old. Though Violet passed by with little note of the paintings, she stopped in her tracks. The sight of a marble statue, a ten-foot-tall naked man, brought a gasp. Why wasn't there a naked woman companion piece, I wanted to know. It was only fair, after all.

Holmes, on the other hand, walked head down, eyes focused on the floor. I knew he was counting paces. He seemed especially interested when we came to the passageway from the living room where a long stretch of metal grill replaced the wood.

"This is a large vent. Are you still using coal to heat your house?"

"No," Margery said. "We have oil. This opening to the basement was sealed two years ago."

"The fuel of the future, I'm sure. Will your son be joining us?"

She hesitated in her step, obviously nonplussed by the question. "No. He's not allowed at my séances. Why do you ask?"

"I was just curious to know if he has your talents."

"He may. If he does, he keeps them hidden. Our room is up this stairway on the fourth floor."

I wrapped an arm around Violet's waist as we climbed the marble stairway. Our shoeless feet barely made a sound, and slight irregularity of the edges of the steps meant many others had passed our way.

Violet and I were wheezing when we reached the landing. Margery and Holmes seemed unaffected by the ascent.

I heard voices coming from beyond a half-open door ahead of us. One I recognized. The other, a cultured baritone with a Boston accent, I didn't.

Margery opened the door the rest of the way and stepped in. "Darling, three of our guests have arrived. This is Dr. Claybrook, Sir Arthur's friend. Mr. and Mrs. Wiggins are friends of Dr. Claybrook. Dr. Claybrook and Mrs. Wiggins were the ones who were kidnapped from our limousine."

O'Neal and Dr. Croydon got to their feet.

Croydon, lank and more than six feet tall, stood head and shoulders above the relatively diminutive police officer. The doctor's ramrod straight posture and severely trimmed russet mustache reminded me of a colonel I once knew in the Royal Marines. Instead of khaki, his uniform was a green tweed three-piece suit. "Ah, yes. Officer O'Neal and I were just talking about that. Terrible thing to happen. Welcome to our humble abode."

Holmes and I nodded acknowledgment. Violet curtsied.

As we entered, I felt a chill breeze coming from the heavily brocaded wall opposite the door, though the room itself seemed quite warm.

Gesturing in Holmes's direction, Margery said, "Dr. Claybrook is from England."

"Really? Which part?"

"Sussex. The Wigginses are from Detroit. Not far from where Albert Becker lives."

Margery looked toward Croydon.

"Sergeant O'Neal and I were just talking about him."

When did O'Neal get promoted?

"Albert is a fine man and never would do anything illegal. I've known him for more than twenty years. I'm sure everything that's happened is nothing more than an enormous mistake."

He sounded so sincere, I almost believed him.

Holmes wasn't about to give up. "Even so, there's a good possibility his underlings were the ones who crashed into your car. You must be furious."

The doctor's face clouded. He glared at Holmes. "Wouldn't you be?" He gestured toward the chairs. "Everyone please find a seat. I always sit at my wife's right, but you are welcome to take any of the other chairs."

Seven chairs surrounded the circular table. I moved around until I found a seat where the chill wasn't as noticeable, and Violet sat next to me on my left. On the table in front of each chair lay what appeared to be an oversized playing card, face down.

Curious, I started to pick it up.

"Please don't touch anything yet," Margery said. "You'll have an opportunity when we start."

Holmes's features had settled into an expressionless mask. "Where and when did you meet Albert Becker, Dr. Croydon?"

"In June of 1904, at the World Exposition in St. Louis. Germany sent an exhibit, and we both had an interest in the discoveries her scientists had made in genetics in recent years. Even then, we knew how important these advancements were to the future of the German people, and ours as well. With land becoming scarcer, the race has needed to develop superior animals and foodstuffs to survive. Albert and I struck up a conversation and immediately became friends. I realized what he lacked in education, he more than made up for with keen intuition. Men like him will be the leaders in building a new and better world."

I started to open my mouth, but Violet squeezed my hand. Hard.

"When was the last time you saw him?" O'Neal asked.

"Yesterday. We breakfasted together before I boarded my train to New York. We were discussing how to conduct a fundraiser to promote Spiritualism in Germany."

"Sir Arthur tells us you had held one earlier," I said. "He said he happily contributed a thousand pounds himself. That's more than four thousand American dollars. Do you know how much you raised in total?"

"Nearly twenty-thousand dollars, wasn't it?" Croydon asked with an inquiring look at Margery.

"Don't you remember? It was exactly that. We made an additional contribution of four hundred dollars to make it an even amount."

Holmes's eyebrows arched. "Twenty thousand dollars is a substantial amount of money. How was it spent?"

"Albert has a foundation in Munich, *Spirintiritisen Gemeinde*. He has a full-time staff of six and an abandoned church we purchased on Alramstrasse."

"A staff of six? That must be a very affluent organization. Only the businesses that deal in hard currencies, like Britain and the United States, would have that much working capital. Why does Becker think he needs to raise more money?"

Croydon hesitated a moment. "He wants to expand operations to Berlin. We both think our efforts will be more successful there."

"I see. That'd certainly be much more expensive. Berlin is the London of Germany."

Croydon scowled. "You mean London is the Berlin of Britain."

The conversation ended with the sound of a bell.

"That must be Sir Arthur and Lady Jean," Margery said, turning on her bare toes. "I'll be right back."

Time seemed to drag. Though she could only have been gone a couple of minutes, it seemed like an eternity before Margery returned, clutching Sir Arthur's arm with Lady Jean a step behind. "We're all here," she said in a sparkling voice. "When everyone is seated, you can turn over your card. They're Tarot, if you've never seen them before."

"I have!" Violet volunteered shrilly, waving her hand. "My neighbor lady uses them."

Her outburst brought a tight smile from Margery and a moment of embarrassment to me.

A smiling Sir Arthur waved at everyone before sitting. Lady Jean merely nodded at Holmes and ignored Violet and me completely.

"The cards will tell you something about yourself while I get into my cabinet to summon Walter."

Despite my skepticism I could hardly wait to see what was on the face of my card. Violet exposed hers first. It showed two children in what appeared to be a medieval town. I wasn't familiar with the cards and had no idea what it was supposed to represent.

"It's the six of cups," Violet said. "It means harmony and contentment. I've had that all my life."

"Very good," Margery said with obvious admiration.

Mine showed a man in a red cape with his back turned, standing amid three trees or stakes.

"That's the two of wands," Violet said, beaming. "It means success through hard work. Timothy has worked hard all his life, and he is very successful."

I could tell how much she enjoyed showing off her knowledge and rejoiced at her success. Even Margery raised an eyebrow in admiration. At the same time, a tiny thought nagged at the back of my mind. *Had I been married to a witch for twenty years?*

"Neither of the cards is inverted," Margery said. "That's very good."

With Violet, Margery, and Dr. Croydon between me and Holmes, I couldn't see which card Holmes had exposed.

"Oh, dear. Death, inverted. We'll have to ponder on that, Dr. Claybrook. It can have several meanings."

An uncomfortable-looking O'Neal covered his card with his hands.

Did he know what it meant? Or was he embarrassed or otherwise uncomfortable to be involved in the proceedings? I wasn't sure what a staunch Catholic would think of a séance.

Lady Jean, on the other hand, looked pleased with the cards she and Sir Arthur had drawn. "Look, dear. You have the Six of Swords. It means we'll have more converts all the time. And it'll all be because of you."

I had to swallow watching Sir Arthur beam.

"How wonderful. What does your card mean?"

"The Nine of Cups means satisfaction, contentment, and well-being. But I already have that."

I glanced to my right where O'Neal still sat forward in his chair, covering his card with his palms.

"Show us your card, dear," Margery cajoled. "Don't be shy."

With reluctance he moved his hands away and sat back in his chair.

"You have the Strength card. You have great courage and self-control."

She paused and circled behind him. Patting his back she spoke in a soft voice. "Certainly nothing to hide."

He answered with an embarrassed grin.

My estimation of Margery's abilities grew by the moment. The lady was a consummate show person, the very top of her profession as a medium.

She returned to stand behind her chair. "We've all seen our cards. I dealt them out just before you arrived. You didn't choose your card. Your card chose you. Each has a message for you in particular. The only ambiguous one is Dr. Claybrook's card. The card upright means positive change and innovation. Inverted it could mean resistance to change and an error in judgment. Perhaps something you may have to reconsider."

"Indeed?" Holmes said. "That's quite possible. Are there any cards that refer to gender?"

"Yes, of course. There are the King and Queen of each of the four minor suits."

"It seems strange no one drew one. What would it mean if a man drew a Queen, or a woman a King?"

"Nothing in particular," Margery said. "Everyone has a masculine and feminine side. And remember, this wasn't intended to be a true Tarot session. If it were, I would deal out seven cards. Then the placement of each card in relation to the others would have to be evaluated. My little exercise was meant to show the power of the Tarot cards to describe your personality."

"Powerful indeed. But couldn't each of the cards apply to everyone here, no matter what seat they chose?"

Sir Arthur and Lady Jean threw sharp looks at Holmes, but Margery refused to rise to the bait. In an even voice she said, "They could, but in this case they do apply to each of you in particular. That may be the area where you need to change your views. Now, are we all ready to meet Walter?"

CHAPTER 37

The lights went out. After a few moments of darkness, two others, much dimmer, came on. Just enough light to illuminate our faces, and to show Margery, now sitting in her cabinet. It reminded me of a packing crate with the front and top missing.

I caught a scent of something burning, a mild odor, spicy and less distinctive than incense.

Margery must have heard my sniffs, and said in a friendly voice, "Yes, something is burning. Sir Arthur and Lady Jean already know what it is, but for those of you making your first visit, what you smell is sage. We burn it as tribute to the ancient Indian tribe, the Massachusetts, who called themselves 'the people who lived on the hill.' Sage is sacred across the entire continent. The Indians and their rituals are part of the source of my psychic power."

Violet sighed, and Margery continued in a soft, soothing voice. "So you see, you have nothing to fear. Now please join hands."

Though Violet's hand trembled, Margery's seemed especially warm and relaxed.

"Everyone just take deep breaths."

I immediately became suspicious. *Was she trying to hypnotize me?*

After my second breath, I felt a chill that didn't come from the wall. The collective sounds of the seven of us breathing together seemed to merge into one unnerving death rattle similar to the one I heard when my father passed away. Violet must have noticed it, too. Her grip tightened.

Margery's grip relaxed and the sound disappeared into complete silence.

This lasted for only a few seconds, ending abruptly and spectacularly with the blare of a trumpet. A jazzy version of the first riffs of Taps came from somewhere in the house. "Is that you, Walter?" Margery asked, her voice unrecognizable.

"Who else would it be?" a mocking tenor answered in a quavering tone. "Valentino's case is still in court, and Warren Harding had to find a different location because Satan can't stand having him around."

Though it was nearly complete darkness, I looked around to see where the voice was coming from. It certainly didn't originate from Margery. It sounded as if it came from thin air.

"Please try to behave yourself, Walter. Sir Arthur and Lady Jean are here. And we have other guests, too." As she spoke, a shimmering white thread began to waft outward from somewhere near her waist. Soon there were two, then three, then dozens.

"Of course I know we have other guests, stupid. Just because I'm dead doesn't mean I'm blind."

Violet giggled nervously.

I watched, transfixed, as the threads now began to coalesce into the outline of a distinctly human form floating above the middle of the table with arms akimbo.

Margery's nails dug into my wrist.

"Sir Arthur and Lady Jean are here to see you. They say they haven't heard from Pheneas for quite a while. Have you seen him recently?"

"Pheneas? That old bag lives in a different pit, so we don't encounter each other very often. But, since it's Sir Arthur and Lady Jean who are asking, I'll tell him."

"One of our guests is a police officer, Walter. He has some questions he wants to ask you about your friend Albert Baker."

"Is that so? What does he want to know?"

"Do you know where he is?" asked O'Neal.

That brought an unpleasant laugh. "Of course I know where he is. He's just a short distance away. I could lead you right to him, if it were possible and if I wanted to, that is. He's still very cold from being outside all afternoon in his shirtsleeves, and he's busily warming himself. He isn't as lucky as I am. It's always warm and toasty here in hell."

I sat up straighter in my chair. Only the police and I knew that Becker had left his coat in the stolen car and might be cold.

O'Neal obviously thought of that, too. "Enough of the banter. Where is he?"

The ectoplasmic outline pulsed brighter as Walter broke into peals of wild laughter. "You must call an exterminator, dear sister. I'm sure I just heard a rat."

"Please do not speak unless called upon, Sergeant O'Neal," Dr. Croydon cautioned. "He won't answer you, and he'll either do something unpleasant or simply go away if he gets angry."

The officer refused to be put off. "Either he answers my question, or I'll have the whole first police zone come here and search the house. Captain Campbell is waiting for my call."

The outline glowed like a neon sign at the words, followed by a thunderclap. Then it began to fade.

"I warned you," Croydon said. "He's leaving."

Mr. Holmes spoke up. "No, please. I have some questions, too."

A new voice rose from the darkness. "Please tell Walter we're sorry about the confusion, but I would like him to stay," Sir Arthur said from across the table. "Dr. Claybrook is a dear friend of mine, and I know he will be polite."

Margery now sounded unsure. "You heard him, Walter. Sir Arthur is asking you to stay."

The blinking continued, but the light didn't dim any further. Then it gradually became brighter. "I would gladly strike Officer O'Neal dead if I had the means, but I will stay, out of my friendship with Sir Arthur. My fellow spirits would be unhappy with me if I didn't heed his request."

Violet and I sighed in relief.

"Thank you," Holmes said. "I have to know whether Mr. Houdini was poisoned, or whether he died a natural death."

"I can't answer that," Walter replied in a voice that suggested he actually could. "All I can say is that it was destined. I want you all to know that now Mr. Houdini has joined us. He's sorry for his actions. He wants everyone to know all his accusations against my sister are totally unfounded."

Sir Arthur and Lady Jean applauded.

"Many people will be interested to hear that, I'm sure. His wife, especially. Bess intends to conduct yearly séances on the anniversary of his death for as long as it takes to hear from him. Is he with you now?"

This brought another laugh, more unpleasant than the first. "Mercy, no. He's out cavorting in the sulfur pits with some of his Kike friends. They're all clannish and constantly plotting something together, you know. Even here. And they stink worse than brimstone."

"I wasn't aware of that. Does Mr. Houdini know he was poisoned by thallium?"

Everyone caught their breath. Even Walter, if he actually breathed.

Before he could answer, Holmes continued. "I understand you and Dr. Crookes had a very interesting conversation about that metal's properties and uses."

The ectoplasmic outline flashed more brightly, then Walter's voice erupted into another bout of laughter. Angry, this time. "Are you silly enough to suggest I had something to do with his death? Quite impossible you know, much as I would have enjoyed being able to do it."

"Not you, but perhaps someone else who was present when the discussion took place."

Like Margery or Dr. Croydon. How I wished I could see their expressions more clearly.

Dr. Croydon's quickly became clear. "What are you insinuating?" he growled. "My wife and I and three of our friends were the only other ones present."

I bent forward, barely able to wait to hear what Holmes would say next.

"Do you recall their names?" Holmes asked Dr. Croydon. "It's possible one of them could have learned of the metal's darker properties and resented Mr. Houdini's treatment of your wife."

"NO. And the idea is preposterous," Dr. Croydon replied. "Besides, even if it were true Houdini died from thallium poisoning, it wouldn't necessarily have been an intentional act. He could have been knowingly taking it as a depilatory without being aware of its poisonous nature. Or he may have accidentally ingested rat poison."

I was amazed. Dr. Croydon's words sounded very much like those from someone who wasn't sure how much we knew, and where we got our information. To me, it represented a clear admission of guilt. Even O'Neal's suspicions must have been aroused. "I've heard enough," he said.

"Please tell them you're joking, Walter," Croydon pleaded.

Walter answered with a laugh. His outline dimmed and disappeared.

Margery's hand jerked away from mine. "Turn on the lights, LeRoi," Margery said, apparently coming to from her trance. "This séance is over."

CHAPTER 38

D r. Croydon got up first and started toward the door. "I'll have to ask everyone to leave immediately."

O'Neal stood. "I'm afraid that isn't possible. Please wait for a moment, sir."

Sir Arthur and Lady Jean murmured angrily, and I could imagine psychic sparks flying in O'Neal's direction.

O'Neal paid no attention to them. "As much as I dislike what must be done, I need to use your phone, Dr. Croydon."

"He already knows where it is, LeRoi," Margery said in an unhappy voice. "If you're calling in other officers, make sure they take off their shoes before they come into the house. I won't allow them to track up my floor."

O'Neal snorted. "I'll be sure to tell them that. I can't guarantee they won't forget, though."

"Then I'll be the one to meet them at the door to see that they don't forget. Otherwise, Mayor Nichols will hear about this. I will tell him personally."

Apparently properly chastised, O'Neal turned on his heel and followed Croydon out of the room without further comment.

Soon after, Margery stood. "Well," she said with a smile. "It seems as if we're the only ones left. I can put a pot of tea on, and I have cucumber sandwiches in the refrigerator."

"If I might have a word with you before you do," Holmes said.

"Just a word then," she said, eyes narrowing.

Violet and I followed them through the door to the hallway. Sir Arthur and Lady Jean looked bewildered but remained in their chairs.

"There are some things about the kidnapping you probably have not heard," Holmes said. "Do you know an Isaac Bradford?"

To my surprise, Margery answered without hesitation. "I recognize the name. I think he's a new convert who wanted to contact his wife. She had passed beyond some years ago."

"Yes. That would be he. Mr. Bradford has a farm in Framingham and currently is in England. The man who calls himself Albert Baker somehow got use of the gentleman's house and automobile. Do you have any idea how that could have happened?"

I expected her expression to change. It didn't, and she replied in a surprisingly matter-of-fact voice. "No. But as I mentioned in my lecture, LeRoi often attempts to find accommodations for visiting church members within our local Spiritualist church. I think Mr. Bradford may have joined our cause after my husband introduced him to a church member who worked at his hospital. I understand they became close, and went to England together. If Mr. Bradford knew he was going to be away for an extended period, it's quite possible he would have left the keys with LeRoi. You'll have to ask him about that."

She stiffened at the sound of a doorbell. "Who can that be? The police can't be here already. Please excuse me."

"What do we do now?" Violet asked.

"Examine the room, of course," Holmes said. "I have to know how Margery did her tricks."

"Are you sure they were just tricks?"

"Very. I'm convinced her son is involved in some of the effects. The bugle blast, for one. The young gentleman must be quite a trumpeter."

"That may well be. I don't see how she could make Walter appear, though."

"Neither can I. At least, not yet. I expect there may be a magic lantern or some other projector such as a *camera obscura* about somewhere."

He opened the door to the séance room, and we followed him back in. Sir Arthur and Lady Jean were still waiting, looking confused.

"Margery said she'll be right back," Holmes said. "We have some things to attend to here in the meantime. We were so impressed by her performance, we're very close to joining the movement."

That brought applause and warms smiles from the Conan Doyles.

"Walter's appearance is indeed a formidable poser," he said, dropping to his knees and looking beneath the table. When he backed out, Sir Arthur called to him in an angry voice. "Whatever are you doing, Holmes?"

"Merely removing our last reservations. I'm pleased to announce, there is nothing under the table."

To everyone's amazement, he crawled up on the table top and searched the ceiling on his tiptoes. Then he shook his head. "Quite remarkable. If there's an opening, I don't see it."

Sir Arthur got to his feet, huffing. "Your actions are reprehensible, Holmes. I'm ashamed to have gotten you invited."

Before Holmes could respond, the door opened, and Margery stepped in. Catching sight of him, her eyes opened wide. "What in heaven's name are you doing on my table?"

"Looking for Walter's footprints," Holmes said, dropping to his knees and sliding to the floor. Flashing an innocent grin, he wiped the tabletop with his sleeve.

"You won't find any up there" Margery said, eyes riveted on her unmannerly houseguest.

"I apologize for my friend's actions," Sir Arthur blustered. "He told me he is very close to converting to the Faith. I swear I didn't know the lengths he would go to remove his remaining doubts."

"Of course, Sir Arthur," Margery said in a patronizing voice. "I understand. Rose Mackenburg is at the door. She asked for Mr. Holmes. I didn't know we had a Mr. Holmes among us. Until now, anyway. Now I understand why you seem to be the most curious of my guests."

Holmes raised an eyebrow. "Curious? Yes. I expect some people do consider me odd."

That brought a glimmer of a smile. "I meant inquisitive."

"Once again I must apologize," Sir Arthur broke in, his face now the color of port wine. "Mr. Holmes asked me to conceal his identity because he was involved in an investigation. Please forgive me."

"There's nothing to forgive," Margery said with a laugh. "Having to reveal Mr. Holmes as a real person would have been an unnecessary chore that could easily be avoided by changing his name. Come along, everyone. I'm locking the séance room now."

FULL DARK HAD FALLEN. At the entryway, Holmes slipped into his shoes without tying the laces. Opening the door, he stepped outside. Violet and I peered out from behind him.

"I'm sorry Margery didn't invite you in," Holmes said to Rose. "I hope you didn't get too cold."

"I'm fine." Coming forward to stand close to his ear, she spoke in a barely audible voice. "I hope I'm not interrupting anything important, but your young spy named Sam just called. He said he wanted to try to make some more money by keeping watch on the Croydons' house. He was right across the street when Albert Becker showed up. Someone let him in."

My heart skipped a beat. I expect Holmes's and Violet's did, too.

"What time was that?" Holmes demanded.

"It must be a bit more than half an hour ago. Sam had to run home to use the phone, and it took me ten minutes to get here from the hotel."

"That'd be about when Walter appeared," I said. "He created such a stir we could have easily missed hearing the doorbell ringing."

"Yes, and I don't believe in coincidences," Holmes replied. "Did the young man observe how the miscreant gained entry into the house?"

"He says a woman opened the door for him."

"That must be the housekeeper," Holmes mumbled. "I'm sure Margery must have a policy for Lucille to answer the door when she's in séance. I'm equally certain she's found him a place to hide at his request. Our roast pig is nearly ready to be carved, my friends. We want to be on hand when it is."

Margery appeared to lock the door. I had to ask myself how she knew we were done talking to Rose.

Wretched, he returned to the kitchen. "What now?" I asked.

Holmes threw me a withering look. "Once again, you amaze me, Wiggins. We find the housekeeper and ask her."

Once again, I was left with rosy cheeks not caused by the cold. "Of course," I mumbled, catching myself before hanging my head. "The three of us are the only ones who know about her complicity. If the police ask her about Becker, she undoubtedly would deny it."

Five non-uniformed police officers waited outside. The doorbell rang, and Margery reappeared to unlock it. From my knowledge of police procedures they would have wanted to avoid attracting undue attention, and had come from two different autos parked at opposite directions from the Croydon residence.

Margery let them in after demanding they remove their shoes. I had never met a sterner schoolmaster in the years I went to lower forms. Soon the hallway was filled with shoes. Sorting them out when they left would be an interesting matching puzzle. Once unshod, the five officers headed for the stairway with guns drawn as Margery relocked the door. After they were out of sight, Margery opened the door to the dining room.

Glancing out through a window, I noticed the cab across the street and wondered why it was still parked there. Could Becker have arrived by taxi and asked the driver to wait? If so, the police would have to act quickly to catch him.

Forcing a smile, Margery asked, "Is everyone ready for tea and cucumber sandwiches?"

"Perhaps we should be getting back to our hotel room," Lady Jean said. "We've imposed on you enough for one evening."

"Don't be silly. You haven't done anything to make yourselves unwelcome."

Violet reacted quickly, so quickly I couldn't stop her. "I'll help you in the kitchen. You have a wonderful house, and I want to find out more about it. I expect the bedrooms are on the third floor."

"They are. We have five," Margery said.

"I remember you have a housekeeper. Are there are any other help?"

"No. I enjoy doing housework. It keeps me busy between séances."

Sir Arthur and Lady Jean sat at the dining room table. I could feel their anger towards Holmes, who had returned to the table and sat opposite them with a placid smile.

My attention wandered between the silent drama at the table, and the events taking place in the kitchen. Violet ran water into a tea pot and put it on the range while Margery retrieved a tray of sandwiches from the refrigerator.

"How do you start the stove?"

"Turn the white handle and light a match from the box on the shelf."

I caught a whiff of gas, then an explosion as flames flared wildly. Violet had never lit a stove before.

Margery rushed to her side. I was sure she could smell singed hair as easily as I could. "Are you all right?"

"I-I'm fine," Violet stammered. "Really I am. Just a little frightened."

"You're supposed to light the match first."

"Of course. How silly of me. No harm done."

Holmes got up and moved to stand in the kitchen door. "Does the chauffeur live in the house with you as well as the housekeeper?"

"Yes. He lives in the basement."

"Is he around now? There were some questions I wanted to ask him about the kidnapping."

"No. He took his sweetheart to see 'What Price Glory.' It's supposed to be a smash hit, if I have the expression right. I know he was looking for sympathy for his injuries."

"I love the movies and read *Variety* all the time, but I haven't heard anything about it," said Violet. "If you'll tell me where you keep the napkins, I'll set the dining room table for you."

"They're in the pantry to the left. The silverware is in the drawer behind you."

As the domestic scenario played itself out, Holmes and I traded admiring glances at Violet's masterful wheedling of information from Margery.

Even Margery seemed impressed. "How did you know the bedrooms were on the third floor?"

"The housekeepers usually live on the second floor to be close to the kitchen and living room on the floor below, and the bedrooms on the floor above. Where do you keep your tea?"

"I'll get it. You have your choice of Darjeeling or Jasmine."

"Whichever Sir Arthur and Lady Jean prefer," Violet said. "Either one is fine with me, I don't expect the men will want to join us, anyway."

"Regrettably not," Holmes said, pushing away from the table. "If you will excuse us, we'll find Officer O'Neal and your husband. We're both anxious to join in the search."

CHAPTER 39

I felt a thrill of excitement as I got to my feet. The path to the end game now lay open. And all because of Violet. I was sure Margery wasn't happy about having two additional unaccompanied strangers joining the posse already tramping about in her house, but she had no choice. The biggest hurdle had been cleared, and mostly because of my amazing spouse.

Holmes read my mind.

"She indeed is a wonder, Wiggins. The only woman I know who even came close was our beloved Mrs. Hudson."

"Except Violet isn't a saint. Mrs. Hudson must have been one to put up with you for so many years."

Holmes snorted. I thought in humor. It wasn't. "Certainly you could have come up with a better line than that, Wiggins. You're a professional writer."

"And you are a professional snob."

"Heh heh," he said.

My heart beat faster as we climbed the spiraling marble stairs, our pathway shining brightly from the medieval sconces dangling high on the wall beside the stairway. Once lit by candles, then by gas, they now furnished steady, unflickering electrical light. Too much light, to my taste. For all the years I stood on the sidelines and reported the battles of the Detroit police, I was now a warrior myself, albeit unarmed. This was a castle, and I wanted shadows.

We reached the second floor landing. Halting, we listened for voices. All I heard was the drip of a faucet somewhere in the expanse. We stood at the edge of an enormous Persian rug that covered the heating vent and led to the Croydons' version of an attic. It could have been a library or an art gallery, with glass-fronted bookcases, furniture, statuary and piles of oil paintings neatly arranged to form aisles. This was no medieval castle, it was a damned antiques shop!

I stopped in my tracks. "We may have some difficulties. Lucille may remember seeing us at Margery's lecture at the Bell in Hand."

"No matter. If she does, she still has to account for being seen by Sam. The threat of exposure may be enough to prise loose what we want to know."

"I don't understand why we're working alone. Why don't we just find O'Neal and have him take over? I'm sure he's more than capable of nabbing Becker without our help."

"Of course he is, but he'll have Dr. Croydon with him. I want to find Herr Becker alone and hear the whole story from him without others present. Especially Dr. Croydon, for obvious reasons. Over the years I've developed some highly effective interrogation tactics of oriental design the police may not find acceptable."

"We won't have time for the Chinese water torture."

"That's merely the technique everyone knows about by the penny press. There are others at least as effective that take far less time. Unfortunately, they would make a polite western European cringe."

I had to smile. "I see. Then you better let me do the talking. Lucille will know you're not a Boston cop the minute you open your mouth."

"Fair enough. I know I can trust you to ask the right questions."

There was only one door in view. And it was straight ahead.

I rapped.

"Who is it?" a woman's voice asked.

"Police. We have a few more questions to ask you."

"Come in. The door's open."

"Not open, silly goose!" Holmes whispered with a roll of his eyes. "Unlocked."

I ignored his linguistic jingoism and turned the door handle.

Lucille Dougherty, who was sitting on a sofa reading, swung her bare feet to the floor and stood. Though she was wrapped in a flannel robe, the top of a pink negligee peeked out as she laid her book on the coffee table before her. "Who are you? You aren't the ones who were here before."

"We just arrived from headquarters with some disturbing new information. You said you haven't even seen Albert Baker. We know otherwise. He's a desperate man and we need to find him before he hurts someone."

She blanched at the words. "I can't help you."

It was time for a bluff, one that even would impress Holmes. "You obviously didn't know it, but we've had the house under surveillance." I took out a scrap of paper—a receipt from buying razorblades at the hotel sundries shop—and pretended to read.

"At approximately seventeen thirty-eight hours, suspect Albert Becker, wanted on charges of kidnapping and attempted murder, approached the house at 10 Lime Street and rang the doorbell. A young female answered and let him in. Suspect has not yet come out at this time. Report signed Officer Liam Reilly, and called in at seventeen fifty-one. Received by the dispatch sergeant, Felix Barnes."

Dead silence. After all my years working with the Detroit police as a reporter, I had the script down to a fare-thee-well. If it worked with hardened criminals in the Purple Gang, I was sure a naïve young flapper had no chance whatsoever.

Holmes added an exclamation point to my statement by opening the bathroom door and peering inside. Lucille's eyes flitted nervously towards him and widened.

After letting her stew in her own juices for a few seconds, I said in a kindlier voice, "We know Mr. Baker has visited here many times, and he is a good friend of the Croydons. I'm sure he's been nice to you, but he isn't at all what he seems to be. For one thing, his real name is Becker. You know about the kidnapping and what happened to Simon. He could easily have been killed when Becker's accomplices threw him out of a speeding auto. Don't make it necessary to arrest you for aiding and abetting a fugitive."

A look of panic came to her face. "I'm sorry," she said with a sniffle. "I . . . I didn't know, believe me." Breaking into actual tears, she said. "I was only doing what Dr. Croydon told me to do."

"What do you mean?"

"He said there's been a terrible mistake, and that the police think Mr. Baker has done something illegal. He told me Mr. Baker might appear at the door during the séance. He did, and I let him in. He said he wouldn't be staying very long, just long enough to borrow one of the doctor's coats and get some money for a train ticket. He told me to say I hadn't seen him if anyone asked, and said I wouldn't get in any trouble. I'm sorry. I know I shouldn't have lied."

"Where is he now?"

"I swear I don't know. I showed him to Dr. Croydon's room and he took a black leather jacket, a scarf, and a derby hat from the closet. When he started to go through drawers, I made him leave. I told him I couldn't give him the money he needed because I only had a few dollars and the Croydons keep their money in a wall safe. I even told him I had a friend who might have enough money to buy the ticket, if he wanted to come with me, but he refused to leave. He said he would wait until the séance was over."

"Where did you last see him?"

"On the stairway down to the first floor. I didn't like the idea of him wandering around in the house, so I told him he could wait in my room, but he was worried someone might find him there. I watched him until he disappeared around the bend."

Holmes glanced at me, and I shrugged. "There's nowhere to hide on first floor," he said. "Did you have any idea where he was going?"

"No."

"Where are the stairs to the basement?"

"Behind the kitchen. Simon has his room in the basement. The Croydons never let me go there." She paused, then continued with a thin smile. "I think they're afraid we might get involved in scandalous behavior, and it would affect their social standing."

"I'm glad you told the truth. We'll do what we can to see you don't get into serious trouble. When we leave, lock your door, and don't let anyone else come in. Not even if they say they're police."

"Okay," she said with a final sniffle. Tears had made her mascara run down in twin streaks through her rouge. Her appearance reminded me of the time Violet dragged me to see Pagliacci.

Holmes wasn't ready to leave. "Do you have to go through the front door to enter the house?"

"No. There's a fire escape outside of my window. I never use it, though. Why do you ask?"

"The element of surprise is more valuable than the purest gold. Where does the fire exit go?"

"To the back yard. There's a fence with a gate that has to be opened with a key when coming or going. Simon uses it."

"Do you have a key to the back door of the house?"

"No," Lucille replied with a trace of suspicion in her voice. "I told you, the Croydons don't want me back there."

"No matter. I think we'll use the fire escape, if you don't mind."

Lucille moved forward to take a closer look at Mr. Holmes. Then, eyes flashing, she said, "You're not with the police. I remember you. You were with the Conan Doyles at the lecture last night."

"You're mistaken, young lady. And even if that were true, you would still be in serious trouble for lying about not seeing Albert Baker. We're only trying to spare you the consequences of your actions. Now if you will kindly open your window for us, we will take our leave."

That brought a laugh. "You're going outside without shoes?"

Holmes's singularity of purpose had run away with him, but he remained unflappable. "Unless you have American size twelve extra narrow shoes I could borrow, that's quite true. No matter though, it's just a minor inconvenience."

Minor inconvenience? Speak for yourself, Mr. Holmes.

She opened a window. Hell-bent on carrying through with his scheme, Holmes climbed through it. "Are you simply going to stand rooted in place, Wiggins, or are you going to join me?"

"Let me think about it."

"Very well. I'll not wait any longer. My feet are already starting to get cold."

Lucille loosed another laugh, this one more of a giggle. She opened a door and squatted. "You may be able to get your toes and half of your foot into these. I don't like to admit it, but I do have big feet for a woman. I have another pair your friend can use."

Happily, both pairs were flats. I set them on the floor and wiggled inside them as far as halfway up the insteps.

I felt like an idiot walking on tip toes, but the shoes stayed on. When I got to the fire escape railing, I dropped the other pair down to Holmes. "See how these fit."

I could hardly wait to see him wearing them. Of all the disguises he used in his investigations, women's shoes too small for his feet certainly would be among the most humiliating. It was a scene not to be missed.

Luckily, the metal steps weren't icy. I clung to the railing for dear life as I lowered one foot followed by the other on each step. Having to go down stairs leaning forward scared me silly.

Holmes was waiting; in stockinged feet. "It took you long enough, Wiggins. Can you unlock the door?

"I certainly hope so," I mumbled.

Without much hope of success, I pushed the lever and gave the door a nudge. The door didn't move. The ancient hunk of oak was a true piece of art, a remnant of the days when the back of the house was expected to be as decorative as the front. More than half was taken up by a decorative leaded-glass window. Its enormous keyhole would require an equally sizable key to unlock the door. I could only pray that the picks in Houdini's extra finger could find the mechanisms in the dim light because I couldn't feel them as I should have. Right off, I seemed to have trouble aligning them.

I fumbled stiffly until my fingers were numb, then gave up. Houdini himself might have done the same thing. "It looks as though we may have to go back to Lucille's room."

"Absolutely not. We're not going to give up that easily, my friend. There must be another way in."

There was: a window eight feet above my head. Even if standing on Mr. Holmes's shoulders, I could never reach it. And even if I could, I would end up in the Croydon's kitchen.

"Maybe this will work better," Holmes said, gesturing toward a wide metal flange imbedded in the stone wall of the house.

"A coal chute?"

Holmes seized me by my shoulders. "Precisely. Mrs. Croydon said they don't use coal anymore. The opening is more than large enough for us to crawl through."

I didn't share his optimism. "There may not be anything on the other side but a ten-foot drop. It would have taken a lot of coal to heat a house this size."

"Without doubt. Unfortunately, the chute door seems to be locked."

I fondled the lock in my hand. It was small, old, and relatively fragile. Not a Yale, by any means. Probably even unnecessary if they kept the gate locked. "That's not a problem."

My heart tripped happily as I readied the picks. A child could handle this one.

My excitement lasted mere seconds. "Blast! The keyhole's plugged."

Holmes sighed. "Then I guess we'll have to admit defeat and go back the way we came."

It was my turn to be enthusiastic. "Not at all, sir. We have another, even better, string for our bow."

Prying the false finger open with a fingernail, I shook the gigli saw into my hand.

Even at rest, the blades seemed as fearsomely sharp as they had when embracing Schultz's neck. I could imagine Houdini smiling as he used it. Cutting through metal would be slightly more difficult than cutting through flesh, but it could handle either job equally well.

Mr. Holmes held the lock for me as I wrapped the flexible saw around its hasp and pulled. I didn't expect a miracle, but the blade merely slipped on the metal. On the second try, the teeth dug in. Soon it was spewing filings with every stroke.

Even so, my face was damp with perspiration and fingers cramping from the effort when the lock finally swung meekly into my hand.

"Well done, Wiggins," Holmes said as he pulled on the now unlocked coal chute cover.

Though rusty and groaning, the flange swung upward to reveal a darkness even deeper than that which surrounded us. And, instead of a metal chute, there was only an impenetrable, inky abyss. We had only one way to get inside—feet first and on our bellies, and the hope we wouldn't break our necks when he hit the floor.

Holmes insisted on going first. "When you come down, land with your knees flexed, hands clasped together, and arms extended in front of your chest. If you fall, you'll fall forward, so you'll have the wall to support you. I should be able to judge the distance to the floor as I go, so you'll know how far it is."

I helped him lift his legs through the aperture, then supported his torso as he inched his way inside. Finally he was dangling with only his chin hanging on the bottom of the flange, one hand holding on to the metal and the other tightly gripping mine. Only then did I notice how slight my friend had become. Slight, perhaps, but certainly not fragile.

"Oh," he grunted, "don't forget to take those idiotic shoes off. You don't want to break your ankles when you land."

Those were his last words before releasing his grip.

I held my breath, waiting for a fearful crash or scream of agony. Instead, a loud whisper wafted through the opening. "Have no fear. It's less than twelve feet to the floor."

Twelve feet sounded like Everest to me. I pushed my legs through the opening and wriggled backwards until my feet dangled over nothingness. Then, remembering Holmes's instructions, I took a deep breath and pushed off.

I got a brief sensation of floating before I landed in a crouch. My feet felt as though they were shattering. Otherwise, as Holmes had said, I merely squatted more deeply as my forearms and elbows bumped against the wall. I bounced backward, landing on my derriere.

"Made it," I whispered, stumbling to my feet and shaking my poor aching dogs.

"Excellent," he whispered back. "Stay where you are for a moment while I get my bearings."

I had no difficulty staying put. I had no idea where I was, or where I was going. And my feet hurt, besides.

"Excellent. I believe I've found the door."

I headed in the direction of his voice. Wood scraped against concrete, and I felt a warm breeze against my face. Otherwise, we still were in total darkness, soundless as a tomb.

I took a step forward and bumped into something that turned out to be Holmes. In the silence, his testy whisper sounded like an angry shout. "Enough needless collisions. Grab the hem of my cape."

"Fine with me. Do you have any idea where we are?"

"According to my calculations, we must be directly beneath the kitchen. I followed the cellar wall to the door. A right turn should bring us to the stairway. Before we continue, I have a slight chore to tend to."

With that I felt him reach into his trouser pocket. A Lucifer flared to illuminate several large packing crates. Holmes headed for one before shaking out the match.

"I'll need your assistance," he whispered. "Watch your step."

The warning proved vain. I bumped into the crate and landed on the floor.

"I can plainly see you're too clumsy for this kind of work," Holmes said. He lit another match. "Help me push this crate around to block the doorway. Since we can't leave through the coal shute, I want to be sure no one can enter that way and escape back into the house."

Once again we were plunged into darkness.

I heard the cellar door close. "Push, my good man."

I did.

"Now, let's find our way to the stairway."

I have experienced his navigational skills on many occasions and would confidently follow him to Timbuktu, or anywhere else I needed to go. Eagerly seizing the bottom of his cape, I said. "Lead on."

He moved confidently for several feet with me in tow, then stopped. I felt him turn, and heard the sound of cloth rubbing against wood. He had found the stairway with his foot.

"Voila."

My mind finally kicked in. "There's a huge window in the back door. Since we can't see it from here, there must be another door at the top of the stairs that's closed. I could open it. Even ambient light would be better than this mud."

"Indeed," he murmured. "Excellent suggestion, Wiggins. I'm weary of playing blind man's bluff, and any natural light would be preferable to striking a match. The decision is entirely yours, my friend."

I had already made up my mind. I found a handrail with my right hand, held out my left in front of me, and noiselessly climbed the risers.

After what seemed an eternity, my lead hand found the door. With a bit of fumbling, I located the knob. Taking a deep breath, I turned it and stepped back.

My heart skipped a beat in surprise. Bright moonlight poured in through the window. Startled, I leaped aside into the minimal darkness the partly open cellar door still provided.

Heart pounding, I took a deep breath, I turned to look down the stairway, certain I'd see Albert Becker leering at me in the distance. I sighed in relief. Though barely visible, another door stood some distance away from the bottom of the stairs. Closed.

I wanted to take the steps three at a time, but I still came down slowly and as far away from the surprising illumination as I could manage. The chauffeur's door could open at any moment.

Holmes gave me a hearty slap to my back. "Well done, Wiggins. Are you ready to storm the dragon's lair?"

"Not yet," I replied, surprised he still was so strong.

With light, I now wanted to find a weapon. Everywhere I looked I saw outlines of packing crates and shrouded figures I took to be statuary, but nothing else. At last I spied a barely visible push broom leaning against a support beam. I couldn't prevent an evil smile as I unscrewed the handle and took a practice swing. Babe Ruth had nothing on us.

"I am now. Lead on."

Destiny seemed to be upon us as we reached the door. Taking another deep breath, I swung the rod behind my ear like a batter waiting for a pitch. "Open the door," I whispered.

CHAPTER 40

The knob turned without a sound. I leaned forward, arms twitching with anticipation. With a vigorous push from Holmes, the door swung open. I swung wildly.

And connected with air. Other than an open wardrobe and an unmade bed strewn with clothes and magazines, the room was empty.

"Where in blazes is he? The so and so is Houdini incarnate."

"By 'so and so' you must mean male offspring of a female canine," Holmes said with a sour look. "Unfortunately, I have no idea."

He strolled to the bed and hoisted a long red-and-white knit scarf with two fingers. "Scarlet, if my memory serves me. Harvard's school color."

"Lucille said Becker took a scarf from the doctor's room. I wonder why he left without it."

"A totally irrelevant point. All that matters is that he's eluded us once again. He must have fled before the police arrived."

Eyes closed, I held up two fingers.

Holmes noticed my expression. "What is it, Wiggins?"

I first saw a fleeting glimpse of Sheriff Peabody at the Bradford Farm, but it passed quickly. Then a much stronger memory took over. I watched Margery at the front door to answer the bell. Then I envisioned the officers filing in one at a time and removing their shoes.

Why should I remember that?

I gathered up the scene again, this time concentrating on watching Margery's movements, especially her hands.

Then I remembered! She had unlocked the door from the inside with a key! Unless Becker had a key to the front door, which he clearly didn't when he first arrived, he couldn't have left that way. The only alternative possibility was so remote it wasn't worth consideration. Lucille was too obviously unnerved when we confronted to have omitted telling us she had given him hers.

"He's still within our grasp," I said. "There are only two ways out of the house. Margery had to open the front door with a key, so he couldn't have left that way. And, as you recall, the back door was locked when we came down the fire escape to enter the basement."

Holmes's eyes lit. "Brilliant, Wiggins."

"I know," I said, enjoying a rare victory. "And not only that, I'm willing to give substantial odds that the back door can be and Herr Becker is somewhere in the back yard."

"Then I suggest we find something for our feet. My toes are still trying to thaw from our last trek across the tundra."

We settled on wrapping them in underwear from the bottom of the chauffeur's wardrobe.

"To the siege," Holmes said.

I hadn't seen him move as quickly since we were together at Baker Street, as he darted up the stairway. And I was a mere step behind all the way.

At the top of the stairs, we both stopped in our tracks at the sounds of voices—clear and very close. I quickly sorted them out as belonging to Sir Arthur, Margery, and Violet chatting merrily away. Realizing we hadn't been discovered, Holmes gallantly stood aside to let me turn the latch on the back door.

Spirits soared as the door moved outward when I pushed on it. Bending low, we slunk out into the yard. The bright moonlight easily showed there was no one in sight.

My first glance showed a tranquil snow-covered arc from the right side of the house to the gate in the distance. As Holmes closed the back door, I whispered, "I'll check the gate."

An owl hooted somewhere in the distance, and some tiny land creature scurried away from me as I dashed forward, but everything returned to dead silence as I reached the gate. A thin layer of undisturbed snow on the path meant no one had come in or left for some time. Even so, I still felt a jolt of pleasure when I turned the handle and found the portal locked.

Waving a thumb in the air, I rushed back and whispered a victorious shout. "He's here somewhere!"

Instead of a show of pleasure, Holmes seized my shoulders and roughly shook me. "Then calm yourself, Wiggins. Your blood is running high, so we must proceed with extreme caution. We already know he's highly dangerous, and we have no idea what else he may have found in Dr. Croydon's room."

Euphoria ended with a thud. "Quite so. Why would he have bolted from the chauffeur's room?"

"I expect he heard the commotion upstairs when the police arrived and decided he needed to find a new hiding place. He may not even have realized there was a back gate when he left the house."

I freed myself from Holmes's grip to survey the lay of the land. Unless Becker had taken our route through the coal chute and trapped himself in the coal bin by so doing, the only direction he could have moved was to the left of the house. Since the front of the building was connected to the adjoining houses, there was little out of eyeshot from where we were standing. The only impediment preventing a clear view was a large coniferous bush next to the house some ten feet away.

I pointed to it, and Holmes nodded. "Gather up your bludgeon," he said. "I have a strong suspicion we're going to need it."

Snow squeaked under our bundled feet as I led us forward in a knee-torturing crouch. When we reached the bush, we halted.

Holmes surprised me by dropping to his hands and knees. Brushing the snow away with bare fingers and breath, he looked up at me with a Cheshire cat grin. An unmistakable shoe print disturbed the snow.

I saluted him with two upraised fists.

Then, instead of getting back to his feet, he turned and continued to follow the new-found spoor like an overly-long basset, belly dragging in the snow, nose millimeters from the ground, and paws burrowing away at the snow ahead of him as he went.

As I watched, I had to swallow hard to keep from laughing. It was a picture worth a thousand dollars to any newspaper or magazine in the world that could afford to buy it.

He disappeared for a moment. Then an arm appeared, gesturing for me to follow.

With a sigh, I shoved my broom handle in front of me and pushed forward with my knees.

I found Holmes standing erect in front of a closed wooden door. A root cellar or storage area for gardening tools, I expected.

"Treed," I whispered. "Shall we call in the constabulary?"

Holmes shook his head violently and pulled me several feet away from the door before answering. "The obvious action, but I want an opportunity to question Herr Becker in private. Perhaps I'll use a Spanish invention, the bastinado, far more effective than Chinese tortures. Your broom handle will work perfectly."

I winced. When I had read Don Quixote, I didn't think that having the bottoms of the feet repeatedly beaten sounded so frightening. Then I found out it could kill you.

"Assuming it's possible he's armed and will come out with guns blazing, how do you intend to collar our villain?"

"Ah, Wiggins. You've obviously forgotten my encounter with the venerable Mr. James Oldacre, in the case of the Norwood Builder. Never mind. I'm sure you will remember soon enough."

The first task was to scour the yard, kicking away snow in search of leaves.

Easily uncovered, they were cold and stiff, but not sodden. Ten minutes labor yielded a knee-high pile beside the wooden door.

Holmes fished his box of Lucifers from his trouser pocket. Before he could remove one, I told him to wait. I remembered a small stack of newspapers sitting on a ledge just inside the back door of the house. They crumpled nicely and nestled among the leaves.

I stood over him as he crouched, shielding him from the wind. The match blazed, paper flared, and leaves quickly began to smolder.

He got to his feet and ran to the opposite edge of the yard. "Fire!"

The back door opened at his second call, and Margery came out. "Who are you? How did you get into our yard? What's going on out here?"

"Nothing to be concerned about, dear lady," Holmes said blithely. "Just go back into the house."

"Mr. Holmes?"

"Yes. Now please go back in."

She didn't move. With a shrug, Holmes again shouted "Fire!"

Seemingly for the first time, Margery caught sight of the billowing cloud. "Good heavens!" she screamed, rushing back inside.

Holmes's next call brought results. The door creaked forward and Albert Becker stepped out, coughing. He didn't see me until the broom handle slammed against his right hand, sending a pistol flying to the ground.

He dropped to his knees, writhing in pain. I kicked the pistol away before he could reach for it. Holmes joined me, pulling the stunned miscreant to his feet. I immediately caught his right arm in the policeman's elbow-breaker I had used on him at the Baker Estate. He hooted in pain, but made no resistance.

I glanced back toward the back door and saw Margery pointing in our direction. I was sure the police would arrive in a matter of seconds.

Holmes opened the door. Instead of darkness, we found a railroad lantern burning brightly atop a bench inside the room.

Holmes pulled the iron latch down into the bracket to lock the door from the inside. "This won't hold anyone out for very long, but certainly long enough. Everyone will need to put their shoes on before they leave the house. I'll clear a space. We need to lay Herr Becker on the floor."

"This is outrageous," Becker cried. "What do you intend to do with me?"

Holmes answered in a quiet voice dripping with menace. "Nothing worse than what you would've done to me as your captive."

At the words, Becker's eyes opened wide. "*Mein Gott!*" he screamed. "*Helf!*"

"I fear only Satan can help you. And he only works when he can avoid blame. Drop to your knees."

A little tug from me was all it took. Becker slowly knelt, fighting hard to stifle a panicked sob.

"Now face down on the floor. I want you to be able to speak. If you choose not to, well, I've heard it takes but two minutes to suffocate if you can't inhale. Survivors say it's the longest two minutes of their lives."

"That's murder!" Becker panted. "You'll never get away with it."

"No one will ever be able to prove it isn't myocardial infarct. Sources tell me you have a weak heart."

Holmes was making even me squirm.

"We don't have much time. Either you answer me, or you'll choke on your own saliva. Did you order the poisoning of Harry Houdini?"

"No," Becker grunted. "You fool, everyone knows he died from a ruptured appendix."

"We know otherwise. You pursued him for more than a year, poisoning him with thallium and making his hair fall out. The fatal dose was administered in Schenectady by your henchman Jurgen Schmidt, when Mr. Houdini was eating at the Stockade Inn. He's admitted to it, and when the police get the autopsy report, they'll have confirmation. We have your briefcase and the newspaper clippings. You will be arrested and tried for murder. You can either be executed, or cooperate with the police. Did Dr. Croydon furnish you with the thallium?"

Becker coughed, but didn't answer. I watched in amazement as Holmes sat on Becker's back. "Well?"

"Can't breathe," Becker gasped.

"Last chance," Holmes said. "Tell the truth or die."

Worried as I was at Holmes's cruelty, I nearly passed out at the loud hammering on the door, and O'Neal's threatening voice.

Becker gurgled, then went silent.

My heart thumped crazily. "I think you killed him!" I said in a normal voice.

The hammering on the door became louder as Holmes arose to a crouch and reached down to feel Becker's carotid. "Yes. It appears you are correct."

"But why? This was entirely senseless. Even if Becker was brought into court, he couldn't be convicted on a forced confession. Certainly Croydon would never even stand trial."

He answered in a detached voice. "That's exactly why I did it. I can't explain now. Open the door."

Hand shaking, I moved the latch. O'Neal and Dr. Croydon stood outside, O'Neal with gun in hand. I stood aside, and he inched in around Becker's body. Croydon and another officer stepped in and shut the door.

"What's going on?" O'Neal asked.

"Mr. Becker was hiding in here, and we surprised him," Mr. Holmes said. "He had a gun and we had to subdue him. Apparently the shock was too much for his heart."

O'Neal glared. "If you knew he was here, why didn't you find me? You had no right to interfere."

"We didn't know he was here until he tried to escape."

O'Neal snorted. "You were certain enough to build a fire."

"True. But I also knew Albert Becker undoubtedly was only at mid-level in the conspiracy to murder Harry Houdini. I wanted a chance to find out who the others were."

O'Neal stared down at Albert Becker's body. "Even if that were true, we have no way to find out now. I'm sure you must already know the trouble you've caused. And if I didn't know what you went through when you were abducted, I'd arrest you for obstruction of justice. Under the circumstances, I won't treat this any differently than an accidental natural death. You say he had a gun?"

Holmes led him to where it lay partially covered in snow.

"That's my three-forty-eight Beretta," Croydon said. "I keep it in my bedroom. I'm astonished Albert would steal it."

O'Neal turned to stare at him. "That's only one of the questions I want answered before I leave. I especially want to hear more from you about why he came here in the first place and how he managed to make his way out of the house to here."

"Surely you can't . . ."

"But surely I can. Ed, will you take the Wigginses and Dr. Claybrooks to their hotel. I'll need to talk to them again in the morning."

Violet threw me questioning looks all the way back to the hotel, but a very awkward silence prevailed. Officer Ed escorted us into the hotel and to the elevators. "Officer O'Neal will be calling you in the morning," he said with a nod. Everyone in the hotel lobby watched him leave.

All the while, the engine in Violet's imagination furiously took on coal. It finally exploded when the elevator arrived and we stepped inside. "Now! Will someone please tell me what has happened?"

"Mr. Becker is dead," Holmes said.

"I wish I could say 'poor man.' How did he die?"

"Mr. Holmes killed him in cold blood," I said. "Don't look so surprised, dear, he said he has good reason. I'm anxious to hear what that might be myself."

Holmes remained silent. Violet glared at him until the elevator stopped at our floor. With a strangely dispassionate face, Holmes strode to our door and knocked two times and then four.

Rose appeared. Noticing our expressions, she asked, "What's wrong?" as she stood aside to let us in.

"We'll let Mr. Holmes explain," I said.

"I'll be more than happy to do just that," he said, fetching his pipe from his pocket.

With Violet and me steaming, and Rose frowning, he calmly took out his pouch of Latakia, filled the bowl and struck a match. "Where were we? Oh, yes. You wanted to know why it was necessary for me to end of the life of Mr. Albert Becker."

After taking a big puff, he continued. "Please sit down everyone. I have much to tell you."

Three frowning faces stared at him and found chairs. All wanted him to get to the crux of the matter quickly. I knew that wasn't his style.

"Very good. To continue, as I'm sure you're aware, murder is not my usual *modus operandi*. I view my investigations as scientific inquiries only, leaving rightful retribution to the judicial system. In fact, other than the well-deserved demise of Professor Moriarty, I've resorted to intentional homicide on only one other occasion before tonight. It was one of my un-recorded cases, and the deeds of the fiend I dispatched could never have been properly weighed in the scales of justice of Old Bailey. He undoubtedly never even would have been arrested. In some ways, there are many similar-ities between the three instances."

I knew of Moriarty's death at Reichenbach Falls, and remembered cases where Holmes or Dr. Watson had to act in defense of their own lives, but never even suspected another instance of Holmes committing an intentional murder. My journalistic ears could hardly wait.

"All three cases involved individuals who would eventually have found a way to kill me, had I not killed them first. All three executions involved issues far greater than the crimes they committed, and for that reason, all three were absolutely necessary."

I fidgeted as I waited for him to take another puff. Holmes's carefully detailed scientific explanations made me glad the blessed Dr. John Watson was the raconteur of the famed adventures.

"None of you have ever heard of Sir Alistair Gordon of Carsworth Es-tates in Brighton, and it's a very good thing you haven't. Sir Alistair was a very handsome young widower who posted bills in that city advertising gov-erness positions for his four-year-old daughter. There was nothing extraor-dinary about needing a governess, but his method of finding candidates certainly was. Nonetheless, he never was at a loss for applicants. And, with his fair looks, I'm sure all were more than happy to accept employment from him when offered."

"I don't like this already," Violet steamed. "The poor girls."

"You're way too far ahead of me, my dear. But, unfortunately, you are quite correct. Had Sir Alistair used the normal channels to find his employees, his continual requirements for replacements would eventually have been noticed. Most of the unfortunates were working class females, and sworn to secrecy at their application for work. The advertisements he posted merely stated the position, a starting salary—a very generous one at that—and a place to meet to interview for employment. Each note invariably disappeared before the end of the day it was posted. Sir Alistair merely hired the first one who appeared at the interview point, and sent the others away. In a matter of weeks someone usually would file a missing person's report, and after a brief investigation producing no clues, the matter was dropped."

Violet snorted. "You're making me angrier with every word. What was he doing to these poor creatures?"

"Yes," Rose added in an equally testy voice. "I want to know, too."

"Not what you might suspect, my dearests. Something far worse. But please try to control your feminine sensibilities long enough to let me relate my account at my own speed. As appropriate as your anger is, it makes the telling all the more difficult."

Violet flung herself back against her chair with a loud sniff. Rose still sat forward, cradling her head on hands with elbows burrowing into her knees. "Hmph!"

"Thank you. As you can easily see, Sir Alistair was so guarded in his actions that it's very unlikely I would ever have become involved with the beast at all had it not been for the actions of a young constable in Brighton who, for personal reasons, became more curious in the missing persons cases than his fellow officers had been. It seems his betrothed had filed one of the reports and was unhappy about the lack of progress. She urged her fiancee to investigate more thoroughly. When he did, he was dumbfounded to realize there had been seven similar reports involving other young women over the course of less than a year and one half."

It was my turn to interrupt. "Isn't that a rather large number of similar missing persons, even in a city the size of Brighton?"

"Yes and no, Wiggins. Even today it isn't uncommon for a woman to run away and marry, even though they usually eventually contact their families after a while. And, as you may have guessed, more than one of the young women was hopeful their prospective employer wouldn't delve too deeply into their background. Most of all, everyone knew Brighton wasn't East London. Now, may I continue?"

"Of course," I said with as much irony as I could muster. "Please forgive the interruption."

"Forgiven. Let me see. It was in late summer of '96, and Watson and I had experienced an unexpected drought of work. I hadn't been to Brighton for quite a while and welcomed the opportunity to revisit the bustle of the rides at the Pier and the joys of the Pavilion, so we caught a train on a Friday morning.

"All the way I wondered what would entice a young woman to possible danger in a city with so many attractions. From the young constable I had learned that all the missing women were residents of the city. There might be others unknown, visiting from other parts of the country, but the fact that all known were from Brighton seemed to narrow down the scope, if just by a whit. It also occurred to me, that most of the women absent seemed to be honestly employed in laundries or as seamstresses and shop keepers or involved in similar labors. All were single, and likely to want to improve their station, either by marriage or better employment."

"I'm sorry, but I do wish you would come to the point," Violet said with a forced yawn. "Any woman would have come to same conclusion years before you did."

"Perhaps it would be better if I stop at this point entirely. I seem to be doing a terrible botch job of enlightening you."

"Stop it, both of you," I said. "I hate to put it this way, Violet, but go suck on a lemon. Please continue, Mr. Holmes."

"Perhaps I can shorten the narrative a bit," Holmes said with amazing good grace. "I only include so much detail to illustrate our extreme good fortune in detecting the plot at all, and to show how many other harmless creatures could have perished but for what almost appeared to be divine intervention. How it relates to Mr. Becker will soon be clear enough, I promise you."

"Then I apologize," Violet said in a much friendlier voice.

"Apology gladly accepted, dear lady. As luck would have it, Watson remarked about the number of handbills he noticed as we walked from the railway stations. Offers of furniture for sale, clothing, men seeking work as bicycle messengers, employers looking for a day's strong back to move building supplies seemed to be posted everywhere we looked. One that particularly caught my eye advertised for a young woman to assist in tending three children at the Pier on the coming Saturday morning, offering an astounding two shillings in compensation for a few hours' work. Something about it captured my attention. That, and the almost unbelievably favorable bargain prices advertised on nearly all of the postings.

"Inspired, I asked a young toff on the street if there was any particular area where young working women would gather to lunch. As luck would have it, he said there was indeed such a place, a square less than half a mile from the Pavilion. We found it easily enough and discovered several young lasses nibbling on sandwiches and luncheoning together in laughter and gay conversation. Better still, it was impossible to miss that all the trees and walls of the surrounding buildings had disappeared under a motley assortment of paper.

"A quick scan netted nothing promising. As was my wont, I quickly hired a lad off the street to visit the square first thing each morning, and alert me if he ever found anything that at all seemed promising. Better still, I offered him a crown if he would bring me the posting, and a guinea if I was especially pleased with the find.

"A fortnight later he called me, and I was sure he had earned his guinea. Watson and I were on the next Southern Railway train from Charing Cross. Our young agent decided to endure the pains consequent to dodging school for the chance of gaining such a fortune and promised, and met us at the station."

"Go on," Violet cooed. "This is starting to get exciting."

"It is indeed. The poster offered the outrageously high wage of five pounds per month as well as room and board. I knew we had found what we were looking for. A cab took us to the address on London Road where the interview would take place. The room was already dark, and the proprietor said the gentleman who had rented it had concluded his business and left two hours before our arrival. A steady stream of young women had been arriving all day. He said the gentleman had paid cash for rent a week beforehand, leaving a postal box in southwest Brighton as his business address.

"We weren't too surprised to discover there was no such box, and no Cecil Enright living in the city. Needless to say, we were impressed at the lengths to which our suspect had gone to cover his tracks."

"Don't keep us hanging," Rose said, unmistakable excitement in her voice. "How did you trace him?"

I had to wink at Holmes. He had become a fine performer at his particular brand of magic.

With a faint smile he continued. "How did we locate him? By the handbill. It was professionally printed on a peculiar shade of pink paper. I was certain it was especially designed to attract a young female's attention. As luck would have it—or perhaps again it was the hand of Deity—we passed an advertisement printed on just that shade of paper on our way back to the railway station. The advertiser had left his phone exchange."

"Was he the monster?" Violet squealed.

"No. Merely a merchant offering to provide flowers for upcoming nuptials. But our florist gave me the address of the printer who had done the work. The printer recognized our handbill as a printing job he had performed for Dr. Alistair Gordon. Using pink paper was the printer's idea, bless the deity. His client, Dr. Gordon, a noted physician in South Sussex, and a supplier of cadavers to the medical schools in Cambridge and London, would never have permitted anything so incriminating."

Violet cried out. "Cadavers? Oh, God, no! The poor girls."

"As strange as this may sound, I would have been much happier if Dr. Gordon had turned out to be just another William Burke. Selling cadavers was a far less odious crime than what we uncovered. Sufficient to say, there are far greater horrors, and I shall spare you the details."

Violet and Rose began to cry and grasped hands for consolation.

"Take cheer, my dears. There is much better in the offing. In brief, Watson and I discovered Dr. Gordon had recently purchased an antique clock at Christies. I had a friend at the company who hired us on to make the delivery. The doctor was very affable, and even introduced us to his daughter, Clara, and his newly hired governess, a pretty young red-haired nineteen-year-old named Phoebe."

"Did she die, too?" Violet asked, nearly sobbing.

"No. I'll spare you that heartache. It was a near miss, but she survived. It was for the sake of the two innocents that I had to resort to such extreme measures in dealing with the doctor. We made our delivery, and before we left the manor, I made sure I had unlatched a window in the music room where he wanted it placed."

"Good!" my dear wife thundered.

"It was indeed. I learned that the estimable doctor had regular billiards tournaments on Tuesday nights, leaving the estate in the hands of the governess and Clara. The following Tuesday, Watson and I hid on the grounds and watched him leave. After he did, we easily found our unlocked window."

Though both women had tears in their eyes, Violet grabbed one of my hands and squeezed, and Rose the other. Even I was joining in the rising excitement, though I couldn't imagine what his narrative had to do with Albert Becker. I could tell Holmes was enjoying at center stage.

"Watson, carrying his bag of tools, led the way. The house was dark and silent, though a central chandelier provided more than enough illumination to light our path and we had to use our torch for only a short time. We had earlier decided to limit our search to the first floor of the manor. It was, it turned out, a wise decision. A heavy door at the extreme eastern end of the building was securely locked. I also could hear muffled angry barking from within."

"Whatever was in there, Dr. Gordon intended to keep secret," I said.

"Stop interrupting!" Violet snapped. "Get on with it."

"As you wish, my dear. Watson had no difficulty with the lock, but we didn't know what we would encounter with the dog. Watson's kit included a metal-reinforced sleeve that would protect him from being severely bitten, but we also didn't know if the governess or her charge would suddenly appear."

"Forget the dog," Violet interrupted. "What did you find?"

"A sinister laboratory with an operating table with manacles, surrounded by miles of hoses connected to gauges. I expect there were well over a hundred dated bottles with preserved specimens of what I couldn't even imagine, though I did recognize a fetal kitten. The room also had a large refrigeration unit. I could tell the floor had been covered with newspapers because there were pieces still stuck to the floor, but there were splotches of blood wherever you looked. The lab in Mrs. Shelley's *Frankenstein* couldn't have been more grotesque. Watson discovered scores of handwritten notebooks describing the experiments Dr. Gordon had been performing."

He stopped, obviously overcome with emotion. "Do you know how much blood a person can lose before the loss causes death? Dr. Gordon did. He knew how much skin could be removed, and the areas where removal caused the earliest and most painful deaths. Some of his other experiments involved female violation so abominable I refuse to even call them to mind, now sealed away from the pains of torture anyone could inflict upon me. Monster was far too mild a term for the evil creature who bore the honored title of doctor."

"Show us some mercy," I whispered. "You've proven how much the demon deserved his end. Give us the joy of finishing the story, and showing how it relates to Becker."

"Gladly. As feared, we were interrupted by the governess and the doctor's daughter. I had Watson push them back into the hall. He stayed with young Clara while I escorted Phoebe into the laboratory, and shut the door.

"I daresay I hardly expected her to believe me, but she told me that Clara had said how much she liked Phoebe and hoped she wouldn't get sick and have to leave, as all the other governesses had done in the past. Phoebe also told me she had recently been falling into deep sleeps and waking up feeling weak. I noticed a bruise and small puncture mark on her left arm at the inside of the elbow and knew it was from a hypodermic needle.

"As much as I loathed having to do it, I showed her the diaries and let her inspect the specimens and devices. She finally told me she realized what I said was true. I told her she had to stay with Clara and make sure she didn't come downstairs from her room until Dr. Watson led them out of the house. I found several canisters of petrol in the carriage house—Dr. Gordon owned one of the pioneer Arnold automobiles in Britain at the time—and doused the entire laboratory as completely as I could, then awaited the doctor's return."

Violet and Rose stopped crying and sat with angry anticipation. I found myself craving the arrival of the pending blazing inferno as impatiently as they.

"I saw the lights of his vehicle in the oval in front of the manor an hour later. He was greeted by the sight of his dog with its leash wrapped around the figure in the fountain in the front yard. As expected he dashed directly to the laboratory.

"I pushed him through the door, leaving it open far enough so he could hear sentence passed on him. Tossing a match wasn't nearly sufficient. He needed to know there was no point in my confronting him about the unbelievable cruelty of what he had been doing. I told him I knew his position in society put him beyond the reach of ordinary justice, as did the existence of his innocent child who didn't deserve knowing what manner of devil she had for a father."

Showing uncharacteristic emotion, Holmes said, "I also told him I knew I couldn't continue my life in London if he were allowed to live, and that vows I would be safe were a waste of breath. Most of all, I made sure he understood he couldn't continue to exist unpunished with the souls of all the innocent young women he had brutalized awaiting their deserved justice. His only defense was an indignant statement that he was doing nothing more than a scientist performing research that would help the future of humankind. I told him he was incapable of knowing what a human being was."

Holmes paused, seeming to realize the depths to which he had descended. "In the depths of the greatest anger I had ever known, I lit a match and tossed it through the door. The blaze nearly scorched my arm in the process. I closed the door and locked it."

He was interrupted by cheers from the women. I didn't join them. Tales of avenging angels always were told on the sharpest angle of a double-edged sword.

"To conclude, Watson and I left before the fire brigade arrived. John told me later he had told Clara we were very bad men who had been paid to murder her father, and she could have done nothing to stop us. It seemed the best way for her to deal with her loss."

The women were weeping again. Even I had to swallow hard.

"I can see some similarities to the story about Moriarty, but how does it apply to Albert Becker?"

"It seems Herr Becker wasn't a mere anti-Semitic spiritualist medium. I received a wire from Mycroft informing me that Becker's mother and father were involved in active espionage during the Great War. Sometime afterward, Becker apparently learned Houdini had been working as an agent spying for England on his various tours of Germany and Russia."

"I always wondered why Houdini seemed to enjoy his cinema role as spy as much as he did. He actually was one. "

"Indeed. But that, in Becker's eyes, wasn't the greatest affront. The famed magician's actions also threatened Hitler's fund-raising mission in this country. It seems that was Herr Becker's primary job, and essential to Hitler's plans. Fortunately for Becker, Houdini had antagonized the entire Spiritualist population around the world, and there was no shortage of individuals who wanted the man dead. It gave Becker the opportunity to kill Houdini without arousing suspicion. When the doctors diagnosed appendicitis, Becker was sure he never would hear any more about it.

"Houdini the spy was dead. More important, the man who most threatened Hitler's plans had been stopped before he could cause irreparable damage. Dr. Croydon undoubtedly provided support and the poison. Proving anything at all now is likely impossible. Bess refused to order an autopsy."

I groaned. "You didn't tell me that. My once in a lifetime story is gone."

"It appears so, but lamentable as Houdini's death is, preventing the damage Becker could have caused to the world if Hitler succeeds is many times more important. As with Moriarty and Dr. Gordon, Houdini's murder was only the least of a number of unspeakable crimes. Hitler's fund-raising machine will undoubtedly be rebuilt, but it no longer will have the same imprimatur or potential support of the entire Spiritualist community, not only Sir Arthur and Margery. If the world is lucky enough, he may never rise to the level of his ambitions."

The room fell silent.

I turned to Holmes. "I don't know how much you've done to prevent the rise of Adolf Hitler, but I do agree it needed to be done. You are a far braver man than I could ever be. I would never be able to bear the burden of my actions for the rest of my life."

"Being a fictional character has its advantages," Holmes said with a wry smile.